Betrayal
The Divine, Book Two

M.R. Forbes

ISBN: 0615829023
ISBN-13: 978-0615829029

DEDICATION

This one is for the bears.

CHAPTER ONE

I couldn't remember the last time I slept. I couldn't remember what it felt like to have a mattress beneath me, to close my eyes and dream of something that had some kind of importance, or at the very least provided relief from the emptiness of being awake. I couldn't fathom the idea of finding peace in the darkness, quiet for my always waking mind or comfort for my weary soul. Sleep was for people, not for me. Now it was just wishful thinking, a memory veiled in the darkness that never came.

Memories. They dragged on me like a thousand ton anvil. Except, I could move a thousand ton anvil. I was stuck with the memories.

I was crouched on the extended precipice of an office building, a neo-gothic behemoth of steel and glass and reflection. In front of me were mirrored windows that were meant to hide the inside world from the outside world. I suppose it was apropos that I could look right through them. I could see the angels gathered inside. I could feel the demons headed their way.

They were coming from the basement, scaling the inside of the elevator shafts with ease. Three dozen at least, summoned from Hell by a fallen angel who had been tipped off to the meeting. I didn't know how. Maybe if

Obi and I were still speaking regularly, I could have asked him. I'm sure he had the answer. It didn't matter. One thing at a time.

In my mind, I always returned to the same place. I wondered how things might have been different if I had been as Aware as Dante had claimed I was. I never saw Rebecca's betrayal coming. I was blinded by her beauty, taken by her artful deception. She hadn't even needed to use her succubus wiles on me.

Dante had warned me, and I had blown it, big time. He hadn't saved any breath in reminding me that he told me to be careful trusting her. Yeah, I had gotten the Grail back, and had hid it someplace that I hoped nobody would ever find it. What I had lost in payment for my efforts, that was a bigger bitch than she had turned out to be.

The angels were gathered around a simple desk, staring at a computer monitor. There were four of them, three I recognized. They were wearing business suits, carrying briefcases, looking like a quartet of ordinary human MBAs gathered for a quick presentation. Their wings were little more than slight bulges under the clothes, their swords banished to their hiding place in Heaven. They were experienced, long term seraphim. Like Josette had been.

Sitting in a leather executive chair in front of them was a Touched woman, Rachel Taylor, a Bruce Wayne type philanthropist and businesswoman. She was showing them how her charities were performing, and they were grinning and nodding in their pleasure. I was sure they had to know the demons were coming, but maybe they didn't. I had lost that perspective a couple of years ago.

Five years. That's how long it had been since the betrayal. I had to remind myself sometimes, because lately all of the days just seemed to coalesce into one another; into a single never ending mixture of color and grayscale. I liked to tell myself that it had been Rebecca's double-cross that had brought me here, but I liked to lie to myself these days. That had been the icing, the cherry, and the straw. I had lost Josette, Obi had never been the same, and frankly, having the long term memories of an angel and a demon rattling around in my skull full-time still made it a challenge to keep my sense of self. In the quieter moments, I could hear their whispers in my mind, their conflicting alignments arguing like a bad cliché.

I stopped peering through the mirrored glass and looked into it instead, at my reflection. My eyes had changed that day. Once upon a time they were both blue, but now one was the amazing dancing gold of an angel, the other the burning red of a demon. Balance. I nearly spat at the thought. Balance was the Universe's cruel joke. I guess I was the punchline.

One of the angels swiveled their heads, looking out of the window, turning directly towards me. I leapt up and grabbed onto the rope I had secured to the rooftop, my feet tapping lightly on the floor above them. I didn't care if he had seen me or not, but it would sure make things easier if he hadn't. He hadn't.

Josette. I had tried to speak to her after she had given her soul to me. I could hear those whispers and so many times I thought I could whisper back. I had tried to whisper back, but she had never answered. That hadn't stopped her memories from flooding into me, usually triggered by a thought, a word, the environment, anything. In that moment I was her, in that time and place, losing myself completely.

I let go of the rope and landed back on the precipice without a sound. The angels were distracted now; they had finally picked up the signal of the onrushing evil, and had taken up defensive positions. One stood on either side of the elevator to ambush the demons when they burst in, the other two took position in front of the desk, protecting Rachel. For her part, she had pulled a pair of revolvers from her desk drawer and had them trained on the elevator. Silver bullets, I was sure. They were poorly prepared.

The demons were only a few floors down now, a mass of heat to my senses. Thanks to Ulnyx, I could pick them out by scent. It was a standard assault group, a front-line of fodder demons to get killed in the ambush, a second wave of devil warriors, and a fallen angel Commanding them. Thirty six against four and a half. It would have been a pretty fair fight, not really the demonic style.

Rebecca. The last time I had seen her, she had left me paralyzed on the floor, waiting for my spinal cord to re-attach itself while she had taken a rift-ride to Hell. Initially, I had thought that it was because she knew it was the only way to escape and keep me from following. I had told myself that she would come back, that the power she had taken from Reyzl had left her confused. It was a stupid conjecture meant to salve the emotional wound, a stubborn denial that the demon who had made me feel more alive after death than I had during life wasn't a slave to the promise of power like all of the others. But the years had gone by and she had remained in perdition. Mr. Ross had reported as much to Dante, though he knew only that she was seeking some kind of knowledge that couldn't be gathered in the mortal world. What kind, he couldn't say. Dante had total faith in his Collector, but over the years it had seemed to me that his reports were always a little bit short, that there always seemed to be something missing. Or maybe that was just my general paranoia.

Her absence hadn't been a total loss. Without the transferred memories and power of generations of Solen offspring, the family had fallen into a state of disarray, a shadow of their former glory, caught in the middle of a power struggle that had left them squabbling over scraps. Reyzl's death had created a similar power vacuum amongst the higher order demons, and even now fiends and fallen angels alike were vying to take up the role, while at the same time hoping it was captured by someone else first to see how I would react. The impending attack on the angels was a standard sortie to flex some muscle. At least, it was to them.

The demons had reached their floor. The elevator doors would slip open any moment, and the battle would begin. I knew why the demons were there. I didn't need Obi for everything, after all I had my share of experience hacking networks and surfing the black oceans on the dark side of the Internet. It was time for me to act.

I focused my will on the mirrored glass. My technique had improved over the years, and where once I would have just blown the crystals to shards or dust, now I superheated them, liquified them, and watched the window melt away. I slipped in behind Rachel at the same moment the elevator doors were thrown open along their tracks. Before the angels could start hacking at the fodder, I allowed myself to be Seen.

It was like a shockwave that burst out from my physical displacement, causing the angels to stop all thoughts of attacking the demons and turn my way, and making the incoming fodder stumble into the room, and then change course in a desperate effort to get back out.

Five years had been plenty of time to pick up some new tricks. One of them was being able to close myself off from being sensed by other Divine. Acquiring the trick had been an interesting exercise, since it required first an understand of how Divine Sight worked, and second an extremely fine control over the strands of power that fed into my physical representation through my soul.

In the beginning, it had been a source of confusion that the Divine struggled to recognize me correctly, in some cases thinking I was a demon, in others an angel. I had learned since that each form of power had its own unique signature, in some ways like how you could use radar to tell what kind of plane you were looking at, even though you couldn't see it. Except, in the early days the Divine had been picking up my nascent output, the purgatorial balance of the powers fluctuating ever-so-slightly depending on my current state of mind.

Later, I had learned to control the output, and could neutralize it such that I still appeared as Divine; my true identity as a diuscrucis. The real fun had come from my experiments with mixing Josette and Ulnyx's energy into the general flow. After a lot of trial and error and with Sarah's help, I had discovered I could effectively negate myself entirely to the senses of other Divine, and just as importantly, I could mimic different signatures. It wasn't very useful against the more powerful players, but it had its moments.

I waited while the fodder demons retreated. I stood motionless until the fallen angel had made his way into the room, his devil warriors lining up behind him. I glanced over at Rachel. She had put the guns onto the desk and was facing me with a look of fearful apprehension.

"Diuscrucis," the fallen angel said. I knew this one too. Alyle. "Who are you fighting for?"

I looked around the room, soaking in the smell of fear and uncertainty, the smell of hopefulness. It was the burning question whenever I showed up where both factions clashed. Which side would I be aligning with today? Where did the balance rest? For the first two years, I had been a staunch ally for the angels. I had killed more demons than I could count. I had freed them up to take on their more peaceful pursuits in the name of goodness. The killing had been great for them, but had left me tired and empty. The idea of my eternal future being predicated by violence was less than appealing.

For two years after I had declared peace. I had disappeared from the fight, an observer to the balance that kept mankind in control of their own destiny. I had spent much of that time seeking knowledge. The knowledge that Charis had told me I would seek. The Demon Queen. I had solved that riddle after I had seen my eyes. I still hadn't solved the mystery she had so desperately wanted me to. I still didn't know how to find her. After she had given me the Grail she had vanished again. Even Mr. Ross didn't know where to.

It was Dante who had pushed me to get back out into the field. He was worried that both factions were getting too comfortable again. I had spent a year picking sides, at first with a clear goal in mind, and then almost randomly depending on my mood when the fight broke out. Tonight I was trying out a new tactic.

I looked at Rachel again. "Please get under the desk," I said.

She glanced over to the angels on the other side of the workspace, then dropped to her knees and crawled under it.

"Diuscrucis?" one of the angels asked. Silas. He had replaced Moses as the elder seraph at the Catskill Sanctuary. An old, wise angel, we had worked together a number of times.

I reached behind my back, unclipping the simple, mortal sword from its sheath and holding it up in front of me. I traced the polished steel with my eyes. No runes, no magic, just straight up sharp, pointy metal.

"Myself," I said, leaping over the desk and removing Silas' head. In the same motion I pulled one of the revolvers to me, firing a bullseye right between Alyle's eyes. It wouldn't kill the demon, but it sent the desired message.

The angels turned on me. The devils turned on me. For a moment they forgot about their own war. For once there was a more important threat. I let off the remaining five rounds in the revolver, perfect hits on five of the devils, and then roared, my body shifting and growing, turning into something wholly inhuman; a massive form of muscle and strength and bone. I felt a sword dig deep into my thigh, but I ignored it. I pounced forward and ripped into the devils, my massive claws shredding them.

They tried to run, but the elevator shaft was small, and it made a lousy escape route. I smothered them with my size and speed, tearing and ripping into them with a visceral fury that rose into my consciousness whenever I took the Great Were's natural form.

I could smell the angels regrouping behind me, organizing themselves for a combined attack on my flank. Alyle was with them, joining in their fight against me, accepting their wordless request for help. It was an interesting development. It wouldn't help them. I crushed the final two devils, and then gave up Ulnyx's form, becoming man-sized once more. I pulled my sword to me and stood stiff straight before the remaining angels.

"Why?" the fallen angel asked. I knew the question would be echoing through all of their minds.

"Balance," I said. I had learned that it was the answer to everything that didn't make sense.

I danced forward, a black clothed blur through the line of angels. They fought well, but Josette had been the best of them before she had become part of me, before my own power had been mixed with hers. It was over in a blink.

I took a cloth from my jeans pocket and wiped down the blade, and then dropped it to the floor. I returned the sword to the scabbard on my back. The angels were already dissolving, first to dust, then to nothing.

I walked over to the desk. "You can come out now," I said to Rachel. I could hear her knees sliding along the floor, and then her head popped up over the edge of the desk.

Forty five years old, short brown hair cut in a bob, brown eyes, a little overweight. She was intelligent, compassionate, and a staunch supporter of good. She put her hands on the desk and pulled herself to her feet. She knew I wasn't going to kill her, so her fear had fallen to the background.

"Balance?" she asked.

I sighed. "The cause and the effect," I said. "I've been thinking about how to resolve it."

She tilted her head. "So you've decided to just kill everything?"

"Not everything. You're still alive," I said.

She frowned. "What happened to you?" she asked.

Where should I start? I had met Rachel only a few months after I had recovered the Grail. She had been instrumental in providing the resources I had needed to reset the balance - finances, transportation, information when she had it, and something more.

"I always told you that things would change when the balance was reached," I said.

"You know that's not what I'm talking about," she replied.

I knew, but I didn't want to talk about it. Rachel had been there for me when I had needed a friend more than anything. No, not a friend. A mother of sorts. She had done a better job in the few years I had known her than my biological mother ever had. She was one of the few who could even pretend to understand what it was like to be me. That I was unable to relate to her, to be close to her, to even remember what that was...

"Landon," she said, her voice concerned. It snapped me out of my useless introspection.

"Memories," I said at last. "I've tried to fight them, but I can't escape. I'm tired of trying."

Charis had known what would happen. She had known because she had gone through it. Maybe it had taken her almost two hundred years, but she wasn't me. I had never handled it well. I tried so hard to handle it, but I was drowning. I knew the knowledge she was waiting for me to find would be my salvation. It had to be.

"There's something else I need," I said, shaking off the heaviness. "Your database."

Rachel looked back at her computer monitor. "My database? What for?"

Whispers and hope. My search for information had brought me to Shanghai, China, where I had spoken to a minor fiend who also happened to be one of the Asian archfiend's top spies. He had told me of the whispers. That the angels were passing encrypted messages through the most benign pathways. That not all of the angels knew about it. I suspected that Rachel's charity's financial transactions might be one of their transports.

"Research," I said.

She looked back at me. "Let me help you," she said. "I know I don't understand what you're going through, but you need someone to ground you."

"No," I replied. "You can't help me like that now that the balance is steady. Even if you could, if you did you would fall. I know how old you really are. You wouldn't survive." I reached into a pocket and pulled out a thumb drive. I handed it to her. "Please, just copy your database to the drive."

CHAPTER 2

I walked out of the Taylor building through the front door, a loaded USB drive tucked away in my leather jacket's inside pocket. I slipped across the street and looked up towards the top of the building, expecting to see Rachel standing at the window, waiting for me to step out into the night. She wasn't there. Unexpected, but not surprising.

I had been holding two bases of operation for the last five years. The first was the hidden excavation beneath the Statue of Liberty, where Rebecca had once lived. The second was my original room near the top of the Belmont Hotel. Rachel had spent months of her life trying to talk me into moving to a different location - she had gone so far as to offer me the penthouse of one of the residential towers her corporation owned. It had been tempting in the beginning, but what kind of mortal comforts did I need? I didn't sleep. I didn't eat. I didn't even void. I was a ghost with mass and kinetic energy.

The Belmont was familiar, and I could still feel the charge in the air from the night I had spent learning swordplay with Josette. I didn't know if it was real, or my memories making it real. Either way I didn't care. It was comfortable. The Statue... Everything about the Statue oozed Rebecca, right down to the bottle of perfume she had kept in the nightstand drawer next to her bed. I didn't sit there and sniff it or anything as forlorn as that. What I had done was study her books, study the runes, and keep up the hope that one of these days I'd go down there and she'd be there waiting. Waiting to explain what she had done, and why. It was almost as big of a mystery to me as Charis' words.

"Survival," she had said. It could mean so many things. I had thought she had allied with me because I was her best shot at it. Obviously, I had been wrong.

I had been too sensitive. I had cared too much, too quickly. I had gotten burned by mortal fire, burned by hellfire, burned by trust. You couldn't fight the Divine and care about anything. The alternative was to suffer pain and loss over, and over, and over again. When it was one of the only things that could hurt you, feelings became the enemy. Like I said, I liked to lie to myself.

I felt a slight pressure in my head and a tingle that floated down my spine towards the place that I identified as my soul's cage. I couldn't help but smile. I sat down cross-legged in the center of the street, ignoring the cars that swerved smoothly around me.

"I'm here Sarah," I said, opening myself up to the connection.

"Hey, Landon," Sarah said, her voice clear in my mind.

She had changed so much since the first time we had met, when she had helped me find the answers I didn't even know I was seeking. She had been a child then, but never just a child. She was a true diuscrucis, the only one in existence, born of the non-consensual union between a demon and an angel. The angel was Josette. The demon was Gervais, her brother, an archfiend operating out of Paris, France. I had never confronted him for fear of revealing Sarah. That didn't mean I didn't know where he was.

Josette had asked me to protect her. Sarah herself had named me protector before I had even known it would come to be. Could she see the future? She said she couldn't, but she was the one person who could lie to me. If she could, she never let on.

"What's up kiddo?" I asked.

The only time I could feel my soul breathing was when Sarah connected to me. I was her protector, and I would never let her see me sweat, never let her see what my world had become.

"Just checking up on you. When are you coming by to do some more of that ninja training of yours?" she said.

Her voice was light, cheerful. So unlike how she had been the first time we had met. Knowing she was safe had allowed her to grow, to blossom, and to live as though she were almost normal. She was still residing underground with the other Awake, but she went to High School, had mortal friends, and even mortal crushes. Nobody in the world knew she was different except me, though she needed to be more careful about not revealing her ability to See.

I reached into my pocket and touched the USB drive. "I'm doing great sweets," I said, pushing my mental voice up an octave to sound more chipper than I felt. "Maybe tomorrow night? I'm on my way back to the Belmont to do some research."

I had spent hundreds of hours over the last three years teaching

Sarah everything I... no, her mother knew about fighting. I found a certain measure of comfort in being able to give her something of Josette's that she could hold on to, even if she didn't know, or at least didn't say she knew, where that particular skillset had come from.

Her laughter boomed in my head. "You're sitting in the middle of traffic," she said. "Do you have to do that?"

It was one of the differences between a directly descended diuscrucis and a facsimile like me. She knew exactly where I was, all of the time. All she had to do was think about me, and she could See me. I couldn't do the same, but I knew it brought her great comfort to always know where I was.

"To be honest, I hadn't even thought about it," I admitted, getting back to my feet and finishing my trip across the road. I had become so accustomed to the mortal world circulating around me, at times I almost forgot it even existed. "How was school today?"

"It's always an adventure," she said. "Katie Winslow and her gang tried to prank me again by swapping my Coke for a can of urine. Somehow it ended up on Katie's head. Just because they think I'm blind doesn't mean I have no sense of smell."

I laughed. A rarity these days, unheard of unless I was talking to Sarah. She had gotten into a couple of scrapes with the school princess already, mainly owing to her perceived disability and the complete lack of imaginative mischief that stemmed from it. She had always gotten the upper hand, and her payback was well measured and deserved.

"What did the principal say?" I asked.

She laughed again. "He said I should have made her drink it. I'm not the only one she tries to torment, I'm just the only one who fights back."

"I'm sure you'd love nothing more than to put your foot up her ass," I said. She had expressed as much in the past, but doing so would risk giving up her faux blindness. How would she explain *that* away?

"I've been thinking about that. What I'd love to do even more is Command her to put her foot up her own ass."

The statement made me raise an eyebrow. Even though she was a diuscrucis, she had always leaned good. The way she took care of the Awake down in the tunnels, her desire to help her fellow targets at school. Commanding was a demonic ability, and not one to be used lightly. It was out of character.

"Are you okay?" I asked.

There was the slightest pause. Just long enough for me to know she wasn't. "I'm fine, brother," she said. "I'm just getting fed up with that witch and her cackling minions. Anyway, I'm headed to bed. I wanted to check in on you and say goodnight."

I could feel the temporary relief waning into the background at the words. It wasn't as if I didn't know they were coming. "Goodnight, sister," I said. "I love you."

"I love you too," she replied. I expected her to break the connection, but there was a pause. When her mental voice returned, it was hushed. "Brother, be careful. You may find the answers that you seek, but you may also wish you hadn't."

I wanted to ask her what she meant, what she had seen or felt about my future. I couldn't, because she broke the connection. That was something else she had me beat on. The call was one way. I briefly considered heading underground, but there was no point. If she had wanted to say more, she would have.

"I love you too."

The words echoed in my mind, bringing back a familiar memory that didn't belong to me. I found desperate purchase against the wall of the nearest building, trying to ground myself before the past could overtake me. My vision went dark, the sounds of the city fading out and history, terrible history taking its place.

I'm on a bed, my thighs are bloodied. The Archfiend takes my newborn baby and hands her off to his servant Izak.

He rounds on me, smiles and laughs. He is handsome, with a mop of curly black hair and delicate features. His nearly naked body is lean and strong and covered in runes. He's carrying a wicked looking dagger in one hand, a decanter of water in the other.

He puts the tip of the dagger at my foot and eases it upward, the tip digging in just enough to make me bleed. When the poison begins the spread he pours the holy water over it, filling my senses with the smell of frankincense, filling my body with even more pain. I'm already healing from the birth, my stomach shrinking so unnaturally, my muscles tightening and reforming back into my petite young visage.

"I have heard that the diuscrucis were banned by Heaven and Hell because of the power they hold as mortals, and the infinite power they can command as Divine," he

says. The dagger reaches my inner thigh. "I am eager to see how I might use such a tool."

I don't move. It isn't because I can't, but because I know that resisting would be useless. This is his home, his domain, and if I want to live to see my daughter again I have to be cautious. "Please don't hurt her Gervais," I say, tears welling in my eyes.

He stops the motion of the dagger and leans in close, his blood-red eyes only inches from my own. "Sweet Josette," he says. "I won't hurt her."

His words are a lie. I know it, but I'm powerless. The tears flow more freely. The knife moves up my abdomen, coming to rest over my heart.

"I'm not going to kill you," he says. "Even I'm not monster enough to kill my own flesh and blood. I want you to know that I could have. That I have shown you mercy today. I want you to know that you have a daughter, and that she is in my care."

The words are worse than a dagger in my heart. He lifts the blade and places it and the decanter on a small table. He leans in again and puts his lips to mine. I return his kiss, knowing the consequences for denial. He moans. I cry. He breaks the kiss and puts his hands under my small body, careful not to damage my wings. He carries me over to the window. I can see the city off in the distance.

"Do not come back here," he says. "I will kill her if you do."

He throws me out the window.

At first I move horizontally, and then I begin to fall. Instinct takes over. My wings spread, catch the currents of air, and lift me back into the sky. No longer trapped by his power, I close my eyes and will myself back to Heaven.

When I regained myself, I was holding crumbled mortar, my

tension causing me to dig deeply into the cement. The tears were streaming from my eyes, the same way they had the dozens of times I'd been assaulted by that memory. I fought the emotions, forcing them back down into my soul.

"Josette," I whispered, hoping that maybe this time she would respond. She didn't. I steadied myself, wiped my eyes, and took a deep breath. I had work to do.

The Belmont Hotel hadn't changed much in the five years I had been there, outside of the police tape cordoning off the entire 'penthouse'. I had put the tape there to keep the druggies, alkies, and whores away from anything they could hurt themselves on. I had added runes to the doors to ensure that the deterrents didn't need to be effective.

As usual, I entered through the roof, gaining access from the neighboring building and leaping across the gap. I took the stairs down and put my hand against the hinges of the door, defusing the metal so I could push it open, checking the runes inside the frame, and re-soldering the hinge on the other side. The process seemed complicated, but it only took me half a second to complete.

I had torn down every wall on the floor that wasn't weight-carrying, leaving myself with a large, almost labyrinthine studio which in the early days after the betrayal I had used to practice my craft, refine my control, and make sure I was never left powerless again. The space was nearly empty, with the exception of a small desk with a task chair and a laptop, a mattress on the floor that hadn't been used in years, an old wooden steamer trunk, and a literal pile of weapons. Not just cursed and blessed pointed blades, but also assault rifles, handguns, and a number of other tools of violence. Some might have said that I kept the instruments of pain as trophies, but I had destroyed so many others it made the pile look like a pittance.

The reason I kept them wasn't clear to me, but it was a compulsion I didn't see a need to deny. They came from angels, demons, vampires, werewolves, the Turned and the Touched. They came from mortals too; I hadn't limited my work to the Divine, especially when it came to violence against the innocent. On some level the stack reminded me of my purpose, a unique installation that spoke of what I had become. I unstrapped the sword from my back, and threw it onto the pile. Take the weapons away from the killers, and then use them to kill. Balance.

I looked over at the steamer trunk. I had found it at Obscura Antiques in the East Village, a popular shop that specialized in oddities and abnormal relics. What had made it special to them was the intricately carved series of patterns that when looked at from a certain angle bore an uncanny resemblance to the Virgin Mary. What had attracted me to it was that the carvings were seraphim runes of power. They rendered the trunk both indestructible and secure, able to be opened only by the angel or part-angel who traced the runes on the front in a unique pattern.

I had spent three months tracking its origins backwards. It hadn't always been a steamer trunk; the wood had originally been installed on Pope Urban's carriage, protecting him from danger both mortal and Divine while he would travel the countryside. I didn't know who had reconstructed it in its current form. It's discovery had been a bit of good fortune and a bit of gathered knowledge.

That knowledge had come from the contents of the trunk; hundreds of books, scrolls, and ancient pages that I had spent the better part of my two years on hiatus collecting, studying, and organizing. Some I had stolen from Universities, some from museums, and others I had tracked down in the possession of an assortment of demons and angels. The demons had been happy to trade the parcels for their lives. The angels had been more stubborn, and an unfortunate number had died not even knowing what it was they were protecting. In the beginning, I had felt some semblance of guilt, but Charis had been right; it was all a matter of perspective.

As for the texts, I knew they were a clue to the knowledge that she had wanted me to find. I had happened on it almost by accident. One of Rebecca's books had included a reference to a scroll I now had in my possession. The reference had included an image, and the image had included an emblem, drawn so small on the paper that no human hand could have been responsible, and no mortal eyes could have seen it regardless. The emblem was a rune, similar to the number seven, with a zig-zag on the top line and a sharp diagonal slipping up and to the left from the foot. It appeared on all of the texts I had collected, and nowhere else.

I didn't know what it meant, who had created it, or how to interpret it, but I was sure it was connected to Charis. I had spent nearly three years learning as much about the Divine on Earth as I could. I had followed thousands of dead ends, discovered leads and connections hidden across the mythology of human culture both ancient and contemporary, studied demonic and angelic texts, and learned to read as much of both languages as possible without a complete reference translation. It was the only character I had ever found secretly emblazoned across every level of divinity and humanity, carefully placed on specific pages of specific texts, the resultant strings creating a dialog of some kind. I couldn't decipher it, because there was one string missing. One resource I had yet to find, an unknown item that held the key to learning the truth and finding myself once more. Even if I had it, I didn't know if I would be able to solve the encryption, but I had to try.

I grabbed the USB drive from my pocket, hopped onto the task chair, and slid the device into the laptop. I typed in my password and navigated through to the drive. There was one file on it, a two hundred gigabyte flat file of transaction data. It was going to be a long night. Then again, they all were.

If there was a pattern to the data, I was having trouble finding it. IDs, dates, and dollar amounts streamed down the screen, scrolling for almost forever. I pored through the information, tried to match up dates to dollar amounts, dollar amounts to other dollar amounts, ids to dates and so on. The second most important lesson I had learned was patience. I had eternity to try to work it out.

The pressure in my head broke me out of my digital trance. I blinked for the first time since I had sat down, and opened up my soul to Sarah's request.

"*I'm here,*" I said to her, reaching up and hitting the power button for the monitor. Twenty hours. I was supposed to meet Sarah for training an hour ago.

"*You're supposed to be here,*" Sarah said, her voice trembling. "*Something's wrong.*"

CHAPTER 3

I took a deep breath, a feeling of worry crossing my deadened threshold.

"I'm on my way," I said, already headed for the door. *"What happened?"*

"Kelsie. She's one of my children. She's missing."

The words spilled out in a tumble of fear, worry, and guilt. I slipped through the door and leaped off the side of the stairwell, focusing on breaking my fall, and landing tenderly at the bottom of the steps. I blasted through the lobby and out the front door, not even giving the latest Punkmo a chance to see what had caused the disturbance.

Kelsie belonged to Trish, an Awake vagrant who had learned too late not to talk about the Divine. She had spent three years committed, and had nowhere to go once she had been released. She sold herself on the street to make money, and Kelsie was the result. Sarah had fallen in love with the little girl in an instant, and had taken the pair into her refuge. That had been a year ago. Sarah spoiled the little girl whenever she could, and in return Kelsie had taken to calling her 'auntie'. She loved that.

"*When was the last time you saw her?*" I asked. I bent down and lifted the manhole cover, slipped in and replaced it. It was about a mile down to the village. I focused, feeling the strength pouring into my legs.

"*Before I left for school,*" she said between sobs. "*She said goodbye to me. Trish said they went out to panhandle. Someone distracted her. When she turned around, Kelsie was gone.*"

I turned the corner, not slowing at all when I reached the huge open cavern that was Sarah's home. Once it had housed a hundred people at most, but it had grown in the last five years. Nearly six hundred lived here now, gathering water and electricity from lines run long ago to a now forgotten generating station. The Awake looked up at me, some with fear, some with admiration. They scurried out of the way as I approached.

"I'm here," I said out loud, pushing open the flap to Sarah's tent in the center of the small city. Sarah was sitting on the floor, her arms around Trish. I saw Izak sitting in the back corner of the tent, his body expressionless, but his eyes betraying the sadness that he felt at Sarah's pain.

Sarah dropped her connection to my soul. She looked up at me with her empty eyes. I felt another pang of hurt that mirrored Izak's. She eased herself out of Trish's embrace, stood up, and fell towards me.

The refugee camp wasn't the only thing that had grown. Sarah had gone from a young girl to a young woman; her body lithe and strong like her mother's, her face proud and defined like her father's. Her once pigtailed hair fell to her shoulders in highlighted ringlets, and I was sure the tight jeans and black t-shirt she was wearing were getting her plenty of appreciative looks. I caught her in my arms and held her, kissing the top of her head and stroking her back.

"I'll find her," I said.

I looked at Trish. The emaciated blonde woman remained hunched over on the floor in silence, her body wracked with distress.

"I'll find her," I repeated.

Sarah backed away from me and returned to Trish's side. "Tell him where you were," she said to the woman.

It took Trish a few tries to compose herself enough to speak. "Penn Station," she said. "We were working the afternoon crowd, trying to get some money for the community. This guy bumped into me, I got knocked down. By the time I got back up, Kelsie was gone. I screamed her name. I looked for her. I grabbed a policeman, but he thought I was hallucinating or something. Oh, Kelsie." Her sobs started anew.

I wasn't going to tell Sarah, but that wasn't the first time I heard the story. Young girls had been disappearing across the city for the last six weeks or so, stolen right out from under their parents' noses. I had considered looking into it earlier but hadn't acted. Karma didn't exist, but it was still a bitch.

"I'll go down to Penn and see if I can pick up a trail," I said. "You didn't sense any Divine?"

Trish shook her head. As an Awake she knew we existed, and she could feel when we were around. I hadn't expected her to have sensed one, or she wouldn't have been there. The Awake avoided Divine with even more fervor than they avoided the Sleeping. My killer was a plain, ordinary mortal, which meant he should be easy enough to track down.

"I'm coming with you," Sarah said, her voice firm. She was trying to preempt my objection. She failed.

"You're not coming with me," I said. "You know the stations are dangerous."

I wish I had known how dangerous the stations were when I had asked Obi to meet me at Grand Central that first time. They had only recently re-opened the tracks that had been demolished by my inadvertent expulsion of power.

"I can take care of myself," she argued. It was predictable.

There were only a few kinds of demons who could stay in the mortal dimension full-time without a more powerful demon to keep them alive. Vampires, werewolves, and nightstalkers were the most prevalent of the Devil's children. Then there were the fiends - they had been human once, died and gone to Hell, and had begged to be sent back to continue their dirty deeds.

All of them preferred to stay out of the light as much as possible, but the stations were the hunting grounds of the nightstalkers; powerful humanoids that were more often associated with the term 'zombies'. They weren't the shuffling, stupid, brain-eating variety. They were the Devil's first earthly creation, and while they ran more on instinct than intelligence, they were fast, strong, and silent. They would be a threat to me in a large enough group. Sarah had power, but her body was mortal and couldn't heal.

"I can Command them," she said, either reading my mind or getting ahead of my thoughts.

"How many?" I asked. Nightstalkers hunted in groups. I didn't have the power to Command, but I knew that it meant dedicating a piece of the mind to keeping the target under control, like a computer dedicating memory to each running application. There was a limit.

"I don't know," Sarah said, growing frustrated. Her eyes were still streaming tears. "She's one of my children," she shouted. "I will come with you."

I felt the immense pressure in my head, and I had to close my eyes to fight it. When I opened them, I was angry. I almost didn't recognize the feeling.

"I'm sorry, brother," Sarah said, reading my anger. "Kelsie." Her voice trailed off.

My anger faded at once. "I'll be back soon," I said.

I felt a hand on my shoulder. I turned around, finding myself face to face with Izak. The vagrant demon had a sword in his other hand.

"He wants to come with you," Sarah said. "He wants to be my eyes."

I glanced back at Sarah. Another manifestation of the evil part of her nature, or just normal teenage rebellion? I knew she had a connection to the demon, similar to the one shared by fiends and their familiars. Did she Command him, or did he volunteer?

"Fine," I said.

I didn't care at all if Izak were killed, but I shouldn't have been so callous towards the demon. Memories of his kindness to Josette circulated through my consciousness. He had been her single source of true companionship in the year that the angel was held captive by her sibling. At first, he had only been her jailor, a silent observer to Gervais's nightly visits and their painful results. Over time he had becoming something more, a caretaker of sorts, always there to lend a comforting shoulder to cry on, a kind touch, a calm and peaceful presence to help offset the chaotic violence of the archfiend.

The gentle devotion had transferred from mother to daughter, and Izak had been tireless in his efforts to protect Sarah. He deserved respect for that, and at least a small amount of sympathy. Gervais had cut out the fiend's tongue in fear that he would one day attempt to usurp him.

I put my hand on top of his and looked into his eyes. I could feel his desire to help Sarah, but there was something else there too. She *had* Commanded him. He didn't want to leave her side, to leave her unguarded. It was hard enough for him when she went topside to live her mortal life. I saw something else there that I wasn't expecting. Recognition. He saw Josette.

Sarah and I had never spoken of the events leading up to the change in my appearance. She had known my purpose before I had, and I'd always imagined she knew the outcome. Even so, did she know Josette was her mother? I doubted it. I squeezed Izak's hand, feeling the bones crunching below the skin.

"Don't tell her," I whispered. "Not now."

He didn't register the pain, but he did give me a quick nod.

"We'll be back soon," I said, letting go of Izak's hand and heading for the exit.

"Be safe, brother," Sarah said. She gave me a weak smile, flicked her eyes at Izak, and returned to comforting Trish.

My initial plan was to make my way out of the sewers and back up into the city, crossing over to thirty-fourth and seventh at ground level. Izak had a different idea. I had grabbed onto one of the ladders leading to the surface, but he put his hand on my shoulder again and squeezed it. When I looked at him, he pointed up at the manhole cover and put his hands over his eyes, and then motioned down the tunnel.

"You know another way?" I asked.

He nodded.

I followed.

Izak's route quickly got me lost. The demon led me through a mazelike traversal of twists and turns, through knee-deep wastewater and large brick connection tunnels that were part of the New York underground's original construction. The sheer size of the system was something residents took for granted every day, except when heavy rains would back up the city's pumps and cause sewage to spill into the surrounding rivers. I didn't take it for granted, but I did lament the fact that if whoever had taken Kelsie had brought her down here she would be difficult to find. This was the perfect hiding place for demon or human, a seemingly endless conglomerate of tunnels, tubes, pipes, passageways and doorways, with lots of random egress points to the city above.

I kept my senses focused around us, not wanting to be surprised by anything we might come across. I knew there were nightstalkers down here. I had already destroyed a group that had gotten too aggressive in their abductions and had been pulling people from the platforms while they

29

waited to board the trains. It seemed Izak knew how to get around them, because the trek was uneventful.

We stopped at a heavy metal door. Izak looked at me and pointed at it, making a pulling motion. I could feel the vibration of the subway rattling the narrow, pipe filled corridor we were standing in. The demon stepped aside so I could squeeze by him to get to the door. I grabbed the handle and pulled. The door wasn't going anywhere without some help.

I focused on the hinges, willing the rust that had stuck the door to accelerate in its aging, pushing it past its corrosive half-life and crumbling it to dust. The rumble was growing, and I could hear the train approaching on the other side of the door. I pulled it open.

We were greeted with a blast of hot air, and then the echoing pulse of the subway's horn blasted into the tunnel. I held my arm out to keep Izak from coming through, pressing myself back while the train rocketed past. I stepped out and jumped onto the tracks behind it, watching it roll off into the tunnel ahead. Izak landed beside me and pointed again. We were almost there.

Penn Station was only a quarter mile further up, and we reached it without incident. I leaped smoothly from the tracks to the raised platform, careful not to be noticed by the people waiting for their rides. Izak pulled himself up beside me. If anyone noticed him, I doubted they cared.

"Trish said they were up in the concourse," I said. "I'll..." I stopped talking and focused. I could See a Divine nearby. Obi. "Wait here," I said to Izak.

He shook his head, but the look I gave him in return settled it. I glamoured myself as a businessman and walked briskly to the other end of the platform. Obi was here, and he was in the tunnels. It wasn't a good sign.

Once I reached the opposite end, I floated back down onto the tracks and followed my nose through the darkness. I could smell the former marine now, somewhere in the tunnels ahead. He wasn't alone.

"How did you know?" the voice asked. It was deep and masculine.

"Yeah, sarge," agreed another. "It's not like we're in a random tunnel in the New York City subway or somethin'."

I followed the source of the voices, off the tracks and through another access tunnel, then down a secondary ladder and back into the sewer. Obi and the two patrolmen were just around the corner. Between my Divine Sight and Ulnyx's sense of smell, I had a good idea of the scene. My heart dropped a little. He was kneeling over a dead body - a child's body.

"Just a gut feeling," Obi said.

Obi had been my first real ally, and despite our estrangement he was the one person I still had complete faith in. After the events at the Statue, he had decided to fight for mankind by getting back into uniform – this time as a police detective. We had gotten into a big fight about his role as one of mine, his pledge to help me keep the balance, and my need to take both sides. He wanted to help people, do good for them, balance be damned. I had been angry, still reeling from Rebecca and Josette, and had said a lot of things I shouldn't have.

We continued to collide on occasion, when he would find his way into my world in pursuit of a vampire or other lesser demon. I had helped him out a couple of times, and he had returned the favor, but it was purely professional. I had dropped my anger a long time ago when the rest of my feelings had faded. This one was going to be professional too.

"Do me a favor guys," Obi said. "Head up to the concourse and radio in, get the coroner down here. Also, get Yenys on the line and have her team come work the forensics."

"Yes sir," one of them replied. I ducked into darkness when their flashlight beams turned, then watched them exit out of the tunnel.

"Landon," Obi said. "What brings you down here?"

I stepped out of the shadows and around the corner. My eyes fell right onto the body. It was Kelsie. I felt the anger start to build, then fade. I looked up at Obi.

He was a plainclothes detective, so he was wearing a pair of navy slacks and a navy blazer over a simple white button down. His pumped up form was trying to press its way out of the suit, and he looked younger than the last time I had seen him. He turned his flashlight, bathing me in the glow.

"You knew her?" he asked.

I nodded. "Kelsie Peterson," I said. "She lives... used to live with Sarah. She asked me to come and find her."

He looked back down at the body. "Well," he said sadly. "You found her."

"This wasn't my fault," I said. I knew what he was getting at. "Nobody could have known that I know her."

"She's been drained, man," he said. He reached down and turned her head so I could see the bite mark. "Vampire."

"That doesn't mean it had to do with me. She's a vagrant. That makes her a prime target."

He shrugged. "Either way, she's dead. The question is, why would a vampire go after an Awake girl, and how did he grab her without being noticed?"

He was right. The numbers didn't add up. "I don't like the sound of that," I said. "How did you know she was down here?"

"Her mother reported her missing," he replied. "She was taken from the Penn Station concourse and nobody saw anything. Where else would I look?"

"It's the same as the others?" I asked. The news reports I had been following wouldn't have mentioned vampire feeding as the cause of death. According to Obi, mortals couldn't see the bite marks, and they didn't seem to think anything was awry with the tremendous loss of blood.

He got to his feet and walked over. "Yeah, six other girls killed by a vampire. It's the same em-oh, different location. I've been keeping an eye on freenet. There's no chatter about this at all. Usually if a vamp is going around draining kids, they're selling the blood for a nice profit."

"So whoever the killer is, he's likely just your run of the mill psychotic demon."

"Right," Obi said. "I've got no leads, man. Not a single fiber to give me even the smallest clue about the perp."

I looked down at Kelsie again. She was too young for this. "I'm on the job," I said.

"You should have been on the job two weeks ago," Obi muttered.

I didn't respond to the dig. "I'll have to go and tell her mother," I said. "I'll have her meet you at the morgue. We should work together on this one."

Obi thought about it for a minute. "Alright, man," he agreed. "You carrying a cell these days?"

I had tried not to, but it did have its uses, even for the Divine. I took it out of my coat pocket. Obi snatched it and began keying in his contact info. I was watching his fingers slide across the keys when I caught my first scent of the demons headed towards us.

"We've got incoming," I said to Obi.

He handed me back the phone, and then reached down and drew the gun from his belt. He was probably the only guy on the force who carried a Desert Eagle.

"I've got silver," he replied.

I turned and looked down the tunnel towards the smell - nightstalkers, a lot of them. "Eighteen," I said. "Nightstalkers."

Obi groaned. "Eighteen?" he asked. "I've never heard of such a large group."

I hadn't either, and I didn't like it. Nightstalkers hunted in groups, but they also kept their packs small so they could survive without attracting too much attention. Four to six was average. Eight to ten was a larger family. Eighteen was unheard of.

They sounded like a subway train, headed towards us at a full run. I could see them through the darkness as they entered our tunnel, a mass of pale flesh in ragged, stolen clothes flowing like a corroded river. A booming echo followed, and the lead demon fell forward to be stomped by the group behind it. Three more shots, and three more demons collapsed.

I took a deep breath and reached for Ulnyx's power, weaving it into my own and feeling myself go through the change. I growled deeply and dashed forward, my powerful limbs carrying me to the nightstalkers in ten strides. I ripped into them with razor claws, scattering the group at the same time I decapitated the unlucky one who didn't move away in time. They regrouped quickly, the whole mass of demons leaping on top of me, pulling me down. I could feel their teeth biting into my flesh, and their hands ripping at me. I heard more gunfire and felt a few of the nightstalkers fall away, but the silver wouldn't hold them long.

"Stay back," I shouted to Obi, my voice like gravel in the Great Were's natural form. My body was being ravaged, but I was so accustomed to the defilement that I hardly felt it. I let the weight of the nightstalkers ground me while I changed back to my human form. I always focused more effectively without the demon's power muddying the waters.

I took a deep, calm breath and focused, pressing my hand down on the cold stone floor of the tunnel. It began to vibrate, gently at first, but it became a violent earthquake in no time, shaking the ground below the demons and I. The ride didn't have much effect on their attack, but that wasn't why I had created the shockwaves.

Instead, I focused on the kinetic energy they were producing, pulling it into me, holding it around myself like an invisible singularity. I pulled it tighter and tighter, and as I felt the first hand grab my vulnerable neck, I released it. The energy crashed into the nightstalkers, throwing them away from me, slamming them into the sides of the tunnel or in both directions down the tube.

I rose to my feet as my body knitted itself back together and then ran towards three that had been thrown down the tunnel. They were stunned, and it made it easy to wrap my arms around their necks and rip off their heads.

Once that was done, I turned back around to check on Obi. He had pulled a blessed knife from somewhere on his body and was making quick work of the two nightstalkers that had been thrown his way. Divide and conquer, except the ones that had eaten the walls were recovering. I focused on my legs and threw myself forward, covering thirty feet in one powerful leap, landing just short of the former marine.

"There's no point in sticking around to finish them," I said. "They won't follow us out of the tunnels."

"Back this way," Obi said. "I have to make sure my guys don't come back down here."

I raced over to where Kelsie's body was lying and gently scooped it up into my arms. She had been such a pretty little girl. I wasn't eager to share the news with Trish or Sarah. I looked back at the nightstalkers. They had regrouped, but they weren't giving chase. They just stood there watching us leave.

"Something's wrong," I said, motioning back towards them with my head. "Why are they giving up?"

I hadn't been paying attention. I turned my head back and saw Izak standing right in front of us, his eyes trained on Kelsie, his expression pure rage. He looked up at me, and I could see the fires of his anger dancing in his eyes. I was taken by the threat of his unspoken power, sizzling in the air around him.

Obi had his gun on the demon in a blink, only to have it ripped away by an unseen force. Izak turned it towards him, cocking the trigger with an invisible hand.

"Izak," I shouted. "No."

The demon looked at me, and the gun clattered on the stone. Obi bent down and picked it up, keeping his eyes trained on the fiend.

"Why don't you ever warn me about the company you keep?" Obi cried.

I didn't pay him any mind. I felt a desperate pressure on my soul.

"*Sarah*," I said. Something was definitely wrong.

"*Landon, help me.*" She was scared and in pain. A moment later she was gone.

CHAPTER 4

"Sarah," I shouted. The anger was real. I could feel the heat of it rising from my chest. I could see it echoed in Izak's expression. "Goddamn it," I yelled as loud as I could, the epithet echoing off the walls. I focused on the rock above us, pulling at the stone in desperation. I needed to get to the surface, to get back to Sarah. The earth crumbled beneath my will, dropping to the floor in huge clumps.

"Landon," Obi said, grabbing me and throwing me to the ground. It broke my focus. "You're going to kill us all, man. Tell me what the hell is going on and I'll help you."

"Sarah," I said again. "Something's happened. I need to get to her."

"Come on," he said, grabbing my arm and pulling me up. He led me out of the tunnel, back to the subway platform and up onto the concourse. His patrolmen were there, and he ordered them to keep the civilians out of the tunnel, that a collapse had ruined the crime scene. They looked at me, but all they saw was a homeless man carrying a duffel.

His car was parked right outside the 34th Street entrance. We jumped in and he hit the gas, his siren blaring a path in the otherwise unforgiving crush of traffic. I directed him through the city streets, the car careening in a controlled wildness as he raced along.

I jumped out of the car before Obi could slam it to a stop, had the manhole cover thrown aside, and was underground before he got out of the door. I could sense him following behind, but I didn't care. I had promised to protect Sarah, and now something had happened and I wasn't there. I focused, powering my legs, propelling myself forward. I left Izak and Obi way behind.

Eight minutes. That's how long it had taken me to get from Penn to Sarah's shanty town. It was eight minutes too late. The tents, tarps, cardboard, and plastic had been shredded and thrown around the cavernous room as though a tornado had somehow managed to form below the surface. Cookware, electronics, clothing; all of the Awake resident's worldly possessions lay scattered on the cement. The vagrants themselves hadn't fared much better. The bodies that hadn't been taken were tossed around like discarded old dolls, fresh blood still pooling around them, leaking from gaping wounds and missing appendages.

In the center of the carnage was Sarah's tent. It was the only thing still standing, pristine and innocent, as if it were immune to the reality of the world outside of it. The flap of the tent was drawn closed, and I didn't sense anything inside. Whatever had done this, it was gone.

"Sarah," I shouted. I knew it was useless, but I did it anyway. If she were okay, she would have kept the connection. I looked at the tent with apprehension. I had to know, but I didn't want to.

Pounding feet alerted me that Obi and Izak had finally caught up.

They came to a quick stop behind me, Izak falling to his knees and doubling over with his hands over his face.

"Oh my god," Obi said, his breath catching.

"If it was, I'm going to kill Him," I said. So many feelings bubbling up, strange sensations that I had lost the understanding for. It was violent, calm, and cold. The tent. I started walking towards it. Obi scrambled to catch up, leaving Izak on the ground in despair.

The smell of death inside the tent was unmistakable, and it grew stronger as I approached. One body, a woman. There was another smell too, Sarah's perfume. She had started wearing it a few months ago in an effort to get the attention of a boy in school. Her efforts had gone unrewarded, victim to another immature male that could admire her physical endowments, but couldn't overlook her physical shortcomings.

I stopped at the flap of the tent and glanced over at Obi. My face must have been betraying my feelings.

"I can look for you," he said. Despite our disagreements, he was still there when I needed him.

"No," I said. "Stay out here."

I took a deep breath and focused, pushing the nylon aside without touching it. The inside of the tent was dark, but I could see it clearly in black and white. My eyes traced along the floor, hesitant to make contact with the body that I knew was there. When they did, I breathed out heavily.

It was Trish.

I only had a second to feel the relief. My Sight exploded with heat and pressure, and the back corner lit up in a circle of flame. A Hell rift. I didn't have time to react before I was thrown backwards out the tent by an unseen force. I slammed to the ground twenty feet away, sliding along the blood slicked floor.

I saw Obi turn to watch my flight, and then he dove towards the side of the tent just in time to avoid the attention of the demon that burst out of it. It was a monster I had never seen before, a mass of liquid darkness that undulated and flowed like oil around a black, skeletal face. The undulations molded and changed as it moved, becoming a foot, an arm, a claw, pushing off the floor at an impossible speed, propelling it towards me.

I focused, making myself stronger, spun my body and launched myself off the floor towards the creature, the force of the maneuver pressing the cement down into the earth. I hurtled towards the demon like a bullet, holding out my hand to grab onto the face. Its body changed in response, moving aside, the head disappearing behind the liquid flow. It slammed me with a monstrous fist as I barreled by, changing my direction and sending me crunching into the wall. Pain blossomed through dozens of broken bones, and I sucked in a weak breath. I focused again, knitting myself back together with as much speed as I was able.

The demon was flowing towards me, closing the distance in no time. I rolled away just in time to avoid a blade that formed in its chest and stabbed out at me. Its face surfaced from the mass and leered, enjoying my mad scramble.

Gunshots echoed through the room, passing harmlessly through the demon to put deep chips in the wall behind us. The creature turned its head to look at Obi, then dismissed him. It rounded on me and lashed out with multiple new appendages. I avoided the blade, but a clawed hand scraped across my chest, ripping open my skin. I grunted in pain and backed away from the demon.

I heard a soft rustle, and then Izak was between the demon and I, a sword in his hand, lit up in hellfire. He had shed the heavy coats, revealing a perfectly chiseled upper body coated in demonic runes. The wraith stabbed out at him with multiple blades, but the fiend was faster than I had realized. He circled around the blades, bringing his sword down on one of the appendages. The hellfire burned right through it, and the dismembered end vanished in a haze of black smoke.

The monster recoiled, and then expanded and rose up, liquid legs stretching to allow it to tower over us. Its face rose to the surface and howled, sharp edges sprouting along its entire length. Izak stabbed his sword into the cement and dropped into a prayer squat, putting his hands together. He threw them wide as the demon collapsed onto us, the air above us exploding in flame. The creature shrieked and fell back, the edges of it singed and smoking.

Izak looked back at me with death in his eyes, and pointed over at Sarah's tent. I nodded, focusing my will on the nylon structure and hurling it at the black mass. The demon was recovering, and a pointed limb launched towards Izak like a harpoon. The fiend saw it coming and smacked it away with his sword. A moment later the tent slammed into the hellspawn, covering it in nylon, wrapping it up like a net. Izak looked at me.

"Do it," I said.

He put his hands together again, then spread them out and forward toward the tent. The demon was struggling below it, and tendrils of black were beginning to snake out from underneath. It was too late. The hellfire lit up the nylon in an instant, giving the creature little time to scream before enveloping it as well.

Izak walked over to the smoldering pile of ash that was left behind, and then knelt down and spit on it. I stood there, stunned. I knew so little about the demon that had raised Sarah. I had always imagined he was a minor fiend, a standard underling to a much more powerful archfiend. I should have known better; Josette's brother hadn't cut out his tongue for nothing. Still, the display of power had been shocking. Reyzl had exhibited only a fraction of the control over hellfire that Izak had, and he had done his fair share of damage to me with it.

After being burned by the stuff, I had learned as much about it as I could. It was pulled into the mortal world directly from the fires of Hell, not completely unlike the way angels were able to conjure their swords. It was difficult to create, difficult to control, and extremely powerful; not something that could be mastered by any old hellspawn. I could heal from it, but not quickly, and not without staying completely motionless and focusing on the affected area. Generating the holy water had been a one-off, a gift from Josette. I had never been able to do it again.

"What the heck was that thing?" Obi asked. He had been the odd man out in the dance, but now he rushed over to stand with me.

"I don't know," I said. "I've never seen anything like it."

His face darkened and he looked over to where the tent used to be. "Sarah?"

I shook my head. "She wasn't in there."

Izak had gotten back to his feet, and he walked over to where we were standing. His eyes still blazed red, and his bare chest was coated in a sheen of sweat. As soon as he reached us, he held out his arm, offering me his sword.

"Keep it," I said. "Gervais?"

The demon looked around the room, taking in the destruction. He shrugged.

Someone had taken Sarah, and not only that had left a surprise for whomever returned to find her gone. Josette's brother had every motive in the world to re-abduct his daughter, and to spring something nasty on his former minion. He also would have known the fiend's power, and what type of creature he would have to summon to be a match for him.

"Landon?" Obi reached out and put his hand on my shoulder.

My hand snapped up and I pulled it away, the force causing the former marine to take a few steps back. My mind echoed with anger and rage, so unfamiliar and yet coming on so strong. I wanted to hurt, to kill. I closed my eyes and took a deep breath, trying to steady myself.

"Hey, man," Obi said. "I'm sorry."

I opened my eyes and looked at him. It was like seeing him for the first time in years. He didn't look a day older than he had when I had pushed some of my power into him, giving him some of the strength of the Divine. He had aged though, I could see it in his eyes.

"No," I said. "I'm sorry. This isn't your fault. I appreciate you getting involved like this, but I think you may be in over your head."

He replied with a huge smile. "Man, when am I not in over my head? At least when you're concerned. We might not always see eye to eye, but that's not just a human quality, that's a life quality. It doesn't mean I'm not with you when the crap hits the fan."

"I appreciate that, but I have a feeling the crap hasn't even hit the fan yet," I said. "If Gervais found Sarah and made his move to reclaim her, he has to have plans for her. Archfiends are always scheming, but when they put the wheels in motion... that isn't good for anybody."

"I'm with you on that one. Look, you have my cell right?" I nodded. "I've got to call this in, get these bodies identified. People might have thought they were crazy, but they still had families, and maybe somebody has missed them."

"What are you going to tell them?" I asked.

He looked around, his face blanching at the scene. "Gas leak, explosion, whatever I tell them is what they'll believe. The mojo is funny that way. The good news, if you can call it that, is a bunch of vagrants die like this, we'll identify the bodies, and we'll contact next of kin, but that'll probably be the end of it. The media isn't interested in stuff like this, so it should be easy enough to make it go away."

"Maybe for them," I replied. Sarah was gone. I needed to get her back. "There's a USB drive at my place at the Belmont. It's got a lot of transaction data on it, money in and out. I think the numbers make a pattern, and the pattern makes a message. If you want to help me, look at the data and see what you can find. Just wedge the door again when you leave."

Obi pursed his lips, considering my request. I knew he would do it.

Like he had said, when times got rough he was nothing if not loyal. "Got it," he said. "What are you going to do?"

I looked over at Izak. "I've got to get Sarah back before Gervais can do whatever it is he aims to do with her. My fiend and I are going to take a trip to the City of Light."

CHAPTER 5

I didn't waste any time getting topside, running back through the tunnels and up through the manhole, onto the street next to Obi's squad car. Izak was following behind me, a little bit further back because he had stopped to grab his shirt and coats. As soon as I reached the surface I pulled the smartphone from my pocket and swiped over to my contact list. I scrolled down to Rachel's name and hit the call icon.

It rang six times before her answering service picked up. "Rachel," I said, after the beep, "can you arrange two tickets from JFK to Paris, France for me, and call me back with the flight number?" I hung up.

Izak pulled himself to the surface, one hand still gripping the sword. He had only put one of his grimy down jackets back on, and had lost the snow cap. He was going to have to do better than that.

"Izak," I said. "Homeless time is over. I can't take you on an airplane like that." I could have glamoured him to the mortals, but it was going to be tricky enough to get through the airport without having to worry about that detail. Not when the demon could take care of it himself.

Izak grinned at me. His eyes danced with fire, and his appearance shifted like sand until the person standing in front of me no longer resembled the meek vagrant the fiend had been hiding behind. Instead, I was confronted with a middle-aged, wealthy playboy, with slicked back salt-and-pepper hair and a neatly trimmed mustache and beard. He was dressed in a fine Italian suit under a long wool trench, which he used to hide his blade.

"Better," I said, focusing and changing my own dress to better match the fiend's. It was like a bizarro Rain Man. I pointed to Obi's car. "Let's go."

I had just slid in behind the wheel when Obi climbed up out of the sewer. When he saw Izak sitting shotgun, his face fell.

"Come on, man," he cried, staring at us.

"It'll be at JFK," I shouted. "Tell them it was stolen."

He shook his head. "It is stolen," he shouted back. "Have you ever even driven before?"

"I'll be careful," I replied, swinging the shifter to drive and pulling away a little bit roughly. Growing up in the city, I hadn't had much need to drive, but I had played games at the local bowling alley. How different could it be?

I watched Obi in the rearview mirror as he pulled out his portable radio and called for backup. I knew he wouldn't mention his missing car until later.

"How could Gervais have found her?" I asked Izak while we drove. He shook his head in reply.

48

She had been safe because she believed she was safe. She had insisted she would be able to sense her father coming from miles away, and would be able to either hide or summon me way before he could ever snatch her. I had believed her, I had no reason not to; not after the other things I had seen her do. But something had changed. There was a vampire running around killing children, a vampire who had taken an Awake child, and they had never known he was there. A vampire that didn't give off a Divine signature. I knew the trick, but it couldn't be done without having access to both angel and demon sources of power. Or could it?

What if the vampire was no vampire at all? It wouldn't be hard for a demon like Gervais to make it look like a vamp had done the dirty work. Or, he could have Commanded it. I slammed my fist on the steering wheel of the car in frustration, accidentally blaring the horn. I waved off the driver in front of me when he flipped me the bird.

The traffic was heavy through the midtown tunnel, and never really opened up as we headed along the Long Island Expressway. I had the urge to hit the sirens and lights more than once, but I didn't want to draw extra attention to the borrowed car. Instead, I looked up at the overcast sky, jealous of the angels one more time for their ability to get from place to place without having to deal with such pedestrian things as traffic. Even the demons had me beat there, with their ability to create and share transport rifts to locations around the world. They hoarded the locations of the rifts like diamonds, and no amount of negotiation or torture had gotten me any closer to mapping them. There was one under the Statue, but it was useless without knowing a connecting address, and Charis had destroyed the one on her end sometime after I had met her.

So I was left on the ground, slogging along like a mortal. Dante had said I couldn't fly, but I wasn't so sure. The problem was that it would draw an exponential sum of energy, and I couldn't be assured that the flux wouldn't have catastrophic consequences. Not to mention, I would likely burn out and drop from the sky in a coma, with no assurances that I would ever wake up. It was sobering to think about the chaos I could potentially create if I chose to, albeit at my own expense.

We had crossed the Grand Central and were doing twenty on the Van Wyck when my cell rang. I pulled it out of my pocket without my hands and air-tapped the pickup icon.

"Rachel," I said. "What's the flight?"

She sighed loudly on the other end of the phone. "I don't know why I do these things for you, Landon," she said.

"It's about Sarah," I said. I had never told her who or what Sarah was, only that she was important to me. That was all she needed to hear.

"Air France 7760," she said. "It leaves in four hours. Are you going to make it?"

Even at this pace, we would be at the airport in less than an hour. "We'll make it."

There was a moment of silence as Rachel waited for me to elaborate. When I didn't she spoke again. "Well, I hope everything works out," she said. "I'm not going to get in trouble over this, am I?"

"If everything works out, you'll be in better standing," I replied. I couldn't imagine Heaven not applauding her for helping me take out another archfiend.

"Okay then. Good luck." The phone clicked as she hung up.

"Thank you," I said, a little too late.

I left the car stopped in the center of an aisle in the long term parking garage, and Izak and I made our way to terminal One. It was going to be a little suspicious for the two of us to be taking an international flight without any luggage, so I created a small fire under the wheels of a parked taxi and made off with a couple of suitcases while the mortals around us were distracted by it. Izak gave me a toothy grin in response to the maneuver, and we headed to the desk better equipped to travel.

"Can I help you sirs?" Monique asked. She was a perky older woman who looked like she was overmatched by most of the luggage that she had to toss onto the belt behind her. Her name badge was pinned neatly to her breast.

"Yes," I said. "I believe my secretary called in a reservation for my associate and I on Flight 7760 to Paris. The name is Joshua Meyer." Rachel had given me the moniker the first time I had left the country.

Her fingers clacked along her keyboard. "Ah yes, here we are. Two first class tickets, Mr. Meyer and Mr. Smith. I'll just need to see each of you gentleman's passports, and then I can take your luggage and you can head off to gate D7."

I reached into my pocket and pulled out a plain piece of printer paper, which I tore in half and handed to Monique. She never saw me tear it, she only saw two passports open to the picture. She took each and ran them under the scanner, verifying the identities. Getting into that database had been an awful month of social engineering and brute force hacking, but I had a nice supply of fake passport information to make use of as a reward.

"We're all set," Monique said, handing me back the paper and struggling to move the luggage onto the belt.

"They should have someone do that for you," I said.

"It's no problem," she replied, her breathing heavy. "It keeps me in shape. You two gentlemen have a great flight."

"We will," I said.

Airport security for mortals was a general nightmare, with long lines, crying children, juggling bags and coats and shoes and being exposed to questionable levels of radiation; not to mention the full body scanners. I hadn't flown much while I was mortal. I had flown a lot as a Divine. Getting past the TSA was as simple as walking right by, but that didn't mean that the airport was without its complications. There would be other Divine here, watching out for incoming mortal agents, keeping tabs on the general populace, and just waiting to be able to report that they saw me passing through. If I was lucky, they would leave me to my business and spy from the shadows.

I knew having Izak along was going to make things more complicated. No sooner had we walked unheeded past the metal detectors and backscatter machines than I sensed a pair of angels among the crowds waiting at the end of the terminal. They wouldn't have been able to recognize me from that distance, but they did notice Izak, and were moving towards us before we could take a dozen steps.

"Just let me handle this," I said to Izak. He held his left hand out and waved me forward in reply, and then stopped walking alongside me.

The angels were still out of view when I got my first smell of them.

I knew one of them, and I knew he was no threat. Thomas. I stopped walking and motioned Izak to join me to wait for their approach.

The other angel was unfamiliar, a younger female with short spiked golden hair and a seraph runed ring through her nose. They both looked like they were better equipped for a stage show at Lollapalooza than an airport. When Thomas' companion saw Izak she reached back under her long leather coat to grab her sword. Thomas placed his hand gently on her forearm to stop her, and then looked at me and smiled.

"Greetings, fellow," he said, clapping me on the shoulder as soon as he was close enough to reach me.

"Careful, Thomas," I said. "The balance is even. You can get in a lot of trouble for fraternizing."

He laughed. "I've been in plenty of trouble since I met you," he replied. "Although the powers that be have been pleased with the results of our arrangement. You kept your word to restore the balance, and now we can at least breathe a little easier while we figure out how to get you out of the picture."

I appreciated the young angel's candidness. I had no doubt that Heaven was working non-stop to figure out how to get me someplace where they could put me out of commission. The problem for the good guys was that they had to do it within their moral code. When you couldn't resort to trickery and lies, it made for a tough assignment.

"Leave me to the demons," I said. "That's your best chance."

He sighed. "Except if we focus too much on good works and killing demons, you come around and set us back again."

"You heard about Silas?" I asked.

He nodded. "I've prayed to stay above getting angry for the things you do. Sometimes you don't make it easy."

I wasn't going to apologize. I had my reasons. I glanced over at the other angel. She was deferential to her elder, but it was clear she didn't approve of the conversation.

"Who's your new partner?" I asked.

"Initiate Melody. We thought airport duty would help her break in slowly. I didn't imagine we'd be running into you, although it was your companion who piqued my interest." Thomas looked over at Izak now, trying to gauge the demon's importance.

"Trust me when I tell you that you'll need a lot more backup to handle this one," I said. "In any case, he's helping me out with a complication that I need to clear up."

"Does the fiend speak for himself?" Melody asked, opening her mouth at last. Her name befitted her voice, a sweet tone with proper British inflection.

"Melody," Thomas said. "Mind yourself."

Her nostrils flared, her face reddening. "We have explicit orders not to let any demons out of the airport. Nobody said 'except if they're accompanied by the bleedin' diuscrucis'."

"Melody," Thomas said softly. "Our orders did not need to specify what we should do if Landon came through. If you want to survive, you *will* mind yourself."

I don't know if it was youthful exuberance, loyal zealotry, or plain stupidity that led Melody to pull her sword and try to stab Izak with it. The whole motion happened in the smallest fraction of a second, an impressive move for such a green seraph.

She needn't have bothered. The tip of the blade had only begun to emerge from the front of her coat when Izak stepped nonchalantly to the side, reaching down and putting his hand on the seraph's arm as the sword whistled through the unoccupied space. Her hand spasmed open at the touch and the blade clattered to the ground. Melody shifted her eyes and looked at Izak in fear, the rest of her body paralyzed.

"Izak," I said in warning. The demon just stood there with a light grip on her wrist. All he would have to do is run a fingernail through her flesh and his poison could begin to seep in. It would serve her right for being so impetuous, but it would also force Thomas to act.

"Melody," Thomas said, his displeasure obvious. "You have been instructed in the basis of our laws. This type of rash violence is forbidden, and giving in to such impulses could lead you down a very dark path that you wouldn't wish to travel. Furthermore, you would serve yourself and our Lord well to heed my warnings, and take advantage of my experience. Look at the back of the fiend's hand."

Melody's eyes shifted down, her pupils dilating when she saw the dark etchings of the runes beginning from the back of Izak's hands. No minor fiend would ever have knowledge of such things. It was a testament to the demon's power.

"You can let her go now," I said.

Izak bore his eyes into Melody's for a few seconds, sending a warning about further aggression, and then released her wrist. Able to move again, the seraph took a few steps back and put her hand to her face to cover her tears.

"We have a plane to catch," I said to Thomas, pulling Melody's blade up to my hand and glamouring it as a guitar case. "It was good to see you again."

I started walking around the angels, but when I looked at Melody I felt a sudden, unbidden twinge of guilt. I stood in front of her until she looked up at me.

"Your time will come Initiate," I said, the words familiar on my tongue but foreign in my mind. "Remember that your greatest strength comes not from your skill, but from your faith."

Somehow, the words brought her comfort, but they completely sapped me of mine.

"*Josette*," I said, calling out to her in my soul. I could feel her spirit, her warmth, but it was gone as quickly as it had arrived. I stepped around Melody and continued towards the terminal, my entire being weighed down by the experience.

When we got to the gate, I found a couple of empty seats in the corner by the window and led Izak over to them to wait. The demon eschewed the chairs for the floor in front of the window, taking off his suit coat, bunching it in a ball, and using it as a pillow to rest his head against. He glanced over at me one last time, and then closed his eyes and went to sleep.

The action confirmed everything I already suspected about our alliance. Demons didn't need to sleep any more than I did, so the move was an obvious dismissal. Izak was interested in Sarah, nothing more. The feeling was mutual.

I closed my eyes and took a couple of deep breaths, feeling the river of power feeding into my soul. I tracked it back to its source, my Source, and watched as the mortal world began to dematerialize around me. In moments it was a frozen haze, and then it was gone. I was sitting in the airport again, but my soul was firmly planted in Purgatory.

A wave of my hand, and the glass of the terminal vanished. I stood and ran towards it, kicking off at the last instant and launching into the air. I couldn't fly in the mortal world, but things were different here.

There was no real need to fly at all, I could have brought myself to my destination with nothing more than a thought, but I had found that maintaining a relative amount of consistency between the worlds was useful for normalizing the feedback of the experience to my physical mind. In the early days after Rebecca had vanished I had visited Purgatory often, exploring my newfound power and testing my limits. I had made and remade the world so many times, and when I had returned to my body I had found my power reduced. Like everything else, it was a balance.

I found Dante outside of his eleventh century manse, tending to his garden. He was kneeling over a smaller outcropping of roses, a simple white linen robe resting over his shoulders, with lines of dirt stains slicking down his back where he would wipe his hands. His balding head was shiny under the sun, and a layer of perspiration trickled down through the wafts of hair that ringed his temple. He was picking delicately at the rose bushes, pruning with precision and adoration.

"Biongiorno signore," I said, landing behind him without a sound.

"Ahh, biongiorno Landon," he replied, his voice relaxed. I had never been able to sneak up on him, or surprise him. "It is quite a fine day for tending the garden, wouldn't you say?"

"Gervais," I said.

Dante dropped the shears and stood, his robe changing to a clean, rich red velvet as he turned. "The archfiend?" he asked.

"Yes. I'm on my way to Paris to kill him."

I had never mentioned Sarah to Dante. While I had more trust for the Lord of Purgatory than I did for most, it didn't extend deep enough for me to believe the poet wouldn't have his own designs for a true diuscrucis. Sarah's current life was mortal, and she deserved a chance to live as close to being one as she could.

"Why Gervais? Why now? Come, walk with me." Dante put his hand on my shoulder and guided me away from the rose bushes, back up towards his home. A servant waited there, holding a tray with two glasses on it.

"I told you about the children being killed in New York," I said.

"Yes, of course. A serial killer no doubt. You said you would let the mortal law enforcement deal with it."

"A girl was killed by a vampire this morning. She and her mother were both Awake. They never sensed it coming. It turns out, the other children were killed the same way."

I watched Dante's eyes shift. He already knew about it. I locked my hand on his wrist as he grabbed for a glass of water.

"You already knew," I said, my anger growing. "Why didn't you tell me?"

One moment I was holding his wrist, the next I wasn't. He slipped my grasp with no effort and picked up his water, taking a few swallows.

"Tell you what, signore?" he asked. "That a vampire was killing children? How is that so different to you from a mortal killing children? Such a thing has little meaning on the balance, and the angels will track the demon down sooner or later, if your Obi doesn't first."

He was right, but I hated hearing it. In the beginning I had taken a hard line on certain kinds of evil, and it had been easy to justify because the balance required it. Lately, I had been too committed to my quest for answers, and too ambivalent to make it a priority. Now Sarah was gone.

"We can't wait for anyone else," I said. "If the demons have figured out how to hide themselves, we need to stop them, right now."

He turned and started walking down a cobblestone path towards a small pond. I followed next to him. "I agree, signore. So the question is, why do you think it is the Parisian archfiend? What would he have to gain by killing children in New York City?"

I wasn't about to tell Dante my real motives. "A test," I said.

He stopped and looked at me. "A test?"

"To see if I could sense him. If your goal was to get close to the diuscrucis undetected, wouldn't you test it nearby, with an increasing degree of difficulty?" Dante didn't look wholly convinced. "Besides, only an archfiend can rune and power a Hell rift, and send something truly nasty through it."

"Nasty?"

I described the creature to Dante, and the destruction that I claimed it had caused. I didn't mention Izak's role in its defeat, changing the outcome to make me look oh-so-clever. It didn't matter, it was the results that were important. In the meantime, Dante had walked to the pond and sat down along its stone banks, hiking up his robes and dipping his feet in the water.

"So you believe it was Gervais?" Dante asked. "It is possible, for only a powerful demon such as he could Command a wraith. Yet, I have two questions for you, signore. How do you know the archfiend returned to Paris, and have you considered that it was not Gervais, but the Demon Queen who is responsible?"

The questions caught me off-guard. I knew that Charis wasn't responsible, because she wasn't against me. How could she be, when she had me in the palm of her hand and let me go? But what if that had been a trick? A deception to point me in the direction she wanted me to go, so that I would be easier to manipulate? That was how demons liked to work after all, and there was no doubt that she had the ability to create such complex plots. But what could she want with Sarah, and how did she even know she existed?

"The archfiend is back in Paris," a smooth voice said from behind us. I turned to see Mr. Ross standing there, still wearing the same pinstripe suit and sunglasses that he had been sporting when we first met. "The kid is right to be concerned."

"What do you know?" I asked. I hated how he refused to use my name. I was always 'son', 'kid', or 'boy'. Dante pulled himself away from the water and stood next to me.

Mr. Ross reached into his pocket, pulling out a fine gold antique pocket watch and flipping it open. "There isn't much time," he said, reaching up to lower his sunglasses and look at me with his rich blue eyes. "Something big is going down, and you're at the center of it, son."

"Me?" No, this was about Sarah. Not me. Unless...

"A trap?" Dante asked.

Mr. Ross pushed his sunglasses back up his nose. His response was smug. "An archfiend picks a fight with you and takes off halfway around the world, hoping you'll give chase... yeah, I'd say it's a trap."

Five years, and I felt like I hadn't learned anything. It would be so easy to draw me in by taking Sarah. If Gervais knew where she was, he was sure to know about our connection, if only through observation.

"Do you know anything about demons being invisible to Divine Sight?" I asked.

Mr. Ross shrugged. "I know *you* can do it. Maybe you aren't the only one?" He turned his attention to Dante. "Should I look into it?"

Dante nodded. "Yes, thank you, Signore Ross."

He disappeared before Dante had finished speaking. I stood and stared at the spot where he had been, annoyed that he had left without telling me anything concrete about the demons' plans. The fact that I knew I was walking into a trap would have to be enough.

"Well, signore," Dante said, "I guess it is Gervais after all."

"It seems that way," I said. "See if you can find out anything more about what I may be getting myself into. I know Mr. Ross was thorough, but I want to be sure we cover all of our bases."

Dante smirked at my sarcasm. "Without Mr. Ross, you would know nothing. At least you can prepare."

"Spare me the platitudes and just do it," I replied, and then I did my own disappearing act, riding the river of power back from Purgatory to my body in meatspace.

CHAPTER 6

We boarded the plane without incident, making our way to our seats near the front of first class. I took both Izak and Melody's 'guitars' and stowed them up in the overheads, forcing the other passengers to figure out how to get their own overabundant carry-ons squeezed into the limited space. Our stewardess, Farrah, stopped by to introduce herself, and to take our drink order so she could serve us as soon as possible after takeoff. I was going to politely send her away, but Izak grabbed my arm and pulled on my coat sleeve.

"You want a drink?" I asked him. The demon nodded. I didn't see the point - I had already tried to decompress with hard liquor. It was a fruitless endeavor. "My associate would like a..whiskey, neat," I said to Farrah. Izak grinned, approving of my choice.

Farrah smiled at him, successful in her effort to hide the oddness of the encounter. "Yes, sir," she said. "I'll be able to serve as soon as we've completed our take-off procedures." She moved on to the next passenger.

"Have you ever been in an airplane before?" I asked.

Izak shook his head. He waved his arm at the interior of the plane, then swept his hand back and forth in front of his chest. No such thing as airplanes, at least in the days before he was able to travel through rifts. Based on his scars, he knew how to use transport rifts. Why hadn't he suggested one for us?

"You know how to use rifts?"

His face grew more grim, but he nodded.

"Then why are we flying?" I asked.

He grinned again, then took his hands and clamped them together. Trap.

"Good call," I said. "How old are you anyway?"

He didn't respond, but a flash of flame cascaded through his opaque eyes. It caused me to question whether trapping myself in a metal tube six miles above the ground with him was a good idea. Could I be sure he wasn't still working for Gervais? I'd seen what he'd done to the wraith. We would never be friends, but for the moment I could trust him.

The jet taxied out to the runway and launched skyward without incident. I put my head back against the soft, supple leather of the first-class seat and shut my eyes. There was no sleep there, little relaxation, and no escape from the guilt that was hounding me. Whether or not this whole thing was a plot to lure me in, Sarah being taken was my fault. Maybe if I had met her for training on time, this whole thing could have been avoided.

My eyes were still closed when Farrah returned with Izak's drink. I didn't open them to watch the exchange, but something the demon had done caused the attendant to giggle like a schoolgirl. She returned a few minutes later, and I could hear her handing him another. Maybe I was the only Divine who wasn't affected by liquor.

I opened my eyes when the 'fasten seatbelt' light dinged off. I looked over to Izak, then jerked my head back. He was staring right at me, booze on his breath and his eyes glowing like smoldering embers. Before I could focus, his right arm lashed out and his hand wrapped around the back of my head. He held me steady, forcing my eyes to lock onto his. I found my focus, felt the pull of my power, but held up in taking action. I felt something else, a warmth that calmed me in an instant. My vision began to fade, the interior of the airliner vanishing into the black void, my self being pulled into Izak's dark soul.

The scene that greeted me when my vision returned was unexpected. A table with a white tablecloth, two candles, two plates, two glasses. Behind it, a fireplace with a small flame flickering inside, its light dancing across the stone and wood walls surrounding the room. It reminded me of a ski lodge, only there were no windows, and no doors. I felt a momentary panic when I realized my perspective was off, and then when I discovered that while I was witness to the show, I wasn't driving.

"It worked." The excited voice was deep and a little bit rough, and it echoed around the room.

My vision shifted, turning to face the new presence in the room. I knew it was Izak before I saw him. He was different here, his face and body the same, but with a confidence and handsomeness that was hiding outside of his Source. He was wearing a sharp, solid black suit with a purple shirt and a black tie. His hair was cut short, and a thin beard traced his angled face.

"Izak," Josette said. I could feel her happiness wash through me as her face split into a smile. If my body were my own, I might have cried from the joy of hearing her voice again. The demon took care of that for me.

"I've missed you," he said, stepping forward and wrapping us up in a gentle hug, the tears running off his face and onto our shoulder.

"Come now Izak. Demons don't cry," she joked.

"Only for you," he replied. "I never thought I would see you again. Gervais told me you were dead, and then I found your soul mixed with the diuscrucis. I wasn't sure you would hear me calling you." He began to grow angry when he mentioned me.

Josette put her hand to Izak's chest. "I heard you, and I am here. "she said. "Be at peace. I gave my soul to Landon of my own free will. Some things transcend loyalty to our Lords."

Izak took a deep breath. I could see the affection in his gaze. "They do," he agreed. He reached up and put his hand over hers. "I'm sure you know. Gervais found Sarah. He tricked the dius... Landon, distracted us so he could take her."

"I'm so sorry, Josette," I said in our mind. If she could hear me, there was no indication.

"We're on a plane to Paris right now," Izak said. "I would have taken Landon through the Empire Gate, but I thought it was too risky."

"You did well," she said. "Bring him through the sewers. Gervais will have his toys waiting there too, but he won't be expecting both of you."

Izak smiled, debonair and mysterious. I could picture him using that face on the stewardess, making her giggle. The smile faded.

"I hope he can handle Gervais on his own," he said.

He took his hand away from hers, reached up and unbuttoned the top two buttons on his shirt to reveal a deep scar; the archfiend's name in demonic runes.

"He branded you?" Josette asked in shock.

"I'm surprised you never guessed," Izak said. "Without the brand, I would have killed him many years ago. To think that upstart got the better of me..." His gaze was distant, and the fireplace flared in response to his angry memory. "It hasn't been for nothing. I didn't believe in redemption before I met you."

"And I believed I would die of despair before I met you," Josette said. She moved her hand up to the demon's face, pulling it down so she could kiss him on the cheek. "Please Izak, help Landon. He has a hard road ahead of him, and while his soul is strong he cannot survive alone. If he is lost, Sarah will follow."

Izak softened under her caress, returning her chaste kiss with puppy dog eyes. "You know I'll give my life to protect Sarah. I will do what I can, but he has to deal with Gervais on his own."

"Thank you," Josette said.

"Of course. Will you stay a while?" Izak's face lit up in hope.

"I cannot," Josette said. "It isn't fair to Landon to usurp his consciousness like this without his consent."

Izak looked crushed, but he acquiesced. "Know that I love you, Josette," he said. "You have brought me back from the depths of Hell, and for that I am eternally grateful."

Josette's emotions were a mixture of joy and sadness. They washed through me in a flood. "Know that I love you as well, and that I am with you, even if only in spirit."

Izak kissed Josette on the cheek, and the room began to darken. I could feel myself being pulled away, taken from the demon's Source and returned to my seat on the plane.

"*Know that I love you too, Landon,*" Josette said, her voice a powerful song in my soul. "*You have honored my request to the best of your ability, and her abduction wasn't your fault. We will get her back.*"

"We?" I asked. She knew I was there with her. My heart thudded with excitement.

"I am with you, fellow," she said. "I will always be with you."

When my vision returned, it was clouded over by the tears that had streamed from my eyes. Izak was still staring at me, his black orbs also moist with emotion.

"Another drink, Mr. Smith?" Farrah asked. She was leaning into our aisle a little bit, observing our moment with absolute professionalism.

Izak removed his hand from my head, flashed her that debonair grin, and nodded his head. I watched her walk away out of the corner of my eye. She looked back four times.

"How did you do that?" I asked in a hoarse whisper. Josette's soul, her power was part of me, and yet her voice had been more accessible to the demon. I was comforted by her parting words, otherwise I would have been in despair at the outcome.

Izak sat up straight in his seat, still looking at me. He cocked his head, confused. He hadn't expected me to come along for the ride. He reached down and picked up a crumpled napkin that was laying on the seat next to me, unfolding it to show me the precise runes burned into the center. I looked down and saw that he had positioned the drink napkins all around me.

He pointed at me, and then swept his hand horizontally and shook his head, looked only at my golden angel eye and smiled. It wasn't the same cocky smile, but a softer, gentler grin. He reached out and touched the side of my face, caressing it. I had been there, I had heard his promise. Maybe we would be friends after all.

CHAPTER 7

Izak spent the remainder of the flight tossing back the booze, but as I had expected the stuff did nothing for his physical state. It had been an awkward and overly complicated conversation of words on one side and hand gestures on the other, but in the end I had come away with the understanding that the fiend had initially used the drinking as a ruse to create some kind of summoning ritual with the napkins, and afterwards had continued drinking because he found it pleasurable. At least it had provided a diversion from the macabre thoughts that would cross my mind whenever I tried to work out what Gervais intended to do with his daughter.

Even so, the time I didn't spend conversing with Izak was filled with an anxiety and dread that had nearly consumed me by the time the plane touched down at Paris Orly Airport. It had been so long since I had felt anything at all, and now every emotion was a knife in my soul, a reminder of why I had worked so hard to suppress my mortal shortcomings in the first place. I fought to keep my mind focused on the feeling of immersive warmth that Josette had brought to me. She was sure we would get to Sarah, and I held onto that hope because my own was floundering.

It was a little after two on a windy, cold, rain-soaked morning when the plane began its final approach into Orly. Izak and I had agreed that stepping foot in the airport proper would be a bad idea, and so we unbuckled our belts, grabbed our carry-on, and started heading for the rear of the plane the moment the wheels touched the ground. We had made it back to coach, all eyes on the two morons who couldn't follow instructions, when Farrah rushed through the first-class curtain waving her arms.

"I'm sorry, sirs," she said, "but I'll need you to return to your seats until the plane has reached the terminal, and the fasten seatbelt light is turned off."

Izak turned to face her, and by her reaction I knew this time his smile was no smile at all. Her eyes grew wide in shock, and she fell backwards in fear, tripping over an outstretched foot and tumbling to the ground.

"Seriously?" I asked the fiend. The rest of the passengers began to erupt in a silent panic, suddenly fearful of who or what was walking down the aisle of the plane. I knew that feeling, because I had experienced it once myself.

We picked up the pace, and when we reached the rear exit I focused on the locking mechanisms, spinning it open untouched and flinging it out into the onrushing air. The passengers started screaming, and I turned at the sound of someone approaching. A well-muscled guy in a suit was coming for us, a stun gun held out ahead of him. It figured we were on a marshaled flight.

I grabbed Izak and threw him from the plane, deked to the right to throw the marshal off-balance, and gave him a soft shove back into the plane before he could fall out. I winked at him, and then tossed myself backwards, hanging in the air and slamming the door shut as the tail of the craft passed overhead, then slowing my momentum and putting myself down onto the tarmac. Izak was already back on his feet and headed towards me, his body regenerating from the major road rash I had given him. When he reached me, he punched me in the shoulder.

"Serves you right," I said. "We could have been a little bit more inconspicuous."

The demon shrugged.

I turned to scan the runway, looking for the nearest perimeter fence. I had only made it a quarter of the way around when my Sight exploded in heat, and a moment later the airplane we had just been riding in began screeching and whining, and then burst into flames. I spun around to catch the tail-end of the action, a tremendous hand reaching down and crushing the fuselage right before the rest of the plane vanished beneath the ignition of the remaining fuel and the explosion of the engines.

When Mr. Ross had said something big, I hadn't imagined he was being literal. The demon that had just obliterated Air France 7760 was massive in scale. Easily thirty feet tall, it looked as though it had been born of the earth itself, its face unsculpted but for a pair of beady red eyes, its body an amalgam of stone and mud, with oversized arms and hands.

It looked up from the explosion, quickly finding me standing out in the open, its reaction confirming that it was there to crush me in those massive hands. I held up the blessed sword and dropped into a fighting stance, only to be forced to leap backwards as a second giant fist pounded the earth where I had been standing.

The size of the first demon and the heat of the explosion had been effective at disrupting my senses, and I scrambled to stay ahead of the second monster's attacks even while the first headed my way. I caught a glimpse of Izak out of the corner of my eye, again crouched in concentration, pulling the hellfire through its conduit and launching it at the creature. The flames licked at the demon's skin, but it was unaffected, its hide too thick for it to be fazed.

Izak leaped out of the way of a tremendous earthen leg, and then rushed forward, stabbing his blade deep into the creature's calf. It didn't even notice, keeping its attention on me.

I heard the sirens of the incoming emergency response team as I focused, enhancing my strength and speed and using the power to keep away from the two demons while they mangled the earth and blacktop around me, trying to land the strike that would crush me into a pulp that I couldn't regenerate from. I tried a few quick stabs and cuts with my own blade, but it skipped off the hard carapace in a shower of sparks. Useless.

I focused and threw myself backwards, putting a few seconds of distance between the monsters and me. Immediately they began to lumber towards me, lined up side by side, their footfalls shaking the ground at my feet. I could see the firetrucks and ambulances behind them, the mortals scrambling to find survivors in the wreckage that I had indirectly caused. I shut down the feeling of guilt before I could fully recognize it, opting instead to reach for some of the twisted metal that had been tossed out onto the field. I yanked it towards me as hard as I could, bringing it high up and around the rear of the demons. They were almost on me now, and while I could evade them all night, I couldn't play this game forever.

I closed my eyes, the absence of the scene helping me to focus with greater precision and clarity. I could still See the demons with my senses, and I used my Sight to direct the sharp aluminum and steel, bringing it down from the heavens to pierce the creatures' small red eyes. The beasts didn't waver, their huge arms rising up to make the killing blow. That was when I vanished.

The demons stopped with their arms still raised above their heads, the confusion obvious in their frozen position. I moved out of their path and caught sight of Izak sitting on the grass, an observer to the battle. When he saw me looking he gave a short wave, then pointed back at the demons.

Having lost their quarry, the two giants began hammering the ground with abandon, their huge jackhammer arms leaving the earth around them in total devastation. That wasn't going to work either. I dropped out of stealth mode and rushed forward, leaping up and latching on to one of the monster's necks.

They tracked my movements with precision, and I let go just in time to avoid a knockout punch that would have sent me back to New York. Instead, the demon's fist smashed into his partner, the tremendous force of the blow crunching into the earth and stone, the momentum separating the head from the body. The stricken monster crashed to the ground without a sound, crumbling into a pile of rock and mud as though it had never been animated at all.

The other demon didn't seem to notice, and it continued to hunt me, bringing its massive body to bear and moving with a renewed vigor. Izak had gotten to his feet now, and I saw him out of the corner of my eye, bent over and scratching something out in the dirt. He held up his hand palm out, asking me to wait. I rolled away from a heavy strike, and then danced around to the back of the beast. I could see Izak through the demon's legs as it tried to turn on me, and a moment later had begun waving me towards him.

I scrambled back between the demon's legs, running full speed towards the fiend. I caught sight of the runes below me when I passed them over and came to a stop. The demon tried to follow and the runes Izak had made burst into flame, pulling in power from Hell itself and sending it up into the demon in an invisible stream. The monster disassembled at once, bursting forward in a flood of wet mud and stone, coating us in a layer of muck and pelting us with rock. Even before the shower had ceased, Izak grabbed me by the collar of my coat and pointed to three words he had scrawled in the ground.

Elemental. Witch. Close.

I looked up towards the terminal, nearly a mile from where we were standing. I focused my Sight and reached out, searching for a Divine signature. It was faint, but it was there. I could never have picked it up with the two elementals so close by, and the witch must have known it. She started moving away from us.

Witches and warlocks weren't straight Divine, but rather Turned who had in whatever manner gotten into the higher graces of a more powerful higher demon. On their own, they weren't much more of a threat then any other mortals who had made a deal with Hell, but once you factored in the imbued trinkets, baubles, and jewelry they were often given in exchange for whatever services had earned them the level up to begin with, they started to become a bit more of a hassle to deal with. My dealings with them had been fairly limited - it wasn't common for mortals to be able to ingratiate themselves that well with an archdemon, but judging from the fact that this one had created two earth elementals, she was important, and her master was powerful. It didn't take a genius to figure out who had sent her.

"We need to catch up to her," I said. There was a good chance she would be headed back to Gervais to announce our arrival. He might know we were coming, but I preferred to keep some element of surprise as to when.

We both took off towards the terminal at a run. I couldn't help but glance over at the emergency crews desperately fighting to find survivors in the crumpled up husk of the aircraft's fuselage. Whatever Gervais was planning, whatever was 'going down' to try to trap me, it had already gone too far.

Our pace was inhumanly fast, and we burst into the baggage loading area and through to a maintenance door in the airport proper before the witch had managed to get too far. I focused, changing our attire so that to the small crowd of people taking early morning flights we looked like French military, our swords appearing as assault rifles strapped to our backs. Not that it mattered much, most of the travelers were either glued to the window, fascinated by the carnage outside, or sitting in a chair expelling their horror with tears.

I could See her more clearly now. She was still a fair distance ahead, but we were closing the gap in a hurry. She knew we were gaining, and I could hear her shouting from the end of the long corridor. I felt a flare in my soul, and a moment later a naga burst out at us from the men's room.

One of the First Fallen's failed humanoid creations, it was eight feet tall, with the head and torso of a human and the backend of a snake, four muscular, armored arms holding four wicked looking jagged swords, and an almost handsome dark face. It snapped its sharp, poisoned tail towards my chest, but I dropped my legs out and slid along the floor, feeling the swish of air as the appendage passed within centimeters of my face.

"Izak," I said. It was all I needed to say. The fiend drew his own blade and pounced, leaving me listening to the ring of steel while I raced ahead.

There was a much larger crowd gathered outside the terminal, denied entry by the police while they tried to figure out what was happening out on the runway, unable to comprehend the massive battle that had just taken place. I could still sense the witch, but she was moving away faster, much faster. I looked around until I saw one officer helping another back to their feet. She had taken his motorcycle.

The crowds parted mindlessly around me as I raced after her, in search of a means to keep the pace. When I reached the edge of the throng, I found plenty of police cars and motorcycles lined up in the roadway. I stopped and took a deep breath. I had driven a car once, and a real motorcycle not at all, but I knew which one was faster and more maneuverable. I had played 'Hang-On' at Coney Island when I was ten. How different could it be?

I mounted the bike and tried to ignore the overwhelming number of switches and levers on the console. I found the key and turned it, bringing the bike to life, and then twisted the throttle. The machine started bucking out from under me until I focused, holding it in place until I was ready for it to move. I took another moment to test the clutch a few times, but decided to just put it in high gear and cheat my way through. I held the bike until I was sure I had enough wheel velocity, let go, and did a peel-out Evil Knievel would be proud of, taking off on my rocket.

The landscape was a blur around me, and I kept the rest of the focus that wasn't holding me on the bike holding my sense of the witch. I quickly found myself headed north towards Paris, following behind her but beginning to gain once again. As long as she was out of tricks, I would catch up well before we hit the city limits.

She wasn't out of tricks. I heard the screeching before I saw them; half a dozen small, bat-like demons with razor beaks and sharp claws. They swooped down on me en masse, buzzing my head and doing their best to knock me off the bike. I could focus on the witch and my stability, but it didn't leave me any mind-share to do anything non-physical about the creatures. Instead, I used one hand to reach behind my back and wrench the sword through my jacket and swing it out at them.

The first few slices were wild and ineffective, and my speed diminished as I put more of my energy into staying upright and gaining control of my attacks. The demons circled around me, swooping in to cut open my arms and legs with their claws, screeching in my ears, and trying to tip me off the bike. They almost did when I found myself only inches from an eighteen-wheeler and had to make an impossible left hook around the trailer before I slammed into it. The demons' amused cackling renewed my focus, and I pushed the sword backwards and through one of the hell spawn, and then swung it in an arc that caught two more.

That still left three, and my quarry was getting away. I changed tactics, letting the sword fall to the roadway and putting my attention back on the chase. I revved the bike up to full throttle and slipped across to the other side of the road into the oncoming traffic. It worked in the movies, so why not now?

Traffic was limited so early in the morning, but the oncoming obstacles still proved to be effective at forcing the demons to either drop away from the bike or get splattered on a windshield. I wound my way around the cars, using their natural tendency to subconsciously avoid me to my benefit. Soon enough I was outpacing the demons, and I was almost close enough to the witch to get her in my physical sight.

I did get her in my sight as we pulled off of E50 onto Quai de la Rapee, the highway that ran into Paris along the Seine. As I had thought, she was on a police motorcycle of her own, her long brown hair flailing out behind her as we raced along the river. She turned her head to look back at me, and I could see the fear and anger on her face. She reached down into a pouch at her side, and I knew I had to end the chase.

"Here goes nothing," I said, focusing my will, pulling at the power being fed through my soul, and leaping off the bike. I propelled myself forward as if I had been shot from a cannon, launching straight towards the witch, wrapping my arms around her as my velocity carried me past. Her bike fell out from under her and went skidding along the roadway, as did mine. A moment later I followed suit, turning myself over to protect her from the impact, wincing in pain when the cement ripped right through my clothes and dug deep into my skin. I tumbled along the ground, fighting to keep my body absorbing all of the impact, feeling bones shattering, ribs breaking. It would heal, but it still hurt.

We came to a stop a hundred yards ahead of the bikes. I heard the screaming brakes of cars behind us trying to avoid the abandoned motorcycles, coming to a stop and then slowly proceeding past as though such obstacles were ordinary. I held the witch tight while she struggled to break free of my grasp, even though every move from her petite frame was burning agony. Finally, I wrapped my hand around her throat.

"Stop squirming, or I'll pop your head like a grape," I growled.

She stopped struggling, and instead started to laugh. "Ah, Landon," she said. "You're a fool."

I saw the glint of metal, and watched her stab herself in the heart with a small blessed dagger. She turned to dust in my broken arms.

CHAPTER 8

I picked myself up, climbing slowly to my feet. My energy was sapped, and it had left me more tired than I remembered being in years. Throwing myself like that hadn't quite been flying, but it was close enough to wear me down. If the circumstances had been different, I might have been able to savor the moment, because I really needed a bed.

She had called me a fool, right before she killed herself. What kind of fool? For walking right into a trap? For wasting my energy chasing her down? For leaving Izak behind? I was certain I was a fool, because no matter how much I had tried to make myself not feel, to make myself immune, I was still part human. I could lie to myself and deny it, but in the end it didn't really make it hurt any less.

I looked around, trying to get my bearings. I could see the Arc De Triomphe lit up down the road, and even though my knowledge of Paris was limited, I knew the Arc was near the Louvre, and that meant there were bound to be hotels nearby. I spent a little energy to adjust my style to a more respectable pair of dark jeans and tweed jacket, and then reached inside my pocket to check my cell.

The hardened device had fared well, its rubberized outer shell keeping it intact. I turned it on and opened up Google Maps, and then asked it for the closest hotel. It pointed me at the Mandarin Oriental, north past the Louvre and then hang a right on the Rue de Rivoli. I took a deep breath and started walking.

Paris was an old city, and I could feel currents of Divine power coursing along the streets like a weird radioactive mist of good and evil. I reached the end of the Place du Carrousel and turned right, my sight feasting on the impressiveness of the neoclassical architecture, my Sight blurred by the thrumming of ancient power. My head was aching, and my eyes were heavy, my soul begging me for a respite amidst the chaos. It was only a few minutes walk before I could make out the sign for the Mandarin, lit up in the night. I never made it.

I didn't sense the weres coming, completely missing them in between the cover of the mist and my fatigue. I smelled them too late, and they turned the corner in front of me a dozen strong, shifted into animal form and coming on fast. I reached around to my back for my sword before remembering I had dropped it on the highway, and then crouched in a martial fighting position. I could feel Ulnyx's power flowing through my soul. I prepared myself to use it.

The weres pulled up to a stop in front of me, teeth bared but keeping their distance. Behind them, a dark silhouette of a woman made itself known, stepping out of the shadows and framing herself under the streetlights. I couldn't make out her features, but I did pick up her scent, wafting over to me in the night air. It was familiar; a flowery, earthy smell that some part of me knew. I felt a stirring in my soul, and the world around me grew fuzzy. I dropped to one knee and closed my eyes, trying to shake the oncoming memory.

I see her from the corner of my eye. Lylyx. I can smell her fear, but also her desire. She's unsure if I can win this fight, and the trepidation is an aphrodisiac. I share in the excitement, my senses heightened, my heart pounding. She's unbelievable in her tight doeskin pants and vest, her cleavage heaving beneath it. Her skin is almost as silky as her raven black hair, glistening under a layer of sweat, and it's enough to distract any man with a taste for perfection in flesh. It's worse for a were in the heat of battle.

The claws that rake across my cheek remind me that I'll only get the spoils if I'm the victor. I growl in anger, ignoring the burning pain and putting my attention back on my opponent. Tiberas, a hulking, scarred, soon to be dead werewolf, the current leader of the Mekong pack, and my brother.

The had been a time when we were close. A time when we were the only survivors of the assault on our pack, when staying together meant staying alive. Even as we had been taken in by the Mekong pack, and gone through the trials to adulthood, that closeness had remained. Maybe we would be close even now, if he had stayed in his place. Instead he had challenged and killed her father to take over the pack, and claimed her as his prize. That was the day he decided this fate. I had always intended to be alpha, and he knew it.

"You've always been a conceited welp," he says to me, his voice weak and tired.

His bait is as pathetic as he is. There's only way one to die as the head of a pack, and I'm enjoying knowing how much it must be rankling him to know he's going to be giving the entire bunch up to me.

"And you've always been a bitch," I reply. He comes at me with his claws again, but I'm only paying half as much attention to her as I was before. I catch his swipe

in my human hand, notice how much bigger it has grown than the his claw, and then twist, breaking the limb at the wrist.

I'd waited to long to put an end to him, and to claim my prize as the youngest to ever rise to leader. It had been Lylyx who had asked me to wait, and in my youth I had thought I loved her, so I waited. She was as weak as her father had been, but her body was perfect for breeding. I would exult in taking her, and then I would cast her aside.

Tiberas backs up a step, casts his eyes to her. I see his weakness in them, his wasteful concern for others when he should only be thinking of himself. It's the reason he is Tiberas, soon to be dead werewolf, and I am Ulnyx, the youngest, the strongest, the most powerful. I don't even need my demon form to take this one, and so I kill him as a human, to embarrass him as he has embarrassed himself.

He sees it coming. His face registers fear, and to my surprise acceptance. I expect him to whine like a bitch in heat, but when I maneuver in and wrap my hands around his neck he looks at me with indignation. Even as the breath drains from him and his eyes begin to bulge he looks at me. I squeeze harder, and he uses his last bit of air to laugh.

I howl in fury, shift to my were form and rend his flesh from his skeleton even as it begins to turn to dust. The black cloud of his soul rises from him, and I open my mouth to accept it, gaining his strength and power while I continue to molest his physical form. I only stop when there is nothing more to rip, to tear, to destroy. I feel a hand on my shoulder, and I turn with my claw raised to see Lylyx standing there, a hungry, feral smile on her face. I regain my human form, lift her to me, and put my lips to hers, claiming my first taste. It won't be the last.

When I regained myself, she was standing in front of the pack, looking down on me with a mixture of disdain and concern. Lylyx. She didn't look a day older than she had in the memory, though her sharp business suit was a stark contrast to the revealing deerskins she had sported in her past. How long ago had that been?

"Ulnyx," she said in a whisper. I could smell her surprise. "I heard you were killed by the diuscrucis."

I hesitated to reply. She thought I was the Great Were, and only the Great Were. In my tired state my link to Purgatory must have been weak enough that her Sight was only reading his power. Had his stirring overpowered Josette too?

"Lylyx," I said at last, bringing myself to my feet and pulling on Ulnyx's power to enhance the illusion of my identity, making sure to match my golden eye to the demon's. I was grateful to have the were's memories to guide me. "It's been a long time."

She smiled and stepped forward. "Too long," she said, reaching up and pulling my head down to hers. Her kiss was strong and sloppy, and I could feel the Great Were's soul howling at her call. I went along for the ride, not wanting to give anything away. Finally, she broke the kiss and took a step back.

"So the rumors aren't true? Nobody's heard from you in years."

"I'm here, aren't I?" I asked, trying to say as little about that as possible. "You're a bit far from home yourself."

She smiled and looked at me with big, round eyes, eyes that I could recall from other memories that weren't so clandestine. Ulnyx had tried to pretend he didn't love her. I had his soul, I knew the truth. The creature standing in front of me was the only thing the demon cared for other than domination and power.

"The master sent me here with my strongest. I'm supposed to be keeping an eye out for the diuscrucis. We aren't supposed to engage if we see him, just distract him a little bit." She shrugged her shoulders, and then squinted her eyes and cocked her head. "You know what he looks like, don't you?"

I let out a rough growl. "Whatever you heard, it's wrong. I wasn't with Reyzl in New York. We split months before. He became infatuated with this vampire girl, and was ready to supplant me in the chain." I was proud of myself. It was a good lie.

"Vampire girl?" she asked. She spit on the ground. "You're better off without him, and it looks like you dodged a bullet getting out of town before he showed up."

I laughed. "You think I'm afraid of some crossbreed?"

She reached out and touched my face. "Of course not Ullie." Ullie? "You've always been the strongest, and with the power Reyzl gave you..."

I reached out, wrapping an enlarged claw around her small throat. "Gave me?" I shouted. "I take what I want. I'm given nothing!"

Her eyes widened, but she didn't struggle. After a moment I put her down. Playing the part of the Were was a little too easy for my own comfort.

"You're still the strongest," she said. "Help me keep an eye out for this diuscrucis, and I'll make it worth your while." She licked her bottom lip for emphasis, but I didn't need it to know what she was getting at.

"If I want you, I'll have you," I replied. My memories told me I had before, and she preferred it that way. She was goading Ulnyx because she knew it would get him all hot and bothered. Hot and bothered was the way to get what she wanted. "Save your innuendo."

I took a good look at her pack. They had shifted back to human form, and were standing behind her looking nervous. "Your pack is pathetic," I said.

They may have taken offense, but there was no way they were going to try to do anything about it. Instead, each one of them dropped their heads and looked straight at the ground.

"What did you expect?" Lylyx asked. "Our best stud gone off to try to become an archwere, instead of staying with the pack and breeding?"

Ulnyx's soul was a fire in my gut. I closed my eyes to contain the burn. He had tried to breed, man he had tried. It was the Great Were's secret shame, the reason he had become a servant to anyone. He was sterile.

I opened my eyes, looked Lylyx and laughed. "Look at us now," I said. "I'm here because your master asked me to come. He promised to bring me to the archwere so I could rip his throat out."

Lylyx looked confused. "He?" she asked. "Which master are you speaking of?"

My inhale caught on my throat. I had just assumed she was referring to Gervais – the only female I knew who this one could call master was Charis. "Gervais," I said.

A murmur rippled through the pack, and the weres around Lylyx perked up. I had the sinking feeling I had dropped the wrong name.

Time seemed to stop while Lylyx stared at me, her body motionless, her breathing escalating from calm and even, to shallow and quick. She was deciding what she was going to do with the information I had just given her, and the physical signs weren't positive.

"When I heard about Reyzl, I hoped you had made it out okay," she said. "When I didn't get any news about you at all, I feared the worst." She stepped back and put her hands out to her sides. "At least, I thought I had feared the worst."

Her hands began to turn into claws, and her body began to grow, shifting and elongating. Around her, the other weres began to shift as well.

"I name you, diuscrucis," she said. "I hear your lies, and I see through your deceptions. Ulnyx deserves a better fate than to have his power usurped by a crossbreed."

I felt Ulnyx recoil at the sight of her. Whatever had happened since they had last seen one another, he didn't know that Lylyx had been promoted. Standing in front of me was another Great Were.

Her attack was blazingly fast, and it was all I could do to step back out of the way and take hold of the fullness of Ulnyx's power, transforming myself into a bigger, stronger version of the female opposite me.

"Let me tell you," I said, blocking her next attack and landing a punch that sent her tumbling down the street. "Ullie is an asshole."

I heard the snarls, and a moment later I had a dozen weres circled around me, trying to get past my defenses. I imagined I probably looked ridiculous standing there, this huge beast of a demon crouched into one of Josette's martial stances, lashing out with chops and kicks like a big ugly

Jackie Chan. I sent the weres sprawling, slamming them with feet and claws, leaving deep gashes in faces and abdomens. They howled and rolled back to their feet, growled and yelped and came in again, giving their leader the time she needed to regain her feet and get back into the fray.

I didn't see her return punch coming, and it knocked me to the ground. She didn't waste any time pouncing on me, trying to pin my arms at my sides, hoping that because I wasn't Ulnyx, I didn't have his raw strength. And I didn't have his raw strength. I could draw a lot of power from him, but it was like AC to DC, and I lost something in the conversion. Lucky for me, I had Josette's intimate knowledge of more complex hand-to-hand fighting to back me up. I used Lylyx's leverage against her, and tossed her backwards over my head. Somehow she landed on her feet, and I had a dozen weres back at me before I could stand.

With the power from Ulnyx running through me, my physical fatigue had vanished, but his power was all I had. I could have done one on one against Lylyx, and maybe even as far as six on one. These odds were ridiculous, and even though I put up a good fight, it was a fight I knew I couldn't win. I managed to disembowel two of the weres, rip the throat out of another, and put a massive hurt on a fourth, but in the end Lylyx helped them drag me to the ground, and a well placed stone to the back of my head took me the rest of the way out of the fight.

I lost control of the Great Were's power then, feeling my body shrink, even feeling the cold and wet of the night on my naked skin. I wished I could relish the feelings that had been evading me for so long, but the world grew fuzzy, and then vanished.

CHAPTER 9

I woke up in a small room, a simple room with stone walls, a small square window, a bed, a wooden door, and a clutter of straw-filled dolls that lay scattered around the floor. I wasn't alone in the room. A fourteen year-old girl with a plain face and brown hair was sitting on the bed next to me. An older man with long black hair tied back in a ponytail was leaning against the wall, looking out the room's only window into a pasture beyond.

"Josette," I said, recognizing the girl. Her smile pierced me, and I could feel my heart begin to race. I reached out and wrapped my arms around her, holding her tight while she patted my back.

"Landon," she said softly. "I've missed you."

"You know I've missed you," I replied.

"Touching. Really," the man said.

"Piss off Ullie," I said, breaking the embrace and staring down the demon. "What are you doing here anyway?"

I knew what this place was from the memories - Josette's Source.

Somehow, I had found my way here after the weres had knocked me out. The good news, it meant they hadn't killed me … yet.

"It's your party," he replied. "If you didn't want me along, you never should have invited me."

Not that I had a choice. Now I was stuck with him. "I liked you better when you didn't say anything," I said. "Your power is useful, your mouth isn't."

I was rewarded with a chuckle. Josette squeezed my hand and regained my attention before I could say anything else. She started to speak, but I put my hand to her lips to stop her.

"I'm sorry Josette, but can one of you please tell me what the heck is going on here? For the last five years you've both been silent except for these random memories that leave me struggling to stand, and now all of a sudden I get knocked out, and you're both here? One of you I'm happy to see, but your timing kind of sucks."

"Be glad you have me, Landon," Ulnyx said. "I'm the only reason you're still alive."

"Care to elaborate?" I asked.

Ulnyx bent over and picked up one of the straw dolls. "It's like this, meat," he said. "Lylyx has a thing for me. She always has. Man, no matter how hard I tried to satisfy her, she always wanted more. It's sexy as hell, and so I have this thing for her too."

"She wanted your puppies," I said. "You're sterile."

I knew it would send him into a rage, especially since Josette was there. He didn't disappoint, taking the straw doll and tearing it in half. He tried to come at me, but a thought was all I needed to hold him in place. I still owned his soul.

"Yeah, anyway," he said, his anger falling away in an instant, "if she's been promoted to a Great Were, it means her master has major mojo, at least as much as Reyzl, and probably more. She's going to see if she can have me extracted."

"Can that be done?" I asked, suddenly hopeful. I wouldn't mind ridding myself of the demon, now that I didn't need his soul anymore. I would miss his power, but not his twisted memories.

"It can't be done," Josette said. "Anyone who says it can is lying."

"How do you know, Miss Priss?" Ulnyx asked, leering at the angel. Another thought, and his head turned to look out the window.

"It's been attempted before," she replied. "Gervais has a laboratory where he performs certain... experiments." We both shivered at the memory of the room, more torture chamber than science lab. "I've seen him try. Once a soul is absorbed, it is entwined with that of the bearer. Trying to unravel it destroys both."

Ulnyx sighed. "I wish you angels could lie once in awhile. The truth is crap."

I swallowed my disappointment. "I get that our souls are connected," I said. "I can feel that when I tap your power. That doesn't answer why all this time I've only been able to catch whispers, and now we're all having a pow-wow in your Source."

Josette shook her head. "I don't know, fellow," she said. "I could hear you calling out to me, and I tried to call back, but you never heard me. Ever since I gave you my soul, I've been lost in the dark, aware of your experience, but at the same time cut off from you. When Izak summoned me, I saw a hint of light for the first time in years. I spoke to you, and you heard." Tears began to run down her round face.

"It hasn't been a picnic for me either, sister," Ulnyx said. "I've had to listen to this one pray, listen to her cry, listen to her bitch and moan. 'Oh my daughter'," he raised his voice in pitch and held his hands up in hopelessness. I threw him against the wall.

"Shut it Ullie," I said. "I can make your eternity worse than being in Hell."

The Were swallowed and nodded. "Well, it sucks being here," he said. "Sometimes you're fun, like when you turned on that dude Silas." He laughed. "Oh, and the way you played Lylyx was classic. Damn that kiss was nice."

"Do you have anything helpful to say?" I asked.

"I've been kicking and screaming in here too," he said. "There's this light always shining down on me. Man, it was dim right after you got that witch to snuff herself. Then, when I smelled Lylyx, it just pushed me over the edge. If I had to guess, I would say your own power drowns us out most of the time. You get pooped, we get let out of our cages."

"There's only one of you I'd prefer caged," I said.

"I'm sorry Landon," Josette said. "I believe it is an all or nothing proposition. However; if you can learn to control it, we may be of some use to you. At the very least, it might help with the memories."

"Be of use?" Ulnyx asked. "Don't look at me, I'm not about to help you out."

I threw Ulnyx against the wall again, and then began to compress his body. He cried out as his bones shattered from the force. "I can do this all day," I said. My control over the demon's soul was complete.

"Okay, okay," he begged. I let him straighten up. "I guess if I'm stuck with you, I might as well throw you bone once in awhile."

I ignored him, struck by a thought that had crossed me before, but I had dismissed. "Tell me," I said. "If I were less powerful, and I had absorbed a couple of demons who were much more powerful, do you think I would hear them talking to me all the time?"

They didn't answer right away.

"Landon," Josette said at last. "I know what you are thinking, but it doesn't work that way. Even if Rebecca could hear Merov and Reyzl, she has total domination over them. She could quiet them if she wished."

It wasn't what I wanted to hear, but I nodded. "But maybe they said something to her. Told her some lie, tricked her into leaving."

Ulnyx face-palmed. "Man, you've got to let it go. She's a demon. She lives to take power, not play house. Maybe she cared for you, but you can't deny your nature. Not forever. Face the fact that you were duped and move on."

I hated to admit it. I hated to accept it. I'd been holding onto hope, but it was fading fast.

"That may be the first smart thing I've ever heard you say," I told the demon. "Now, let's talk about Lylyx's master. I thought it was Gervais, but that's obviously wrong. Whoever is Commanding her, they're female."

"It has to be the Demon Queen," Josette said.

"No," I replied. "She gave me the Grail. She told me Reyzl was going to turn on me. She had her blood blessed by an archangel, and she wanted me to win. Why would she do that just to turn on me five years later?"

"You know the answer," Ulnyx said. "How many times do you have to have your balls yanked by a foxy hellion before you wise up?"

Demons were patient, and they were masters of deception and manipulation. I had already been over that thread with Dante. "The Outcast's servant was sure it was Gervais."

Ulnyx shrugged. "So they're working together. Probably having some fun in their spare time. Where's the confusion?"

It was possible they were in it together. I wasn't going to make the same mistake twice by trusting my female alter ego too far. Right now it didn't matter. Even if they were tag-teaming me, if I could get to Gervais, I could get to Sarah. Charis had outmatched me the first time we had met, but that was five years ago. I had learned a few more tricks since then. Hopefully more than she had.

"Okay genius," I said to the Were. "It doesn't hurt to assume you're right. We have one little problem, in that your girlfriend has my body, and I'm unconscious."

"You're going to wake up eventually, and like I said, she won't harm you while she thinks she can get me out. She's a bitch, but she's my bitch, and I don't want you to destroy her." Ulnyx smiled - a vicious, devious smile. "Here's what you're going to do."

CHAPTER 10

When I woke, it was dark. Not that dark meant much to me. It only took me a second to recognize that I was squeezed into a too-small sealed enclosure, my body contorted in a way that would make anyone cringe. I felt the pain of my burning muscles, but I had felt much worse, so I didn't let it distract me. Instead, I focused on my sarcophagus, recognizing the feel of metal, looking for a locking mechanism. I smiled when I found the tumblers. A safe of some kind; it would be easy enough to get out of.

Except, I didn't even try. Ulnyx had given me a plan, and it seemed like a good one. Despite the pain and discomfort, patience was the best course of action.

I focused on my Sight, finding Lylyx without difficulty. She was less than twenty feet away, I closed my eyes and focused on enhancing my hearing. She was on the phone.

"Yes, master," she said. "Yes, I know you said to distract him, but I did better than that. He's nowhere near as strong as you thought. I captured him." She stopped to listen, and I could smell her fear, even through the steel box. "Yes, master. I was only trying to make you proud. I'm sorry.

97

You want me to let him go? I don't understand? What do you mean it isn't time yet? No, master, I'm not questioning you. Yes, master. I'll leave him in Chantilly. Please, I'm sorry. Thank you, thank you. I won't fail you again."

I heard her take the phone from her ear and put it on the desk. The chair slid back on a wooden floor, and a door opened.

"Get the truck," she called out. The door closed again, and then I heard her bare feet whispering along the hardwood. She stopped right outside the safe, crouched down and whispered. "Ullie, if you can hear me, I've never stopped loving you. I want to get you out of there, but if I don't do what the master says I'll be in worse shape than you are."

"If you don't let me out of this safe, you won't have to worry about it," I said. I smiled when she gasped.

"Wasn't being beaten down once enough for you diuscrucis?" she asked, recovering from her surprise.

"I'm afraid not," I said. "Hey, I have a question for you. Do you accept that I've absorbed Ulnyx's soul and have domination over him?" I added the last part myself. I hope the Were heard it.

She paused. "I accept that you've absorbed his soul, but if your ability in a fight is any indication, domination isn't a word I'd use."

The snark didn't matter. What did matter was that she had confirmed Ulnyx's continued existence, which was the lynchpin of the demon's plan. Apparently, there was some odd loophole in were law that I could take advantage of provided she acknowledged him. It was his way of getting me what I wanted, and also something he wanted. A demon wouldn't do it any other way.

"In that case," I said. "As the former alpha, I challenge you leadership of the pack."

I heard her gasp again. I smelled her renewed fear, though it was nothing compared to what she had exhibited when she was on the phone. We hadn't factored that fear in, but it would play right into my hands.

"What kind of trick is this?" she hissed. "You have no right to challenge."

I focused, finding the deadbolts and crushing them. She backed up when the door swung open and I pushed myself out, falling into a lump on the floor. Muscles and tendons popped back into place, my body healing almost instantly. I hadn't realized how drained I was becoming by never shutting down. I felt stronger than I had in a long time.

I rose smoothly to my feet, facing her, and felt a sudden rush of blood to my head. I hadn't expected her to be nude. She stirred something in me that I knew wasn't wholly mine.

"Wow," I whispered, the word escaping me before I could catch it. She truly was a work of art, but that wasn't part of the plan. "Pack laws don't distinguish the meat," I said, pulling my eyes up to her eyes. "Otherwise the strongest wouldn't be able to claim new shells. You just confirmed that Ulnyx's soul is inside of me, and that makes me eligible to challenge. They're your rules, not mine."

She backed up a few steps, her eyes dropping to my own naked form. I fought to stay confident, despite her gaze on my overly cooperative midriff.

"You've put me in an uncomfortable position diuscrucis," she said, looking back up at my face. What about the uncomfortable position she had me in? "When I win, I'll be forced to answer to the master for killing you."

I tried not to smirk, but I couldn't help it. Ulnyx had told me how he thought this would play out, but Lylyx's overwhelming fear of her master was making it much easier. I couldn't communicate with either of them now that I was awake and my energy had been restored, but I knew they would experience the moment. I could imagine the demon's glee.

"You aren't going to win," I said. "In fact, you're going to lose on purpose, because it's the only way you have a chance to survive."

Her anger flared, but she didn't argue. Instead, she walked across the room, rocking her hips suggestively. I ignored the temptation to follow her retreat, instead taking in my surroundings. Judging from the faded yellow striped wallpaper, the worn hardwood floor, the arched wood roofing, the filthy windows, and the pasture beyond, I figured I was on the top floor of an old farmhouse. It must have been the master suite, or an apartment, because there was one door which I knew led out to the rest of the house, and another that led into the bedroom, and beyond it the bathroom. That was where Lylyx was headed.

She returned a minute later in a white silk robe that covered her modesty, but didn't leave much to the imagination. I could feel Ulnyx still buzzing below the surface like the caged animal he was. She tossed me a matching robe.

"Not that I mind the view," she said. "But it'll be easier to do business this way."

I caught the robe, fighting to keep my face from flushing. I slipped it on and focused, re-rendering it into a pair of sweats and a t-shirt. I did the same to her clothes; not a glamour, but an actual alteration. It seemed simple, but that kind of precision had taken months to develop. Judging by a sudden change in the atmosphere, she knew it was no parlor trick.

"I agree," I said.

"Last night?" she said. It was obvious she had just realized how badly she'd underestimated me.

"I had a long day, and was running out of steam," I replied. "You should have killed me when you had the chance."

She looked at me like that was the dumbest idea she had ever heard. "Kill you? Do you know what she would have done to me for killing you? Besides, you have Ulnyx in you, I can see him in your eye. I'm not stupid, I know extraction is a supposed to be a myth, but there are rumors there's a djinn in Moscow who can do it."

I filed that tidbit away. Josette had said it couldn't be done, but there wouldn't be any harm in paying this djinn a visit once Sarah was safe. "You keep talking about your master. I know it isn't Gervais, so who is it?"

Her face blanched. "The Demon Queen," she said.

I tried to stay stone-faced, to not give anything away. My heart began to pound, my mind began to race, and I knew I had blown it. The witch had been right, I was a fool.

"She sent an archvampire to our den with the phone," Lylyx continued, her voice frightened in response to my body language. "She told me if I would follow her, she would make me Great." She smiled. "Of course I agreed. I've been in charge of the pack since Ullie left, but I'm getting old, and it was only a matter of time before I was challenged to a fight I couldn't win." She laughed. "I didn't expect you to be the one to make that challenge."

I closed my eyes and took a deep breath. It was better to know what I was dealing with. It was better to know Charis had suckered me, but to what end? I clamped down on my emotions and opened my eyes again.

"Your time is up," I said. I walked over to the desk and picked up the cellphone. "She calls you on this?"

Lylyx nodded. I looked at the contact list. I wasn't familiar with the country code, but it wasn't the United States. I pushed the call button.

"Nobody's going to pick up," she said. "She calls me, I don't call her."

I let it ring eight times, and then got disconnected. It was worth a shot. "Who was the vampire?" I asked.

"His name is Cho. He's based in Japan. He looks like you can knock him over with a feather, but he laid out ten of my pack and fed on one, just to show me that he could."

Cho. I knew the name, but I had never met him. The angels cut him a pretty wide path; an indication of his power. It seemed Charis was gearing up for war.

I put the phone back on the table, and then heard a ring. Not from this phone, another one in the bedroom. I found my own cell sitting on a dresser. Obi. He'd have to wait.

"So," Lylyx said, joining me in the bedroom. "I think I know what's going on now, but how did you know about the law?" She stepped right up to me, invading my personal space. Her scent had changed again, to something decidedly more enticing. She was close enough that I could feel the heat of her body radiating outward.

"Ulnyx told me," I said, trying to back up and finding only the bed behind me. She knew exactly what she was doing.

"You can talk to him?" she asked, surprised. She inched herself forward, tightening an increasingly small gap.

"Only when I'm not awake, it seems. He's an asshole, but he cares for you. He..."

She leapt at me, pushing me back onto the bed and shoving her lips up against mine. I could feel Ulnyx struggling against me. He was testing me, and whether she knew it or not, she was helping him.

My control over him was absolute. I sealed off my mind to the Were, feeling the loss of his power as I used my own to disconnect us. I overwhelmed him, punishing him for even trying. I pulled myself away from Lylyx, rolling out from under her and getting to my feet. She turned over and spread herself out on the bed.

"If you're going to be alpha," she said, "you have an obligation to breed."

"An alpha is obliged to nothing," I replied. "Now get up, and let's get this done. I need to be in Paris." I left her laying there, heading for the door out into the rest of the house.

"Wait a minute," she said, hopping off the bed and rushing in behind me. I turned to face her. "Let's get this straight before we go down.

You make the challenge, I accept. We go outside, we fight. You're going to pin me, right?"

I shrugged. "Unless you'd rather I kill you."

Her expression was pure lust. "Now you sound like Ullie," she said.

I shook my head and pushed open the door. As expected, it opened out into a short hallway with a couple of doors on either side and a stairway directly to the right. I took the stairs down with Lylyx trailing close behind.

The remainder of the pack, minus the ones I had killed and the two that had gone to get the truck, were sitting in the living room of the house, watching some kind of French 'Three Stooges' rip-off on an old tube television with bent rabbit ears. They were spread out across a beat sofa, a rocking chair, and a worn burlap rug, dressed in their finest jeans, tees, and leathers. Six males and a female, their heads swung around in unison when I stepped on a creaky floorboard.

"Seriously?" I asked, motioning at the television. Their lips curled in response, and they began to rise. Lylyx stepped around me and stayed them with her hand before they could get themselves in trouble.

"What the hell is this?" asked the female on the rocking chair, a too-young girl with short black hair and a large skull tattoo on her neck.

"Relax," Lylyth said. "The diuscrucis has Ulnyx's soul. He knows our laws, and he's challenged me."

Seven mouths gaped open.

"He can't do that," one of the males on the floor said. He looked like a model, with a petite frame and high cheekbones.

"He can," Lylyx countered. "He has Ulnyx's soul - he's already proven it to me. Our laws are clear. Follow me outside."

I could tell they didn't want to go. I could tell they would have preferred to try to rip my throat out. It didn't matter. Lylyx turned and opened the front door, leading us outside onto an old porch in sore need of some paint. The small box truck pulled up a few seconds later, and the remaining two weres jumped out. Lylyx raised her hand to them also, and when they saw their pack mates, they fell in line.

"Where do you want to do this?" she asked me.

I scanned the area. There was a small pasture off to the right of the house. "In the pasture," I said. "That way your pups can wait behind the fence."

She nodded, and we walked over. Once we'd hopped the short chicken wire fence, she turned to her brethren. "You all stand witness to the diuscrucis..."

"Landon," I interrupted.

"You all stand witness to Landon's challenge for leadership of the Mekong pack. I have acknowledged him as the rightful bearer of Ulnyx, the former alpha of our pack, and have accepted his challenge."

There were a few growls and grumbles, but no one said anything.

"Just come at me like you think you can win," I said. "Don't hold anything back."

Lylyx smiled. "I hadn't planned on it. I want to see what you've got."

We separated by twenty feet, and Lylyx shifted, her body growing and elongating until she had the demonic form of the Great Were. I remembered Ulnyx's battle against Tiberas, and how he had remained in human form to embarrass the old were. I renewed my connection to the demon, feeling his power running along with mine once more, and allowed my form to change.

The weres outside of the pasture howled in support of Lylyx as she made her first attack, charging in quickly, faking left, and kicking out at my left knee with her right foot. It might have been a good move twelve hours ago, but I was at the top of my game now. I stepped lightly aside and grabbed her leg in my massive claws, and then pushed forward, forcing her to either allow her leg to break or be knocked onto the ground. She tumbled backwards, and I came down on top of her.

"Not so bad, is it?" she asked in a throaty growl. I was suddenly aware of myself, and she used the distraction to rake her claws across my face, and then knee me in the groin and throw me aside.

I rolled to my feet, just in time to block two more quick strikes. "Clever," I said, catching her wrist and pulling her into my foot. The reverse force sent her bouncing to the opposite side of the pasture. She shot back up and charged again.

She was all teeth and nails, scratching, clawing, and biting at me while I batted her strikes aside with efficient ease. She was skilled, I admit, but I had already been delayed long enough. I ducked under her next blow and rushed forward, grappling with her and taking her to the ground like a linebacker. It was ugly, but it did the job. Once her weight was below mine, it was only a matter of time before I had gotten hold of her arms and pinned her.

"Surrender," I said.

"No," she replied, wriggling and twisting, trying to break the hold.

I hadn't expected that. I leaned in and took her neck in my razor jaws, biting down hard enough to draw blood. I could taste it on my lips, at once exciting and disgusting. She roared in pain, and ceased struggling.

"Fine," she said. "I surrender."

I jumped off of her and shifted, knitting my torn clothes back together. Once Lylyx had changed, I pulled her to her feet, noticing the mark and bruising where I had bit her.

Lylyx had been alpha of the Mekong pack, but she had nothing to transfer, because Ulnyx had already taken it. There was no mojo to make me commander-in-chief, no special powers to bestow. It was kind of anti-climatic. The only real difference was that when we retreated back over the fence, the other weres all followed behind us without a word.

"So, now what?" Lylyx asked, once we had returned to the master bedroom. I had left the pack downstairs, and instructed them to leave the television off.

"Change your clothes and meet me downstairs," I said, grabbing her cell and updating my wardrobe to my standard blacks - leather jacket, polo, jeans, and boots. "I have to make a phone call. Do you have any transportation besides the truck?"

"There's a bike stashed in the barn out back. Am I coming with you?"

Another bike? I wasn't exited about the prospect. We hadn't staged the show just to leave her there waiting for Cho to come put an end to her. That was part of the agreement I had made with Ulnyx.

"Yes. Bring the bike around with you," I said, shutting the door to the bedroom, and heading downstairs.

I stopped at the bottom and whistled to get the attention of the weres, who were talking amongst themselves. They silenced in an instant, giving me their complete attention.

"I have a feeling you won't be safe here," I said. "Lylyx and I are headed back to Paris. I want you to find somewhere else to hang out for awhile."

"How about Versailles?" the model joked. He started laughing, until I stared him down. Take any crap, and they would just keep giving it. I had learned a lot in the last five years.

"There's a small bed and breakfast in Chantilly," the girl with the tattoo said. "We can check in there."

I looked at her and smiled. "Sounds good," I said. Her face turned red in response. "You're in charge. Take these other mongrels and lay low until you hear from Lylyx or me."

The other weres all looked to her. I could feel their jealousy over my favor. Weres were weird. She got to her feet and started barking orders, getting them ready to go.

I pulled my cellphone from my pocket the moment I stepped out of the farmhouse, unlocking it and navigating into my list of missed calls. Obi had tried me three more times while I had been out mud wrestling. I hit the call button.

He picked up after three rings, sounding agitated. "Hey, man, I called you like five times already," he said. "You should try picking up your phone sometime."

My mind flipped through a few witty retorts, but I abandoned them for simplicity. "It's not easy being me," I said. "I assume you have something?"

He laughed. "Yeah, of course I have something. It's a latitude, longitude, and date. The date is today. I put it into Google Maps, guess what I got?"

"Yankee Stadium?" I guessed. Not likely.

"Damn Yankees. I'm a Red Sox fan. Try Eiffel Tower. Aren't you in Paris?"

Eiffel tower? Then it was no coincidence that I was here, now. Or that Lylyx had been sent to distract me, not stop me, and that she had said something about it not being time yet. I was supposed to take that data, supposed to look for the pattern. Whoever had planted it, they had a little too much faith in me. Or maybe they knew I would turn it over to Obi, and that he would be able to crack it?

"Hey, you there man?" Obi asked.

I swallowed my heart. "I'm here. This just got a lot more complicated. What time?"

"Nine o'clock, French. You need me to catch a flight out?"

After everything I had said in my anger, the minute he thought I needed him, he was ready to back me up. "No, thanks," I said. "Listen, I'm sorry for the crap that I dumped on you. It's been tough."

There was a silent pause. I could hear him let out a deep breath. "Don't sweat it, man," he said at last. "I can't pretend to know what it's like, so I won't. All I want is respect for my own decisions."

I didn't know what to say. I heard the rough tumble of a motorcycle coming to life out behind the house.

"My ride's coming," I said. "If you want to do me another favor, track down Thomas and see if he'd be willing to risk his heavenly eternity to help me out. Tell him it could be super important. All I need him to do is trace a pair of fangs onto the front of the chest in the corner. Once its open, take a look at my notes inside, and see what you can do with it. Start at JFK, that's where I saw him last."

I didn't know how relevant the mystery I had been trying to unravel would be to my current predicament, but I was starting to feel like there were answers to something in there, and that I would need those answers sooner rather than later. Still, the contents of the chest were my most closely guarded physical secret, and it wasn't easy to trust Obi to it. It was even harder to ask him to find Thomas. Trust sucked like that, I realized. No matter how many times it burned you, you couldn't live without it, or you'd always be empty and alone.

"Can do," Obi said. "Give 'em hell." He disconnected.

I couldn't ignore how striking Lylyx was when she tore around the house on a fancy Italian pocket-rocket. She had covered her skull in a full black helmet with a wolf's head airbrushed on it, the fangs bared around the front so it looked like it was eating her head, and traded her clothes for a white tee and leathers that accentuated everything feminine. She skidded to a stop next to me.

"I'm ready to roll boss," she said, patting the seat behind her. "Hop on."

CHAPTER 11

I thought about driving the bike myself, but decided I would rather conserve my energy for whatever was going to happen once we got back into the city. I slipped over the saddle and wrapped my arms lightly around Lylyx's stomach, and then clutched her tighter when she launched away from the farmhouse. We rocketed down a gravel driveway and out onto a narrow paved road that split a pair of fields. This really was the middle of nowhere. I was amazed my cell had worked here.

"Any specific place in Paris, or are we just going sightseeing?" Lylyx asked, shouting back at me over the noise of the wind.

"I need to pay a visit to Gervais," I said. "He's taken something that he shouldn't have."

I gripped her tight enough to cause her to squeal after she nearly wrecked at hearing the archfiend's name.

"I'm beginning to question whether or not I should have just let you kill me," she said, getting her nerves and the bike back under control.

I ignored the remark. "He has an entrance to his chateau tucked away in the Paris sewers. I'm not sure where just yet, but I'm working on it."

I closed my eyes and floated through Josette's memories, searching for the path to the demon's hidden transport rift. She had never made it all the way into that part of the sewer because Gervais had rigged it with wards that angels couldn't cross, but she could at least get me that far.

I could feel the warmth of Josette's soul touching my own as I mingled with her, an unseen hand that guided me towards the information that I sought. She had been there every time I had delved into her experiences, I realized. I just hadn't known how to recognize her. I focused, trying to reach out with my soul to touch her warmth, her hand. I felt myself drifting towards it, the warmth growing, until I passed through and discovered I had dove in too far. The darkness behind my closed eyes vanished, replaced with the eerie glow of the past.

"Where did he go?" Shiva asks, shifting his torch back and forth, trying to keep us bathed in at least a small amount of light.

We're standing near the dead end of a narrow alley between two hôtels particuliers in the Marais district. I can hear the clomping of horse hooves and the creaking of wheels as a carriage trundles past behind us, likely bringing a wealthy merchant home for the evening. I turn my head left and right, then rotate it to look up. The walls of the hotels are smooth and clean, the windows still intact. He didn't go that way.

"I don't know," I say, looking back down the alley towards the street. "Perhaps he snuck past in the shadows." It wouldn't be the first time he had evaded me in this way.

"This is getting to be a much larger problem than we thought," Shiva says. "Your brother has been consolidating his power, and now he moves about almost freely in

the night. Even you are unable to keep up with him."

My capitaine was right. He most often was. Gervais had been active in the last few weeks, murdering other fiends in the area and taking their holdings for his own. It had fallen to us to put a stop to him before he achieved the levels of power he so clearly lusted for, power that would make him difficult to challenge directly.

I lower my head, feeling shameful for losing him. Gervais had always bested me, no matter the challenge. I kick a stone in frustration, sending it clattering along the cobblestone and into the darkness. I'm about to apologize to Shiva verbally when we hear a faint plunk rise from the black.

"I've been a fool," Shiva says, running forward with the torch. He lowers it to the ground, revealing an open hole in the ground and a metal grate placed directly next to it. He moves to jump down, but I hesitate.

"What about nightstalkers?" I ask. "We should return with more of our fellows."

Shiva shakes his head. "There is no time, Josette," he says. "We may not have another chance to get this close to him while he is weakened."

Indeed, we have chased him from the home of a nearby Turned noble who had betrayed him to a rival. We came upon them both in the middle of their battle, killing the other fiend before Gervais could take his soul.

I respond by jumping into the hole, fluttering my wings beneath my loose blouse to slow the descent. Shiva is right behind me, and the torch returns our sight.

"Look," I say, pointing at a splotch of blood on the side of the brick sewer wall. Gervais had taken a deep cut to his abdomen from a hellfired blade during the fight.

"This way," Shiva says, heading deeper into the sewers at a full run. I follow along behind, fearful of losing the light from his torch. I know this is a bad idea, but what choice do I have?

We have to stop every twenty yards to check the walls, to follow the trail of blood. It makes following after my brother slow, and with each step I'm more certain he's gotten away. We pass from a smaller tunnel into a larger one, then come to a silent stop. The torch is casting just enough light for us to see the nightstalkers up ahead, leaning over, feeding on one of their own. It has a dagger sticking out of its neck. It's dark, but the size and shape is familiar.

"We're on the right path," Shiva says.

"Capitaine," I say in a whisper. "This is a hopeless pursuit. We can barely even see down here. Look at them feeding, he is minutes ahead."

Shiva looks thoughtful for a moment, considering my opinion. "If we die in service of our Lord, then so be it," he says. "We must take big risks to have big success."

I am a servant, and so I nod and hold my sword out in front of me. "I will clear the path," I say, rushing forward into the darkness before Shiva can stop me.

It's much easier to fight in the dark than it is to move in the dark. I close my eyes and concentrate on my Sight, feeling their presence, registering their every movement while I put years of training into play.

I hear the rustle of a shirt-sleeve and twist, avoiding a pale hand and lashing out with my blade to impale the nightstalker. I kick it back out of the way and duck under a grab, reach into my boot for a dagger and stab back into the demon's knee.

Hot breath on my neck alerts me and I spin, sweeping my leg along the ground, pushing through the impact, following the sound of the creature knocking against the wall and sending my dagger airborne into it.

I leap upward, fluttering my wings to gain more height, and lash out with my boot, hearing the crunch of bone as the last one's head is snapped backwards. I stab this one, and then stand calm in the center of the melee, the smell of frankincense strong in the enclosed space.

I open my eyes.

"Well done," Shiva says, patting me on the shoulder. He aims the torch at the passage beyond. "This way."

I lose track of how long we are in the sewer. We follow a path that appears below us, a worn avenue of motion that keeps the grime of the tunnels away. It speeds our progress, but it doesn't calm my nerves. The path is too worn for a single demon, too worn for even a handful of nightstalkers. What will we find at the end?

The tunnel opens up into a large room, lit by sconces of hellfire. I swallow to try to quell my fear. The room is filled with skulls and bones, stacked neatly along the walls, piled twelve feet high from floor to ceiling. It reminds me of the catacombs, but we aren't in the catacombs. There is a large demon skull on the other side of the room, its mouth spread open in a horrified howl. Through the mouth is another tunnel that vanishes in the darkness beyond. Gervais' torn shirt lays discarded in the center of the room.

"We're getting close," Shiva says. Such is the focus of his pursuit that he seems oblivious to the grotesquery of our surroundings. He reaches Gervais' shirt and bends down to examine it, at the same time I see the corner of a rune sticking out from the edge.

"Shiva, wait," I cry. I'm too late. He lifts the shirt and exposes the runes scratched into the floor. A spout of hellfire rises, the flames lashing into his head, igniting his hair and clothes. He's an effigy, his arms outstretched, his body aflame. He has no time to cry out in pain before he is consumed. Then, he is gone.

My breathing is ragged, and my eyes are streaming tears. I hold my sword in front of me and rush forward, desperate to reach my brother, desperate to make him pay. He knew I would be the cautious one. He knew I would survive.

As soon as I pass into the demon skull's open maw I begin to feel the pressure. I take three more steps, and my head feels as though it will explode. I see the runes encircling the tunnel, carved into the stone as far as I can see before the light no longer reveals it. I cannot pass, so I back up. I sit on the floor and cry, knowing that I still need to find my way to the surface, and the torch is gone.

My vision snapped back into focus, finding itself on the rear of Lylyx's helmet, the traffic sweeping by on both sides of us as she weaved her way towards Paris.

"Landon," she shouted. "Landon."

"I'm here," I said. "Just doing some soul-searching."

I fought to shake off the feelings of despair and hopelessness that Josette had been experiencing while she sat alone in the room of skulls and bones. I put my hand up to my forehead, rubbing my temple to try to shake the hangover. I needed to get better control of my inherited memories, because the reenactments were a serious drain.

"We're five minutes out," she said. "Do you have a destination for me?"

I took a deep breath and gathered myself, reaching gently for Josette and feeling her presence as a feather on the edge of my soul. "Marais," I replied.

CHAPTER 12

Le Marais was one of the oldest districts in France, a former aristocratic section of the city that had once been home to Victor Hugo and Robespierre. Today, it maintained its architectural charm and grace, while also supporting a much more eclectic manner of Parisian. Le Marais held its share of historical hotels, trendy restaurants and posh art galleries, as well as gay clubs and cabarets.

I had kept my senses focused while Lylyx had navigated us through the City of Light. I knew we had passed by a few vampires lurking in the shadows of the surrounding buildings, as well as two or three angels who were keeping an eye on the machinations of the vamps. None of them gave us any trouble, and I had cloaked myself to better match Lylyx so as not to draw any added attention.

My plan for finding Gervais' underground rift wasn't much of a plan at all. Lylyx circled the bike through the streets of Paris while I looked for any kind of visual cues that would either register as familiar, or cause some kind of emotional flood from Josette's past. I was a little worried I would find myself back in her memories, but there didn't seem to be any way around it. It was true that I could have gone straight to the archfiend's chateau; I knew from Josette exactly where to find it, but she had felt it was too risky and I was inclined to agree.

We were cruising past the Picasso Museum when I felt a familiar heat fall into my Sight. A hint of a smile played across the edge of my face, and I tapped Lylyx on the shoulder and pointed her down a connecting street. The roads were narrow in Le Marais, and it took us a few tries to find the right pattern to get closer to the target.

"Where are we going?" Lylyx asked.

I had made her stop the bike, and we had continued on foot, down another narrow corridor to stand in front of a tall wrought iron gate. Beyond the gate was a dark alley, and I knew I would find my quarry at its rear.

"The entrance to the sewers is down there," I said.

"I smell something else down there," she replied. "Something old and powerful."

I focused, pulling the iron gate out of the way. "That's how I know we're in the right place."

The buildings on either side of the alley were tall, and blocked any chance the sun had of making its way down into their depths. The darkness cast by the shadows held a palpable, eerie quality that was edging its way under my skin. Even though Josette's hunt for Gervais had happened hundreds of years ago, I could almost feel the energy of it hanging in the air.

I was about to ask Lylyx if she had a bic, or a match, or something so I could create some light to pierce the blackness. It wasn't that I needed it to see, but something about the darkness was making me strangely uncomfortable. Before I had a chance to, a small flame flickered to life a dozen yards ahead, illuminating its wielder in temporal light. A sharp, devilish grin behind a neatly groomed beard, on a narrow, angled face.

Lylyx gasped, and stopped walking. She started to step backwards, but I grabbed her arm. "Come on," I said. "He's with me."

She looked at me like I was crazy, but she didn't say anything. I held her arm until we reached Izak. I saw he was perched at the edge of a hole in the ground, the sewer grate already placed off to the side.

"Good to see you again," I said, clapping the demon on the shoulder.

He looked at Lylyx and furrowed his brow.

"It's a long story, but I've had a little bit of an adventure since we split up. Izak, this is Lylyx. I'm sure you can See she's a Great Were."

Izak nodded. He cast the hellfire into the air so he could hold out his hand for her to shake. He didn't do it to be friendly, he did it to show the runes running up his wrist.

She tentatively took it and gave it a light shake. "I'm also Ulnyx's mate," she said, casting a sidelong glance my way. The whole thing was some kind of weird demon pissing match. The logic of it eluded me.

"Have you been down?" I asked Izak.

He shook his head.

I focused my Sight, reaching down into the depths, and finding it didn't stretch very far. I guess we were going in blind. I turned to Lylyx. "Stay behind us. We aren't going to have much room to maneuver down there, so hulking up is out of the question."

She didn't look comfortable. "I guess now isn't a good time to mention that I'm claustrophobic?"

"You can mention it," I replied. "But it doesn't change anything. Izak, take the lead."

The fiend jumped down into the hole, his flame trailing behind him. I stepped up to the hole and found the hellfire resting at the bottom next to Izak's face.

"I should have let you kill me," Lylyx said. I jumped.

I landed on a puff of air, creating only the slightest splash in the inch deep run of wastewater flowing through the tunnel. I could See Lylyx standing above us, and I could smell her fear. I knew when it changed from apprehension to determination. I held out my arms and caught her gently, finding her in my arms looking up at me with big, dark eyes. I felt Unlyx stirring.

"Thanks for the catch," she purred, her hand reaching around behind me to find purchase somewhere else.

I deposited her roughly, ignoring the position of her hand on my rear. "Just stay behind us," I said.

"With pleasure," she replied.

I stayed focused on my Sight as we walked, even though it could only penetrate a short distance further than my eyes. The sewers seemed clear, but there was a tangible charge in the atmosphere, a foreboding that this was only the calm before the storm. I was thankful to have Izak with me because he knew where we were going, saving us from a lot of stumbling around in the cavernous maze of tunnels.

As we walked, I was able to pick out some areas of the brickwork where Gervais had passed by so many years before, the dark splatter of his blood still leaving its indelible stain along the surface. I could sense the pull of it through Josette's soul, an invitation to explore in greater depth. I could feel her invisible hand resting on me, feeding me her strength.

"Nightstalkers," Lylyx whispered from behind me. I couldn't See anything, so I stopped and turned towards her. "Ulnyx never did have a very good sense of smell," she said. "At least compared to me. Though I'm surprised, because there are a lot of them."

I still couldn't See them, or smell them. "Where?" I asked.

She smiled coyly. "You mean you don't know? Behind us, but I think they're running."

"Izak," I whispered, causing the demon to stop walking and face me. I pointed back the way we had come. "Lylyx smells uglies, coming this way."

It was only another heartbeat or two before I Saw them, a mass of heat spread down the smaller sewer tunnel. They were definitely running, and fast. Izak grabbed my shoulder. I turned back to look at him.

His arms swung wildly back and forth, and his eyes were wide. He pointed down the tunnel, and then swung his hand back around to point the way we had been going. I shrugged and held my hands out to the side, not able to understand what he was trying to say. After a couple of rounds of this, he growled in exasperation, dug his claws into my arm, and threw me away from the oncoming nightstalkers. He took hold of Lylyx's wrist before she could pull it away, and dragged her after me.

We were running away from the nightstalkers. I didn't know why, because I was certain the three of us could have dealt with them without difficulty. Judging by the focused look of disturbance on Izak's face, I was getting the feeling there was more to the story, something I hadn't caught on to. The fact that it was causing the fiend to run was enough reason to obey.

The stone was a blur, the constant sound of our footfalls kicking up water echoing around us, trapped and reverberated by the enclosed space. I could smell the nightstalkers now, getting closer even with our all-out run. I could smell their fear. They weren't coming to attack us, they were running away from something else. We just happened to be in the way.

We reached a break in the tunnel, where it split off on either side. I knew from Josette's memory that we should have continued straight. Instead, I hit the brakes, swerving to the left, and then reaching out and taking hold of both Izak and Lylyx, pulling them in after me.

"We can't outrun them," I said. "With any luck, they'll go right by." Izak didn't look convinced, and Lylyx looked nervous. "Just be ready."

They came on in a pounding flood, two dozen at least, all herded and stampeding in front of some unseen menace. I tried to See it, tried to smell it, but there was nothing. The only sign that the nightstalkers weren't all hallucinating was that same thick feeling of darkness that had made me desire some light. It was evil and empty, and growing heavier by the second.

"What the hell is it?" I whispered to Izak.

His eyes were aflame, and filled with concern. He pointed to his dancing fire, and then clenched his fist and crushed it out of existence. He pointed at his eyes, and did the same. Then he really unnerved me, when he pointed at the pit of his stomach, the general area where I felt my soul rested, and crushed it too.

We waited for the nightstalkers to arrive. We waited for them to make their rush past. We waited for the sounds of screaming, or pain, or fear, or something. We waited to put our eyes on whatever this creature was that was chasing them.

I kept my Sight focused; the demons should have been here by now, but instead they had stopped running, and they turned and moved in total confusion. One by one, their Divine souls began to vanish.

"They can't see," I said to Izak.

He nodded.

I understood why he had run. I understood we were still too exposed. I understood that whatever this thing was, it didn't matter how strong we were. If we couldn't see it, couldn't See it, couldn't smell it, couldn't touch it, we were dead.

I Saw the last nightstalker vanish, leaving my Sight as blind and useless as my eyes suddenly felt. The darkness was increasing, the hopelessness and despair ratcheting up in intensity. It was coming.

I looked down the tunnel, losing it in the dark distance. I turned back the other way, and saw no escape.

"We have to get to the rift ahead of it," I said. There was no other way.

We started running. I took the lead, letting Josette's memories guide me, following the twisted path through the sewers that she had taken in pursuit of her brother hundreds of years before. The darkness responded to us, the pressure of it nearly overwhelming as it reached out, an invisible but absolute thing.

Still we raced on. I could focus and make myself faster, could add a new dimension of quickness, but it was a feat neither Izak nor Lylyx could match. Maybe I could get away, but I wasn't about to leave either one of them behind. The entity that was chasing us was still gaining, and we were still too far away. We weren't going to get to the rift ahead of it.

I stopped running again, hopping up and turning over to walk back along the ceiling. "Keep running," I said. "I'll catch up."

Izak didn't slow. Lylyx tried, but the demon took hold of her again and forced her to keep moving. With my momentum lost, gravity pulled me back down off the top of the sewer, and I rotated to land on my feet. I focused on the water below me, pushing it back, bunching it up, raising it higher and higher.

Pitch-black tendrils began snaking overhead, and the feeling of death and loss was unlike anything I had ever experienced. My whole body went cold, and I could feel Josette and Ulnyx both withdraw from my consciousness, the power of the oncoming demon forcing them back. Still I pushed the water, leaving the area around me dry while I created a wall of liquid.

I didn't really know what I was doing. I didn't know if it would slow our assailant in the slightest. The pressure was becoming overwhelming, and I dropped to a knee while my body shook from the intensity. It couldn't have been too far away from me now, and I looked forward, expecting to see its physical shape materialize through the water at any moment.

I didn't have to wait long. The darkness was everywhere now, and my eyes were barely good enough to see. It had no real shape, though the form was vaguely humanoid. It had no mass, but instead was like a thick vapor of nothingness. It pushed its way into the wall of water without hesitation, and it was clear that it could move through the liquid without effect. My entire body was rocking uncontrollably, my soul crying out in fear. It was all I could do to stay present, and to find my focus. It was coming, and I wasn't sure I could stop it.

I cried out as I forced my will on the wall of water, demanding it to harden, for the molecules to pull together in crystalline form, for it to turn into ice. I felt the tug in my mind that told me the universe was bending to my demand, and I watched the water freeze.

A high-pitched shriek echoed through the sewer, and my body immediately stopped shaking, the darkness pulling back and grey clarity returning to my world. I saw the black form in the ice, the edges feathering and coalescing, reaching out and snaking through the barrier. I had succeeded in slowing it, nothing more.

I took off down the tunnel at a dead run, finding a new strength in the escape from the cold grasp of the monster. My feet pounded the stone in a quick cadence, and I focused on the water beneath them when I passed, lifting it and pushing it, piling it up to create a series of walls behind me. It was enough to stop the creature for a few seconds each, but right now every second counted.

I found them waiting outside the room of skulls and bones. Izak was standing in the corridor with his back to me, preventing Lylyx from getting past him to attempt a rescue. I was impressed by the were's loyalty, even though I knew it was more for Ulnyx than it was for me. I had no doubt she was still harboring the hope that she could extract his soul from mine.

"Landon," she cried, seeing me appear behind the fiend. Izak turned, quickly masking a look of surprise at my return. She took advantage of the distraction, ducking past the demon and throwing herself into me, wrapping her arms around me and nuzzling my neck.

"Okay, okay," I said, untangling myself from her. "I slowed it down a bit, but we have to get going."

Izak motioned with his arm, ushering us into the final room before the rift. It was almost just as Josette had remembered it, with one major difference.

Standing in the center of the room was a large wooden crucifix. From it hung an angel, an old, grey angel, wings spread and nailed to the ends of the cross, hands stretched above his head, body gaunt and unclothed. His head hung limply to his chest, but it rose as we approached.

"Demons," he said, in a quiet, hollow voice. "Have you come to die?"

"You're the only one who looks like they're going to die," Lylyx said.

His laugh was a wheeze and a cough. "You truly think that, do you were?" he asked. "I don't know how you got past it, but it will be along for

127

you soon. Whatever you're doing here, you should never have come."

"Get past what?" I asked.

His eyes fell on mine, and narrowed. "A diuscrucis?" he said, alarmed. "So she wasn't lying."

"Who?"

The angel looked up at his bonds, then over to his wings. "Release me, diuscrucis, and I'll tell you a tale. When it's done, all that I ask is that you set my soul free from this prison."

"You want me to kill you?" I asked.

"Yes," he replied. "But I beseech you to allow my soul to travel to whatever waits beyond."

I nodded, focusing on the nails that held the angel in place and pulling them from the cross. He would have tumbled to the ground, but Lylyx caught him and lowered him to the floor. The angel took a deep breath and fluttered his wings. Once he was off the cross, I could see the blade that had been affixed to the post, stabbing into his spine and preventing him from escaping his torture.

"Do not underestimate the kindness you have done me," the angel said to Lylyx. She looked surprised, and stepped back away from him.

"Speak quickly seraph," I said. "As you've said, the demon that hunts in these sewers won't be trapped forever."

"Of course," the angel replied. "I am archangel Avriel."

My head nearly burst from the power of Josette's voice in my soul.

"*Avriel the Just*," she said with a mixture of joy and sadness.

"I was ordained by Michael himself shortly after the death of Jesus," he said. "During my years among the living, I was a simple farmer, a layman, known among my peers for my honor and integrity. My sense of justice." His voice strengthened as he spoke, and the years began to roll off, his body finally able to regenerate. Just how long had he been hanging on that cross?

"I found even greater justice in death, volunteering into the Lord's Holy War against the First Fallen's mischief on mankind. As a shepherd of the Lord I was offered the chance to protect the meek, and in time rose to be the greatest seraphim walking the mortal plane. In those days, there were few diuscrucis, and those that walked the Earth were direct descendants, hated by both demon and angel, ostracized and killed when possible."

Avriel had finished healing, and now stood up straight and proud, his seven foot frame rippling with muscle and power. His grey wings had regenerated to a healthy silken white, with golden tips. He wrapped the wings around his front to cover his nakedness.

"So it was that the balance was maintained only through the opposing efforts of both Heaven and Hell, and it was common for the archangels to walk the Earth in response to the growing demon threat. We were the most skilled fighters, the best engineers, the strongest in holy scripture. For many years, we kept them at bay, until we no longer could.

"One day, a blight appeared on the mortal realm that threatened to destroy the balance, to end the reign of humanity and deny the Lord his rightful victory. It was a cold darkness that stretched across the land, bringing hopelessness and death to all that it touched. It was the First

Fallen's greatest creation, culled from the anguish of his many thousands of prisoners. Its name was Abaddon."

"*Abaddon*," Josette cried out. The strength of her fear burst into my head, and I closed my eyes and clutched at my temples.

"Abaddon is a myth," I said, Josette's thoughts reflected in my speech.

Avriel approached me, spreading his wings and wrapping me in them. He lowered his face so it was only inches from my own. "You've taken an angel?" he asked, boring his eyes into mine.

I felt Josette within me, being pulled to the surface by his gaze.

"Not taken," she said through my voice. "Offered."

His eyes softened. "*Why?*" he asked, his unspoken word resonating in my mind.

"A new blight is threatening," Josette said. "The demons move against the diuscrucis. We are not strong enough. If he is removed, we will lose."

Avriel nodded, and looked up at the entrance to the room. "It is almost through your barriers," he said. "Abaddon is no myth. It is the deepest heart of Hell's despair, and it once walked this Earth, destroying all that it touched. Angel, demon, human, animal, plant, it makes no difference. It exists to feed.

"Thousands were killed in its blights, and countless more would have died had we not engineered the creature's doom. A box of my own design, covered in seraphim runes and imbued by all of the disciples. I alone was charged with bringing the box to Abaddon. I alone was charged with approaching the demon, having developed the mental strength needed to combat its message of fear and death. I succeeded in my conquest, and caught the monster in the box, but not without cost. I too was trapped by my design, and spent countless hundreds of years in a war that could not end. We have destroyed one another more times than can be known, but the power of the box is such to repeat the cycle of time, and so we did."

I could feel the blackness begin to creep in. It was taking its time to reach us, unhurried in its confidence. Avriel sensed it too, and he stepped over to the doorway and scratched out holy scripture into the stone floor. As he completed the characters, it took on a soft golden glow.

"That will give me time to finish my story," he said, turning back to us and continuing. "I don't know how long we were inside. I couldn't know what happened to the box, for it would have fallen in the center of the demon's desolation, left lying on the naked ground to be discovered by anyone, or anything. Time passed, impossible to track in the prison of my own making.

"Then one day, it destroyed me. I would have expected to return to my place inside the box, waiting for the demon to find me again, but instead woke here, nailed to this cross, with Abaddon standing before me, no longer contained. For the first time ever, it spoke to me.

"'*You are mine at last,*' it said. '*You can never escape, and I will delight in the years of despair you will feel from my hand, in payment for the years of despair I have felt chained inside your device.*'"

The darkness couldn't pierce the archangel's scripture, but there was a shriek from the other side of the doorway, and when I looked up it was standing there, its vague, black, humanoid form shifting and moving while it tested Avriel's defenses. It didn't sound happy that he was off the cross.

"The demon remains here to torture me," Avriel said. "Each day it forces itself into my soul, and I suffer a fate I would wish on no one. We are bound by the power that returned us from my prison, the power of the Demon Queen. Once I am gone, it won't be able to survive here, and it will retreat to Hell."

"The Demon Queen?" I asked. "She was here?"

"I do not know," Avriel replied. "Abaddon has told me she is the one who set us free, and nailed me to the crucifix."

There was a hissing sound, and when I looked back I could see that Abaddon was defeating the archangel's runes, black tendrils smothering them and erasing them from the stone. I felt the cold despair returning, and I knew our time was up.

"Destroy me now, diuscrucis," Avriel said. "For all our sakes."

I looked at him, and then back at the demon. "If I kill you, Abaddon will be returned to Hell?"

"Yes," he said. He began to grow agitated.

"If he's returned to Hell, he can be brought back to the mortal realm, untethered by your bond," I said. "Do you have any idea what that could mean?"

The glow of the runes began to flicker, and more of the demon's power began to ooze into the room. The hellfire sconces started going out, one by one. Avriel's eyes grew wide, and he grabbed my shoulder.

"Please," he said. "You made a promise."

We were out of time. I took hold of Ulnyx's power and used it to create a single sharp claw. All I needed to do was break the skin.

"Hurry," Avriel cried, spreading his wings wide and holding out his arms to give me a clear opening.

I focused, pulling on the air, creating a massive gust that lifted the archangel. It threw him backwards, returning him to his place of impalement on the cross. I located the nails lying on the ground and pulled them up, pinning his wings and hands anew, leaving him in tears.

"You promised," he cried, his voice soft, hoarse, and filled with despair.

"I'm sorry," I said, and I meant it. I reached out and took Lylyx by the arm, pulling her with me towards the open mouth of the giant demon skull. Izak was already in the tunnel, running for the rift.

CHAPTER 13

"Light it up," I said to Izak as soon as we reached the end of the short tunnel. I had half-expected that Charis would have destroyed the rift, and left us to be devoured by Abaddon. Then again, I had a sneaking suspicion that freeing the demon was precisely what the Demon Queen had hoped I would do.

Izak knelt at the rift and began tracing over the existing runes, making a series of harsh guttural sounds in the back of his throat. Cries of extraordinary agony echoed through the tunnel; the demon extracting payment for Avriel's defiance. I cringed with every terrible vocalization, trying to ignore the guilt I was feeling for leaving the archangel in such a state.

The circular set of runes began to flame, and I felt a slight charge of ionized air fill the space. Izak stepped back from the transport rift and motioned me towards it.

"Be ready," I said. There was no telling what might greet us on the other side.

Lylyx reached out and took hold of my arm. "These things always make me a little dizzy," she said.

I gave a slight nod, and stepped into the rift.

I had only been through a rift one other time since I had visited the Demon Queen and retrieved the Grail. I was chasing a fiend through the streets of Manhattan when he ducked down an alley and into an old, abandoned bar. I followed him into the bathroom, and after shoving my way through the door had found myself in a different abandoned pub in Dublin, Ireland. In the end, I had caught and killed the fiend, and destroyed both ends of the rift. They didn't make me dizzy, but I hated not knowing what I was walking into.

I was expecting a well-laid trap, or at the very least a poorly laid trap. I thought maybe Charis would be there on the other side, as she had those years before, waiting to gloat and tell me again what a fool I was. I considered that Gervais would be there, his own power brought to bare, ready to strike me down before I could gather my wits.

None of that happened. One foot left the rift while the other one entered, and on the other side there was nothing. No Charis, no Gervais, no Sarah, no minions or underlings. Nothing. I had made every effort not to be taken by surprise, and instead I was taken by surprise. I stood there in shock long enough for Izak to bump me on his way through.

He stumbled to a stop, looking as confused as I imagined I did. Lylyx seemed out of sorts as well, but that may have been her reaction to the travel.

"Not what I expected," I said. We were in a simple twelve-foot square room with the rift in the center, an open doorway beyond. I focused on my Sight, reaching out for a sign of an ambush, or at least an indication that there was anyone home. Nothing but nothing. My heart sank. Where was Sarah?

"Are you sure we're in the right place?" Lylyx asked, recovering from her disorientation. She dropped my arm and used it to point at Izak. "Are you sure you can trust this one?"

The demon ruffled at her suggestion, rounding on her with flames in his eyes. I stepped between them.

"I trust Izak more than I trust you," I said. I turned to the fiend. "We're in the right place, aren't we?"

Izak nodded, waving at the room and giving me the thumbs up. This was where he had planned for us to be.

"Okay," I said. "We'll take a look around, and see if we can figure out what's going on." Mr. Ross had said Gervais returned to Paris. Sarah had to be here. "Keep your guard up, they may be able to hide themselves from Sight."

I started towards the door, but Izak put his hand on my shoulder. When I turned back, he pointed at his chest. The brand. He motioned at the floor, and then took a seat.

"What are you doing?" Lylyx asked.

"He has to stay here," I said. "Gervais is his master. He's been branded."

Lylyx's face softened. "How?" she asked quietly.

Izak glanced up at her, and then turned away, embarrassed.

"Leave him be," I told her. "It's none of our business. Let's go."

We headed out of the room, finding ourselves in a long, straight stone corridor that didn't appear all that different from the sewer we had just escaped. There were a few doors spaced along either side of the hallway, but opening them showed the rooms to be no more than standard household storage – cleaning supplies, sacks of grain, tack for horses, and anything else a rich French noble might need to enjoy the comfort of his chateau.

The end of the corridor brought us to a small, open room that split at a pair of narrow stairways headed in opposite directions.

"Up or down?" Lylyx asked. I closed my eyes and focused my Sight, but still there was nothing.

"*Which way?*" I asked, reaching out for Josette. I knew she could hear me, but her response couldn't pierce the solitude. I wanted to search her memories, but the idea scared me. Here of all places, I had no idea what I would find, what I would experience, or what it would do to me.

We had determined it was my power, my connection to Purgatory that was obscuring our ability to communicate. It was a river of energy that couldn't be easily crossed. She had done it on occasion, with help or in moments of strong emotion, and I could always feel both her and Ulnyx's pulse running just below the surface, fluctuating in and out of reach. It was clear that the key to letting her through was to stifle the connection, to put a finger in the dam, but I had no idea how, at least not consciously. All of my efforts up to now had been to learn to amplify the signal, not suppress it.

I opened my eyes and considered the steps. The chateau was huge, at least forty rooms, and that was only the upper floors. I knew Gervais had also built a laboratory somewhere underground, as well as a prison. What else had he constructed beneath the surface that I didn't know about, but maybe Josette did? I could have used her help.

"Down," I said at last. It was the lab that decided it for me. Just the tiniest sliver of a thought that Sarah could be down there was enough to turn me cold.

We descended the stairs, following three narrow flights into the bowels of the chateau. Still, the estate seemed deserted.

The steps finally fed out into a large, unlit corridor that I recognized immediately as the prison. Rows of cells lined the passage, and I stopped to take note of the runes that covered each individual bar. This wasn't an ordinary dungeon. These were cells designed to hold demons.

All except the last one. The last one had runes too, but they were different. The entire hollow was different. It was three times the size of the others, with a soft pillow-top mattress in the corner, along with a recliner, end table, lamp, and a shelf full of books. It was warmly decorated, and strangely homey. I lost myself at the sight of it.

The demon looks in at me with inquisitive eyes. I've seen this one before, I know, trailing along behind Gervais, attending to his needs. I remember chasing him outside of Notre Dame, only to have him vanish around a corner like no more than a ghost.

Izak. That's what Gervais calls him, but when I hear my brother's voice echo through the dungeon I see the demon bristle, and I know that isn't his true name. Why does he call him that, I wonder? Does it have meaning, or is the moniker a flaunt? I can see the runes on the fiend's arms, and I know he has power of his own.

He's standing there, looking at me, his hands wrapped around the bars that bind me to this place, preventing me from returning to Heaven. He's been coming around more often lately, and staying longer to stare at me.

"Good morning Izak," I say. I began speaking to him a few weeks ago out of boredom and loneliness. He doesn't bristle when I say the name anymore. When I say it, he almost looks pleased. "Have you come to check on Sarah?"

He never speaks back, either with his eyes or his hands. I know he cannot use his voice, because he has no tongue. It was taken long enough ago that he doesn't try.

I put my hand to my stomach, feeling the small bump of it. So much fear at the truth of the pregnancy, but I am a servant of the Lord, and the Lord has seen fit to bless me with this child. She is innocent of the crimes of her father. She is innocent of her heritage. I know the others would disagree, but it is my right to believe in a just, kind, and merciful Lord. It is my right to believe He has a plan for Sarah, or she would not be developing in my womb, the first diuscrucis born in nearly two millennia.

The demon is still standing there, staring at me. He looks sad.

"Why don't you come in?" I offer. "It's early, and I'm sure your master is still in bed."

His eyes widen at the suggestion, and he moves to leave, but then hesitates. He looks at me for another minute or so, and then cautiously unlocks and opens the door. His eyes stay glued to me while he enters and locks the cage behind him.

"The Lord has said that the fallen cannot be redeemed," I say, "for hate that has grown in the heart of an angel is hate that cannot be undone."

He walks over to where I am resting on the recliner and kneels down in front of me. I reach out and put my hand on his forehead. He jerks backwards, frightened, and then leans back in. His brow is tinder.

"You aren't fallen, Izak," I say. "The Lord will forgive you, if you but ask."
I am Calming him, but he is letting me. My ability pales in comparison to his strength.

Tears run from the demon's eyes, and he shakes his head in disbelief over the
Lord's forgiveness. I take his head and rest it on my lap, singing softly to him. In
minutes, he is at rest. I could take the keys and make my escape, but I remain. I will not
turn this creature away from the redemption he so desperately needs. The Lord will decide
my fate.

"Landon?"

My vision returned. Lylyx was there, holding me up from behind
while I clutched at the bars to Josette's former prison. I should have seen
that one coming.

"I'm okay," I said, rebalancing on my feet and removing my hands
from the bars. There were imprints in the skin where the edges of the runes
had dug in. I studied them for the few seconds it took my body to repair.

"That's the second time you've gone dark on me," she said, letting
me go and backing up a step.

"Have you ever absorbed a soul?" I asked her.

"Not yet," she replied. "What's it like?"

"When you absorb a soul, it becomes a part of you, but it still
retains its own sense of itself, its own memories. Ulnyx can see everything I
can see, he feels my pain when I'm hurt, and I feel his…uh… happiness,
when I look at you. It's a lot more symbiotic than I expected." Five years,
and I was only now beginning to reach any true understanding of it.

"Different things trigger different memories, and sometimes they're overwhelming."

I shouldn't have mentioned feeling what Ulnyx felt. No sooner had I stopped talking than Lylyx's arms were back around me, and her mouth was pressed against mine. I could feel Ulnyx pushing inside me, practically begging me to return the affection. In that moment I understood that even the most vile of the First Fallen's children was not immune to love. I opened my mouth and returned the kiss, giving the experience up to Ulnyx in payment for his advice. One kiss, and one kiss only. That was the remainder on the balance.

"Don't get the wrong idea," I said to her, breaking the embrace. "That wasn't from me."

Her smile was lustful. "Tell me there was no part of you that didn't enjoy it," she replied.

It was a small part. "Come on," I said, leading her past the prison cells and into a small antechamber. I focused on my Sight again, and started to run.

It was faint, but it was there, the smallest trace of heat, the barest sign of life. It could have been anyone, or anything, the signal was just too slight to know, but even the thinnest hope was better than none at all.

The antechamber fed into a separate large room that reminded me of my own place at the Belmont; a wide open space, a rack of various weapons, stuffed practice targets, and singed walls. I noted the piles of ash as we sped by. They could have been incinerated dummies, or they could have been the remains of Divine.

The training room exited into another, more gruesome space, most easily described as a torture chamber. I only recognized a few of the evil tools, the most popular standards of the middle ages. An iron maiden, a rack, a scavenger's daughter, and a host of other cruel devices lay in haphazard order about the space. They all had some measure of staining from the blood of their victims, though the judas chair appeared to be one of Gervais' favorites. At the end of the room was a metal door, covered in demonic runes that had been painted with blood. Whatever I was chasing, it was behind that door.

I focused my will on it, demanding the bolts to corrode and dissolve, insisting that it crumble and fall to the floor. I watched the runes begin to glow, and felt the feedback building.

"Get down," I shouted, turning my energy to myself instead, using the power to leap towards Lylyx, grabbing her and throwing us both aside as a gout of hellfire launched from the door.

We hit the wall hard, and I heard Lylyx's back crack under the pressure. She hissed in pain and lashed out, catching my shoulder with her fist and rocking me off of her. I prepared to defend myself from her rage, but she wasn't even looking at me.

She got to her feet, growling and shifting, her body growing, changing, healing. With a roar, she rushed over to the door and began kicking it. "Son of a bitch," she howled, each blow leaving a deeper dent in the metal.

I got over my initial stasis and joined her, pulling on Ulnyx's power and using it to become the monster. We hammered at the door together, using brute force when Divine energy wouldn't do. A dozen smites later, the iron flew off its hinges, headed into the room. I focused, pulling in the air behind it, giving it an unnatural density, stopping the bullet before it could hit anything that might be important.

"Nice catch," Lylyx said, returning to her human form. I shifted back as well.

We had smashed our way into the archfiend's lab. Computers ringed the perimeter, interspersed with all kinds of medical equipment and paraphernalia that I couldn't name or understand the use of. Near the rear of the room were a couple of gurneys, and one of them had a corpse on it. The corpse wasn't what I was Seeing.

That was in the center of the room, not ten feet from where the door had come to rest. He was hanging from a chain that had been bolted to the ceiling, his arms bound above his head, his legs swinging freely a foot above the ground. A dagger was sticking out of his chest, dug straight into his heart. It was a cursed blade, so it hadn't killed him. Instead, it was keeping him incapacitated and weak, unable to die, but also unable to heal.

His head lifted slowly, and looked unsteady at the end of his neck. A curl of black hair rested over his right eye, or rather what had once been his right eye, which had been gouged out. In a surely-not-coincidental irony, so had his left. It must have been done by a demon's claw, because that was the only way it wouldn't have healed.

"Gervais," I said. "Where the hell is Sarah?"

.

CHAPTER 14

So many memories. So much pain. In that moment, I didn't suffer one specific flashback, or fall into a single dark hole of Josette's past. In that moment, I went headfirst into a pool of blackness and hurt that was beyond compare. Every memory of the archfiend's torture and betrayal ripped through me, a terrifying primal scream that ran through me like a nuclear blast. I crumpled to the floor, putting my head in my hands, trying to resolve the emotions. The destruction was physical, spiritual, and mental. It was beyond intense, and it felt like it lasted forever.

Behind me, I could hear Lylyx calling my name. In front of me, I could hear Gervais struggling to breathe, trying to speak, or laugh, or gloat. I swam through the maelstrom, my anger building. One thought, a memory of my own. Josette trapped under the weight of the angel Moses, struggling for survival, the elder seraph chiding her for her brother's evil deeds. In that moment, her anger and guilt and pain had driven her to become nothing more than an object of rage, a broken visage of goodness that had brought her to violence and caused her to fall. I didn't have to worry about falling.

The tidal wave pushed me to my feet, and the dagger in Gervais' chest came to my hand with barely a thought. The scream that left my lips was inhuman and cold, more feral and raw than any demon could manage. I wanted to stab, and cut, and tear, and rip, and continue to plunge the blade into the archfiend over, and over, and over again. I wanted revenge, penance, balance. I wanted to put a bloody, agonizing end to the evil creature before me, and I wanted to do it slowly.

I stepped forward and raised the knife, ready to extract my payment, when I was hit from inside for a second time.

"*Landon, no,*" Josette cried, her own shout rising over my turmoil, overwhelming my anger, and breaking my momentum. "*This is not the way.*"

The knife clattered to the floor, and I stood transfixed, staring at Gervais but not seeing him. The chaos of my soul began to quiet, and reason began to filter back in. Sarah. I couldn't help Sarah if Gervais were dead. He was the only one who knew where she was. My body shook at the thought of how close I had come to complete failure. I *was* a fool.

"Diuscrucis," the archfiend said. The hole in his heart had closed over, and his breathing was returning to normal. Still, he didn't attempt to remove himself from his chains.

Josette was a bastion of peace in my soul, sending me soothing thoughts, stealing away the anger that remained. I looked up at the demon.

"Gervais," I repeated, my voice more powerful in its newfound calm. "Where is Sarah?"

He spoke in a soft French accent, his voice smooth and confident despite his situation. "Of course, she told me you would come for her. She told me you would be angry." His head shifted forward, as though he were focusing. "She left me here as a gift to you. She said you would appreciate the state she left me in, before you killed me. Oh, but I knew. I knew my dearest sister wouldn't let me down."

My anger was rekindling, but as quickly as it could rise, Josette's soul tempered it. "Who told you?" I asked.

His smile was mocking. "That vampire bitch of yours. Reyka."

"Rebecca?"

My heart skipped, but I held onto my center. Rebecca? Back in the mortal realm, back from Hell?

"She's used that name before," he said.

My mind began to spin with the possibilities. She was back, and she had taken Sarah from Gervais, leaving the archfiend incapacitated for me to find. I wanted to believe she had returned to help me with whatever was happening, whatever plot the Demon Queen had cooked up for me to fall into. I wanted to think that she had been on my side the entire time, and that the last five years had all been for some esoteric purpose whose meaning I would discover once we were reunited.

I wanted to believe in the dream, but the fact was that I couldn't. I had heard her lie when she left me paralyzed on the floor. I had seen in her eyes that she knew exactly what she was doing. Why would she have done that if she really had cared. Survival, she had said. Survival was about doing whatever it took. Survival didn't leave room for friends.

"She's no friend of mine," I said. It was a hard thing to let out, because I had avoided it for so long. Still, I couldn't stop that small piece of myself that remained naive from holding on just a little bit. "Tell me what happened."

The smile remained, and he shook his hands in their shackles. "I'll tell you everything, mon ami, but I have terms."

Of course. No demon would trade something for nothing. "You aren't exactly in a strong bargaining position," I said. "All I have to do is stick this dagger back into whatever passes as your heart." I focused, bringing the blade up so that the point bit into his chest.

"I beg to differ," he countered. "I've already lost my eyes, and I know you won't kill me. Sweet Josette protects me still. What is it they say about family? The family that lays together, stays together." He paused, allowing the words time to cut. I didn't give him the satisfaction. "No matter," he said. "You need me to tell you where my beloved child has been abducted to. I need nothing from you. I can hang here for a thousand years, someone will be along sooner or later."

"If Rebecca has Sarah, I think I already know where to find them," I said. Where else would she go? "Which leaves you nothing to bargain with, except your life."

"Can you be sure?" he asked me. "Are you willing to risk Sarah's life on what you believe of this creature you say isn't your friend? I have seen her. I wouldn't, if I were in your position."

What did that mean? Rebecca had spent the last five years in Hell. Who could know how she had changed? What I knew for sure was that the Demon Queen was moving against me, and she had employed no shortage of powerful demons to hinder my progress in getting here. Were Charis and Rebecca working together? Or did Charis seek to delay me because she knew Gervais had lost Sarah? In either case, what did they want with her in the first place? Too many questions, and no answers. The archfiend could help me with at least one of them.

I plunged the dagger back into his heart. "I'm done playing games with demons," I said.

He laughed. "You think this is pain?" he asked with his last strong breath.

"No," I replied. "That's just to keep you still for a minute." I walked over to him and tore open his shirt.

His chest was covered in dozens of runed scars, swirls, sigils, pentagrams and crossing lines. It took me a few minutes to find it, and I could feel the demon's ragged breath on my scalp the entire time.

"What are you looking for?" he whispered. His voice hinted at fear.

I reached up and pulled the dagger out of his heart with my hand, leading him to take in a big gulp of air.

"Don't worry, I found it," I said.

The one I wanted was on his right pectoral, and I didn't hesitate to sink the dagger into his flesh and cut it cleanly away.

"What are you doing?" he cried, watching the formerly scarred skin regrow clean. Somewhere in the distance, a shout echoed through the stone.

"It's clear you don't fear me," I said, stepping back away from him. "That's okay. I don't need you to fear me."

I looked over at Lylyx. She was grinning widely, understanding what I had just done. "You should have just told him," she said to Gervais.

A strange coldness that brought back the recent memory of Abaddon preceded Izak's entrance into the lab. The moment Gervais Saw him, he began to wriggle in his chains.

"What did you do?" he shouted, his fear now plain.

Izak looked at me, and then at the archfiend's chest, smooth where the scars of the binding had once been. The fiend's shirt was hanging open, his chest bleeding where he had mutilated his skin to remove the other end of the connection. He approached us, his eyes alight in anger. I raised my hand, putting it between the two of them.

"Not yet," I said to Izak. "I need to know what he knows. Keep him alive. For Sarah."

Izak didn't look happy, but he nodded. A small ball of fire formed in the palm of his hand, and he held it up to Gervais' face. The archfiend tried to move away from it, but the chains kept him static.

"Tell me what you know," I said. "I can't be sure how long Izak can control himself after what you did to him."

Gervais growled. "Fine," he said. "I'll tell you everything, if you get him away from me and let me go."

"Deal," I said. "Izak?"

The fiend punched Gervais in the gut, sending him swinging on the chains, but he retreated.

"Of course," he began, once he had stopped swinging. "I've been looking for Sarah for years. Ever since Izak stole her away. I combed the world in search of her, offering up everything I have at my disposal. Money, sex, power, information… nobody knew anything, or if they did, they were afraid to get caught between he and I. As you may have surmised, this one is quite a devilish fiend."

And Izak wasn't his original name.

"Sixteen years," he continued. "A blink in time under normal circumstances, but Sarah is mortal. Her time here is limited, and there is no chance that the powers-that-be in the other realms will ever allow her to return. I was becoming desperate, and I am ashamed to admit, losing hope. You have no idea of what she is capable of. What she can become with the proper...education.

"She came to me two months ago, your little vampiress non-friend. I could feel the power radiating off of her the moment she stepped through the transport rift. Whatever you think she was before, think again diuscrucis. She's been to Hell, and something happened to her there."

My mind kept returning to the last vision I had of her before she disappeared into the Hell rift. Sad, but strong. Sure of her decision.

"What did she want?" I asked.

"She told me she would help me, if I would help her. She said she knew where Sarah was. I asked her what she wanted in return, and I offered her everything. She settled for my loyalty, and allegiance. It was a steep price, but such is the nature of my desire that I agreed. In any case, allegiance among demons is a fickle thing." He laughed then, a self-defeated chuckle.

"She gave me the means to hide myself from Divine Sight, runes she etched into my back with her claws. She brought me to New York, and showed me how Sarah was living. I watched her walk to school, and I was disgusted. She's wasting her life as a simple mortal when she should be Commanding them like a God." His voice rose to a shout, and his body trembled with anger. "I would have taken her then, right out in the open, but Reyka forbid it. She insisted I had to wait, that it was not yet time. I was a fool. She wanted you to know she was taken. She wanted you to know that it was me. She wanted you to come here, because she wanted you to find me like this. I didn't see her lies until it was too late.

"I found Sarah in her city below the surface, living like a vagabond instead of the princess that she is. She didn't know me, because she couldn't See me. She tried to call for help. I could feel her power reaching out, but I put her to sleep, prepared the rift to summon the wraith, and left. Izak was supposed to be killed. That bitch assured me that Izak would be killed." He started screaming again, shaking on his chains. The anger left as quickly as it had come, and he hung still again.

"Just another deception," he said, his calm and anger exchanging like the tide. "She's quite good at the game. Sarah knew her as soon as we returned here. She asked her if it was time."

Gervais paused and sat motionless on the end of the chain, deep in thought. "Why would she say that?" he asked in a whisper before continuing his tale.

"'Almost,' Reyka had said to her. 'You're safe now.' And then the bitch put her vampires on me."

"You got beat by vampires?" I asked, confused. In the earth-walking demonic food chain, Gervais was near the top, while vampires were close to the bottom.

"Really stretching your head muscles on that one, aren't you diuscrucis," he spat. "She's done something to them. They're stronger and heal faster than any demon I've ever seen. They even healed from my fire."

I was ready to fire back on the first comment, but the second stopped me dead. I couldn't be sure, but I had a feeling I knew what she had done. The Grail, my blood, her blood. It made me sick to my stomach.

"I couldn't defeat them," he said. "Not without risking Sarah and bringing the entire chateau down on us. They chained me up, and Reyka stuck the dagger in my heart. She didn't want my allegiance. She wanted to give you a gift, an apology of sorts. She said to tell you that Sarah is safe in her care and that she's waiting for you."

"Where?" I asked.

"Las Lajas Cathedral," he said. "South America."

He was lying. "Izak," I said, turning to the fiend. "Your former master thinks he can lie to me."

Izak clenched his fist, and it lit up in flame.

"Wait," Gervais cried. "I swear that's where she said she would be." Truth. "I don't believe her." Truth.

I paused Izak. "Why don't you believe her?" I asked.

"Do you know what would happen if she tried to hang out inside a church?" Gervais asked. "She'd be surrounded by angels within thirty seconds, and cathedrals have power of their own. She may be strong, but she isn't that strong."

"Even with an army of super vampires?"

Gervais fell silent. "Sarah," he said finally.

"What about her?" I asked.

152

"Look at my eyes, diuscrucis," he said.

"Rebecca took them," I replied. "You deserved it."

Gervais laughed. "Reyka didn't take them. Sarah did."

I felt Josette's fear creep up my soul, where it was added to my own. "Sarah did?" I asked.

Not that it wasn't understandable after what the demon had done to her, but it was still surprising. When I thought of her, I saw only the innocent, frightened girl who had slept by my side and named me protector.

"If she had tortured anyone else the way she did her father, I would have been proud," he said.

I had another thought then. One that was more disconcerting than any other. Gervais had always wanted to raise Sarah to be evil, to tap into her power and use it for his own ends. Josette had believed that getting her away from the archfiend would be her salvation. What if Gervais' influence was unnecessary? What if she was breaking bad on her own? Sarah had tried to Command me. She had sent Izak with me against his will. She had cut out the demon's eyes, and had asked Rebecca if it was time, as though she were in on whatever was going on.

"Why would Rebecca bring Sarah to Las Lajas?" I asked, gripped with a dread that I couldn't shake.

"If Sarah's power is maturing, she'll be able to Command the seraph. She can make them fall, and she can do it faster than you can balance it. She'll need time though, time to learn to control them. Las Lajas is the sandbox. The Vatican will be the battlefield."

My fear evolved into anger. "Is this what you wanted?" I shouted, walking back over to the demon and planting the dagger deep into his flesh. He didn't react to the wound. "Is this what you raped your sister for? Is this what you imprisoned her for?" I pulled the blade out and stabbed him again, and again. I could sense Josette in the back of my soul, but I still controlled her, and I pushed my power between us.

It was surprising that Izak would be the one to stop my mutilation of the demon. He grabbed me from behind and ripped me away from Gervais, leaving him as a shredded mess, blood streaming to the floor. He immediately began to heal.

"I want power," Gervais said with unaffected calm. "Sarah was to help me control this world, not destroy it. Let Satan have Hell, let God have Heaven, let Dante have Purgatory. Earth could have been mine."

He actually sounded remorseful. It made me sick. Gervais had occupied so much of the pain and anger I had been carrying around for the last five years, his treatment of Josette blasting at me from her memories and my reaction to them. I don't know how many times I had been doubled over by those memories, left leaning or crouching with tears running from my eyes, my heart racing, unable to control myself. He was the boogie man in my nightmares, and like any kid growing up and finding out there were no monsters under the bed, I was discovering that his power was an illusion fed by the very fears that had incapacitated me. Josette's ties to him were too personal to see through the charade, but now that I was looking on him, hanging blind from the ceiling, I almost felt pity. Almost.

"I've told you everything I know," Gervais said. "Now set me free."

"Lylyx," I said, turning back towards the door to the lab, "stay here with Izak. I have to go meet someone." I glanced over at the fiend. "Izak, I'm done. Do whatever you want with him."

Izak smiled. He hadn't pulled me away to stop me. He had pulled me away because he wanted to be the one to destroy the archfiend. I could feel Josette struggling within me, and I begged her for forgiveness. It was the second promise I had broken in less than an hour, but I decided that I could live with that.

I found a Ferrari in the carriage house outside the chateau. I could hear Gervais' screams as I drove away.

..

CHAPTER 15

There was a certain comfort to the sooth purr of the Ferrari's engine that helped me keep my mind in some kind of coherent state while I made the much longer mortal trip back to Paris from Gervais' chateau in Besancon, not far from the Swiss border. It was nearly six o'clock France time, and I could only hope that whatever was occurring at the Eiffel Tower today hadn't happened yet. Since I was running under the assumption that the party was in my honor, I was pretty sure that it hadn't.

Of course, it didn't offer me any more clarity. I had spent the last five years fighting every day to keep my emotions in check, to push them down into the recesses of my soul and try to lose them there. It had made my work maintaining the balance almost clinical, an exercise in efficiency. It had led me to scour the world for answers to Charis' riddle, because the unfeeling soul meant an eternity worse than anything Hell could throw at me. In the end, it had cost me Sarah, because I had ignored the warning signs and plodded on my fixated course.

Now? Now it was all coming back in a flood of anger that was threatening to complete my failure. I had lost Josette and Rebecca that day under the Statue of Liberty, but at least I thought I had won the war for balance. I was beginning to see that I hadn't won anything. At best I had just delayed some schemes for a while, taking the Grail out of the game and causing the forces around me to move on to plan B. The trouble was, I couldn't figure out the game, or even who the players were. Charis was out there, and she had freed the demon Abaddon in Gervais' tunnels. Did the archfiend know about it? In my eagerness to reach Sarah, I hadn't even thought to ask him. She had also sent a witch and Lylyx to slow me down, to keep me from getting to Gervais too soon. Why?

What about Sarah? The fear of her maturation into a powerful diuscrucis who had chosen selfishness and power had been converted and joined with the rest of my anger. If she really had moved in that direction, it was because of what Gervais had dictated she would be. She had grown up in fear and hiding. Suppose she found she had the power to live a different way, to be in control of her own life? Could anyone blame her for using it? How much evil was ingrained by fate, how much by genetics, how much by fear and lack of independence? Her lineage made her the poster child for nature versus nurture, but even there I saw only balance.

Where did Rebecca fit in? She had given Sarah up to Gervais, but then taken her in and left Gervais for me. The archfiend had said it was a gift to me, but why leave me a gift unless she wanted something? What could she possibly want, if she already had Sarah, and with it the means to bring down Heaven? Unless Gervais was wrong, and she had taken Sarah to prevent that very thing. But the demon had said Hell had changed her. I couldn't imagine Hell changing anyone in a good way.

Too many balls in the air, and none of them rotating in a predictable orbit. Trying to catch them all was out of the question, and the powerlessness of that truth fueled my anger even more. Obi had given me the only solid clue I had in anything. A message sent by anonymous, intended to be intercepted and lead me to the Eiffel Tower. I would follow it and let this part of the game play out, and then I would see the truth. Sarah had said it to me plainly the first time we had met - they can't win if you don't play. I wasn't sure I had a choice. I jammed my foot down harder on the accelerator, an angry grimace playing across my face as the car burst forward with renewed force.

It was just after eight when I eased the Ferrari into a spot on the street across from the Tower. The spot had been a little too small for the car, so I had focused, giving the fore and aft vehicles just enough shove to make room. I changed my appearance before getting out of the car; an older gentleman with salt and pepper hair and a neatly trimmed mustache in an expensive dark suit.

I strolled across the street and along the concourse leading to the Tower, my hands in my pockets and my Sight stretched out into the night. I knew right away that I was in the right place, at the right enough time. There were a lot of Divine here, most of them at the ground level, spread out and stationary. Waiting. For me? Or something else?

There was one up on the Tower, positioned at the second deck, their signature a hot beacon burning into my soul. I felt a familiarity to this one, something about them that I recognized some piece of, but couldn't quite place. I had no doubts they were the one I was here to see. There was no motion from the other Divine, and I wasn't hiding. Play the game, but be ready to change the rules.

"Hello sir," the young french girl at the Tower ticket booth said. She was slender, with long, dark hair, brown eyes, and porcelain skin. A math textbook rested open off to the side of her counter, next to a small computer terminal.

I was pretty sure she was speaking French, but I had quickly learned that Divinity granted the gift of tongues. I heard everything in English, and spoke it that way, at least to my own ears.

"Hello," I replied. "I'm meeting someone up at..." I looked over to the board behind here, where the destinations and ticket prices were listed. "Jules Verne."

She smiled. "Of course, sir. Name?" She put her fingers to the keyboard to type in my response.

Except, I didn't know what to say. I wasn't even sure who I was actually going to be meeting up there. Was it Charis, familiar to my Sight but changed somehow? Was it Rebecca, her identity altered by her trip to Hell? I stood silent, trying to do all of the permutations, to guess the right password and gain access to the Tower's second floor. Not that I needed the permission of the girl in the booth, but I preferred to go in quietly.

"Sir?" she asked.

There was only one name I could be sure of. "Hamilton," I said.

Her fingers danced along the keys. "Ah, yes sir. Party of two. I see your acquaintance has already arrived. An escort will arrive momentarily to take you up. Enjoy your dinner, sir."

I stepped off to the side and looked up at the Tower again. My 'acquaintance' hadn't moved. A minute later a tall, handsome man in a tuxedo approached and led me over to the private elevator up to the restaurant.

The Jules Verne was a posh, elegant eatery located on the second floor of the Tower, about four hundred feet above ground level. Of course, it had fantastic views of Paris, and the dark, classy ambience mixed well with just enough chintz to call out the place as both a fine gourmet treat, and an obvious tourist destination. When the escort dropped me off with a second maitre-de in the restaurant proper, I could see that it was a full house. I imagined it always was.

I didn't need the waiter to guide me to my table, but I allowed him to. My Sight was red hot now, though I still couldn't identify who the signature belonged to. Judging by the layout, the table was in the back corner by the window, my line of sight obscured by a support beam. When the waiter pulled me around the obstruction, I smirked.

The man at the seat across from the empty one I took to be mine was a small, lean Asian, with a thick lawn of spiked black hair, a petite, well-defined face, and sharp grey eyes. He was dressed in an expensive suit, a gold Rolex dangling from a narrow wrist. He was playing the part of the businessman perfectly. He smiled and stood at the sight of me, his fangs sliding out to overlap his lower lip.

"Mr. Hamilton," he said, his voice too deep for his size, but smooth as the silk tie he was wearing.

"Mr... Cho, is it?" I asked, going along with the formalities.

He nodded. "At your service, my friend," he replied. "Thank you for meeting me here. Please, have a seat."

I slid into the offered chair, and he returned to his own. "To be honest," I said. "I was expecting someone else to be here."

He put up his hand. "Of course. There is much to speak about, my friend. First, a drink? I know it will do nothing for your senses, but some still find the act itself relaxing."

I thought about Sarah, and Rebecca. No more stalling. "Skip it," I said. "I don't have a lot of time to waste on you."

He laughed. "You have more time than you might think," he replied. "But as you wish."

The archvampire put his hands out on the table and lowered his head, his eyes falling closed. I heard a soft hum escaping from his mouth, a hum that began to morph and change in pitch and timbre. An amalgam of coldness and heat pierced the air, and the smell of a familiar perfume mixed with iron and blood. I could sense the tempo of my heart rising, my body reacting to the change faster than my mind could process it. Cho's eyes opened and his head snapped up, leaving me staring at crisp, blue orbs.

"Rebecca."

The name fell from my mouth and floated between us. She took a deep breath to suck it in. In that moment everything I had wanted to say scattered with the inhale, and I was left in a new type of purgatory, firmly entrenched between desire and disgust. It didn't matter that she was using Cho's body. It was *her*.

Her lips spread into a sensuous smile. "Landon," she said. "I've missed you."

She wasn't lying.

"Where is Sarah?" I asked. "Rebecca, if you hurt her…"

The smile vanished. "Hurt her? Why would I hurt her? Be assured worm, I have no intention of harming your sister. She is with me, and she is safe."

There was nobody else who could make the nickname 'worm' sound like a good thing. "I just can't believe it's you, that you're here. After all this time."

I felt a pinch in my soul, the tiniest little push against me. Ulnyx.

"Did you like my gift?" she asked. "Josette's brother all tied up? I would have added a bow, but I couldn't find one large enough to wrap around his ego."

"It would have been a nice touch," I replied. "Although I think Sarah appreciated it more than me. So did Izak."

There was the slightest twist in Rebecca's expression at the mention of the demon. Another pinch from the Were, sharper this time.

"Gervais' puppet? He's with you?" Her eyes danced around the restaurant.

"No. He's having his way with your gift," I said. "Rebecca, I'm happy to see you, but I'm having a hard time trying to understand what the heck is going on."

In fact, it was more than that. A third hit from Ulnyx, and it was like he had cracked a window, an invisible barrier that was up between Rebecca and I. A new distortion spread from the crack, one that was closer to reality. I saw it, but I didn't understand it. Not yet.

"It is a wondrous time for us, Landon," she said. "Not just for you and I, but for all Divine. A new age."

I raised my hand. I could see it through the crack. I could see the veins running along my wrist, the flesh laid over the muscle underneath. I saw past it to Rebecca. Not just Rebecca, but also Cho. There was something there. Something I was forgetting.

"No. Start from the beginning. You bled me out and took a swig from the Grail. You left me paralyzed. Why?"

Her head tilted a fraction. "I did what I had to do," she said. "In that moment, it wasn't about you, other than the blood you carry in your veins. You could have been anyone, and I would have done the same. When a Divine drinks the blood of a diuscrucis from the Holy Grail, they change. They become more powerful than they could have ever dreamed."

"Reyzl regenerated faster," I said. "He didn't seem like he gained any other power." At least not compared to before he drank the blood.

She laughed. "We didn't let him live long enough for the blood to get through his entire system, to effect a total change. Anyway, Reyzl was a fool. His ambitions were small."

I felt Ulnyx again, and the single crack in the barrier lengthened and began to spider out. I saw Rebecca with my Sight now. I saw how she had changed. I saw the raw power that she possessed, even here, even now when the body and voice she was using were not her own. Through the distortion, I could suddenly see that all the time I had spent lamenting her betrayal had been wasted time. She couldn't have betrayed me, because she had never been with me.

"So you knew what the Grail would do for you the whole time?" I asked, growing angry. "That's why you saved me from Reyzl at your party?"

"Landon, wait," she said. She hesitated, and then nodded. "It's true. When I helped you escape I was taking a risk that you would be able to get your hands on the Grail, and I would be able to use it. Merov told me what it could do. He went on and on about it, about how he wished he could find a diuscrucis to bleed. Anyway, that was how it started, but that isn't the whole story. I care for you. I really, really do."

She wasn't lying.

"Then why didn't you just ask? I was raw enough. I would have done it."

She looked sad. Genuinely sad. "Would you have understood that I needed to go to Hell? Would have have understood why? You were a Divine for all of three days. Even now, I'm not sure you'll understand."

"You went to Hell *on purpose?*" I asked. "You're right, I don't understand. But I guess that's why we're here."

I felt one last pinch from Ulnyx, and the cracked glass shattered. It was like being released from a hypnotic trance, with all of the clarity and understanding flooding into me at once. I don't know how Rebecca had done it, but the Were had helped me escape.

"It wasn't enough to survive, was it? Not for a demon. You needed to become the Queen."

This whole time I had been pinning the title on Charis, sure that she was the one trying to trip me up. Demon Queen was a title, not a name. The most powerful female demon on Earth. But why the glamour? Why try to keep me from seeing it? Another test?

"I need more than that," she said, reaching out and touching my

164

hand. "You once asked me if we could be together. We can, Landon. I want us to. I went to Hell because I needed to learn. I returned because what I was taught will allow us, you and I, to change everything. Angels, demons, and humans living together. A future for all of us. A future for the two of us."

Some of what she said was true, but not all of it. I realized with a start that whatever spell she had put on me, it wasn't to keep me from identifying her as the Demon Queen. It was to keep me from recognizing her lies. That she had told them at all was my hint that she had no idea the charm had been broken. Which part had she been lying about?

"Gervais told me about your plans for the future," I said. I decided to keep dancing to her tune, to see what she might reveal.

"Gervais is almost as simple as Reyzl," she snapped, her eyes flashing empty and black for the barest of instants. "What he thinks he knows, and what is true are two completely different things. There's a war, Landon. A hidden war whose boundaries aren't as clearly drawn as Heaven versus Hell. I know you've been tracking the messages. It's how I lured you here."

'Lured' was an interesting choice of words. Would I have heard it before, or would I have heard something else? "What is the war about? And what do you need me for?"

She smiled again, leaning forward so that her... Cho's face was close to mine. "Change," she said. "Justice. Power. The end of an old, tired God."

Did she say God? I fought to stay composed. "Mankind is part of this new world order?" I asked.

"Of course, my love," she said, her eyes dilating, her voice a coo. "The dark brothers and sisters will need sustenance in the days to come, and all of us can benefit from slaves."

It took all of my will to keep up the charade. She had said 'my love'. It was no lie. She had also said she intended to use humans as slaves and meat. My stomach turned.

"As for you," she continued, "your power is obvious. And there are other things I want from you."

She was standing now, leaning towards me, her lips hungry. I wasn't ready to show my hand, so I leaned forward and joined her in the kiss. It was deep, and emotional, and I could feel her power burning through her saliva and licking at my soul.

"What about Sarah?" I asked, once the kiss had ended. It had taken my breath away, despite the fact that a good part of me was finding her words repulsive. There was still some piece in there somewhere that knew absolute evil, that embraced it and found succor in it. It was the part of me that still cared for her, and it had a strong voice.

"She's our prize," she said. "It's her power that will end the old God, and allow a new one to take His place."

A new one? "How do you replace a God?" This wasn't balance. This was betrayal beyond anything I could have imagined.

"Just say you're with me, and you'll see."

I took a deep breath. I closed my eyes. I focused on Rebecca-as-Cho, mentally reaching for the strand of power that I knew had to be connecting them. It wasn't hard to find, her energy was so great that it writhed and pulsated in a huge, bright, tendon.

"How can I say no to you?" I asked.

"I knew you wouldn't," she said, smiling.

It was time to end the charade. I took hold of the tendon and squeezed it tight, causing Cho's eyes to open wide and his jaw to fall slack. "You're the fool," I hissed. "You either overestimated yourself, or underestimated me, but be assured that I'll stop you. This is the realm of man, and it's going to stay that way."

I pulled the plug on her, and Cho tumbled backwards into his chair. His eyes closed, and then opened. The archvampire laughed.

"I told her you wouldn't do it," he said. "Her love for you clouds her judgement."

I didn't have time to reply, because it was all I could do to duck back away from his fingers that stretched and sharpened into razor claws. His pupils vanished in a sea of black, and his fangs hung out over his lip.

Screams filled the restaurant. Cho came at me, his body a blur of motion, leaping over the table. I focused, lifting the table up and slamming it into him, pushing him upwards into the ceiling. He left a dent in the plaster before he fell back to the ground, landing on his feet.

My Sight exploded as six more vampires revealed themselves. She had hidden them from me.

"Where is she?" I shouted at Cho, rushing forward, leading with my fists. He ducked away from the blows, the smile still on his face.

"You can still change your mind," he said. "Stop this now. She wants to be with you. You saw the gift she left you." He came back with an attack of his own, his claws moving faster than I thought possible, catching my chest before I could move beyond them. It hurt, but it healed.

I could still hear the screams. I twisted my head and saw that the other vampires weren't coming for me. They were attacking the patrons. I looked back at Cho. He stood motionless, waiting to see what I would do.

"You don't need to save them," he said. "You aren't one of them. Not anymore. It isn't your job to protect them. Come with me, be a king and claim your queen."

"I'd ask you to send her a message from me, but you aren't going to live to do it," I said, overtaken by the total calm of absolute understanding. I focused, throwing Cho against the wall and pinning him with solid air. "Wait there."

I grabbed the closest weapon at hand, a steak knife lying on the nearest table. Screams still drowned out any other sound in the room, though the vampires were thinning the ranks in a hurry. I leapt on the nearest one and jabbed the knife into the back of his head, letting the silver blade sink through his skull. He cried out and dropped the woman he had been drinking from, falling face-first to the floor with a kick to the back of his spine.

He should have been out of the fight, a silver shard in his brain more than enough to keep him down. I watched while his hand reached around, seeking the blade. When he found it, he pulled it out, and the wound immediately closed over. I looked back at Cho, who was laughing in his prison. I realized why he had been familiar to me. I realized why all of the vampires were familiar to me. My blood was running in their veins, passed from the Holy Grail to Rebecca's lips, and from Rebecca's body to theirs.

The room fell quiet, the bodies of the people who had been enjoying a quiet night out at a fine restaurant left scattered on the floor. Some had been drained, others just put down like no more than meat. I reached for Ulnyx's power, but I knew I couldn't fight all of them like that. The Were's form was massively powerful, but it was also massive, an easy target and difficult to maneuver in confined spaces. I swung my head in a circle, searching for anything that I could use. There was nothing that would be enough.

"You're fortunate, Mr. Hamilton," Cho said, still trapped in my cage. There was no point wasting my energy on it. I let him go.

"Why is that?" I asked as he walked over.

"She wasn't lying when she said she needed you." He reached into his pocket, taking out a small black box covered in seraphim scripture. It bore a resemblance to a Rubik's cube, one made of polished ebony and inlaid with gold. "It's hard to hold a diuscrucis. At least when they resist."

I didn't need him to tell me what it was, I had met its former inhabitants only hours earlier. So that was why they had been set free. I looked over his shoulder at the window behind him.

"You won't make it," he said, placing the box on the ground in front of me. "Avriel was careless. He didn't ward his trap from use by demons."

My mind was racing, trying to find a way out. I could reach the window, I was sure of it. Whether I would have enough left to survive the fall was the real question. I would have to find out.

Cho started speaking, his voice smoothly reciting the language of God's children. The scripture on the box began to glow, softly at first but gaining intensity. I could feel it pulling at me, beckoning to me. I was out of time.

I heard the elevator door slide open. I heard the boom of a gun, and felt the sting of buckshot rip into my flesh. Cho stumbled backwards, his chest spreading open, his skin hissing. Three more shots fired, and I heard the cries of pain from the other vampires. The smell of frankincense filled the air.

"Well," said a voice from the edge of the elevator. "Are you going to stand there, or are you going to escape?"

I was going to escape. I ran to the elevator, bending down and grabbing the box on the way. When I reached the doors, a meaty hand grabbed my shoulder and threw me inside. Two more rounds fired from the shotgun, peppering the vampires with more of the buckshot.

"How?" I asked. The shot was only slowing them, but it was working a lot better than the silver had. The elevator began its descent.

"Plastic shot," he said, "filled with holy water."

I looked up at my rescuer. Way up. He was a monster of a man, at least seven feet tall, with thick arms, thick legs, and a round middle. His long wool overcoat made him look even bigger, hanging from broad shoulders down to his size twenty something combat boots. He had long brown hair with huge sideburns and a heavy goatee that made his eyes look tiny and lost on his face. He was holding the shotgun in one hand like it was some kind of toy, using his other to reload it.

"We're not going to make it," I said. I focused my Sight above us. The vamps were forcing open the elevator door and starting to come down.

"Take a look around, Landon," he said.

I looked down. The Divine I had Seen earlier were encircling the base of the Tower. Touched, but not like any Touched I had ever met before. Just like the behemoth in the elevator with me.

"If you could get me a clear shot, I'd appreciate it," he said.

I focused, ripping the metal around us away so that he had a good view of the vampires crawling down the side of the Tower. He fired again, and the lead vamp stopped moving as its face was shredded. A moment later I heard an even louder pop, and the demon was ripped from its perch and tossed aside like a rag doll.

"You know my name, but I don't know yours," I said.

"Ezekiel," he said. "You can call me Zeek." He held out his massive ham hand. I took it and gave it a strong shake. "You're lucky m'lady has been keeping an eye on you."

Two more pops, and another scream as a vampire was blasted from the Tower. A shout sounded from the ground, and I looked down to see that Cho had skipped the climb. He was already earthbound, finding the shooters and tearing them apart. The moment our ride touched down, I made to head in the archvampire's direction. Zeek grabbed me.

"I said escape," he said, pointing across the street to a plain grey van.

"They'll die," I said, throwing his hand from my shoulder.

He nodded. "They're ready to die. I don't like it either, but there's no other way. You can't beat Cho right now without bringing the world down around you."

I knew it was true, and it wasn't time to bring the world down around me. Not yet. I let him lead me to the van. I could see Cho watching us as we pulled away, his mouth covered in the blood of Zeek's allies, that damn smile still on his face.

.

CHAPTER 16

We drove in silence for the first ten minutes, Zeek's mind surely on the fate of his comrades, my mind reeling from the discoveries I had made. The biggest one, the one that was twisting the knife in my gut deeply enough to be twisting Josette too - Rebecca was fighting for the wrong team, and Sarah was with Rebecca. No, that wasn't it. Sarah was helping Rebecca. I had no proof, but I was sure of it.

I could have agonized over what I had done wrong in watching out for her, and helping to raise her. Too much 'ninja training'? Not enough attention? Not enough affection? I knew it was none of those things. She was a real diuscrucis, and like it or not evil was in her nature. So was good, which meant there was still hope. Just as much as I was sure she was helping Rebecca, I was just as sure that the new Demon Queen had manipulated her into doing it. Maybe all it had taken was to put her in front of Gervais with the opportunity to get even.

Still, I longed for a minute to breath, to try to relax and close my eyes, to get back to Josette so we could work our way through everything together. I'd even welcome Ulnyx at this point, to lend me his demonic perspective. There had to be some benefit to having his soul mixed with mine beyond an enhanced sense of smell and the ability to shift into a huge smelly monster. I had a feeling minutes to breath would get harder to come by, not easier.

"Where are we going?" I asked Zeek, breaking the silence at last. I could see the guilt and pain written on the man's giant face. I could smell the intensity of his emotions.

"I'm taking you to m'lady," he replied. "Two hours to the airport, another two to Zurich. We'll be there before dawn."

Back the way I had come. We'd likely be flying over Gervais' chateau, where Izak and Lylyx were waiting. "I need to make a phone call," I said, reaching into my pocket and pulling out my cell.

It rang twice before Lylyx picked it up. "Lylyx, it's Landon. You've got to get Izak, and you've got to get out of the chateau. Tell him to take you somewhere safe, I'm sure he knows where."

"Landon, are you okay?" Lylyx asked. Her concern was sincere.

"I've been better, but I'll survive," I replied. "I want you to survive too. Where's Izak?"

"He's still down in the basement with Gervais, but at least the screaming stopped a while ago. I came upstairs. I can be evil, and I can be cruel, and I can kill anything that tries to stop me from getting what I want, but this was something else. What's going on?"

I couldn't imagine anything that would rattle a Great Were. It made my skin crawl. "I don't have time to explain. Just get him and get out. I'm pretty sure there are some nasty demons headed your way, and I don't think even Izak can take them all. I'll call you again when I have more time."

"Okay," Lylyx said. "Stay safe."

I looked over at Zeek. Something told me that was going to be a hard request to grant. "You too," I said. I hung up.

"Lylyx is working for them," Zeek said.

"Not anymore," I replied. "That's why I need to get her someplace safe. Once Rebecca finds out I took over the pack, she's going to be out for blood." Not to mention, she had been surprised that Izak was still alive. There was no way she wasn't going to try to rectify that miscalculation.

He raised his eyebrow. "You took over the pack?"

"I absorbed the soul of their former alpha, a Great Were named Ulnyx. He told me about some loophole that let me challenge for position."

Zeek's laughter boomed and echoed in the van. "M'lady is going to love that one," he said. His mirth spent, he returned to glowering. "You said Ulnyx?" he asked after another breath. "I knew a were once who went by that name. It was a long time ago." His small eyes rotated towards me. "Ulnyx is a pretty uncommon name, even for a demon. Maybe he knows me? I went under a different name back then. They called me Tobias the Grand."

I felt Ulnyx kick, hard. Zeek smiled, a friendly but malevolent smile. The demon's power surged in me, and I sensed the memory flooding forward, overwhelming my defenses, and dropping me towards darkness. Zeek's smile faded, his brow furrowing. I heard him say my name, but then he vanished in the present.

"Uncle, look!"

Rolix is excited when he sees the red flag raised high in the center of the village, a signal to the outlying properties that the King's Fair is in town. I look over at the pup and smile, the fair always means good hunting.

"Do you think they'll have acrobats, like the fair back home?" he asks.

At nearly sixteen, Rolix is barely a pup any longer, the time for his first hunt upon him. It's the reason we've travelled so far, from the familiar humidity of the Delta to the coldness of the west. Along the way I have taught him all that I know about survival, and some of what I know about thriving in our world. It's rare for the alpha to embark on a First Hunt with any of the brood, but Rolix is his father's son, and his father is the only one in the pack I can trust. This is the depth of our bond, forged in the blood of our enemies and strengthened by domination. Rolix is also the closest I'll ever come to offspring of my own.

"You are a pup still, Rolix," I say. "But come nightfall you will have outgrown acrobats and magicians. If you haven't, you won't survive for long." It's a cold reality, one that all of the pack must be prepared for if they're to survive.

Rolix growls and nods in agreement. "I know that Uncle. Since it is my last day to enjoy it; I want to savor it one final time, before I cast it from my mind forever."

I fear for the length of his life, the way he clings to his childhood. My own First Hunt came when I was only seven, when I demanded the right to kill for myself. I know he'll never be an alpha, and that he'll never take a mate. It's better this way, I tell myself. I will never have to defend myself from him. I will never have to kill him.

"Fine," I say. His fate is not my fate. "Let's see if there are acrobats."

The fair is crowded with peasantry, all centered on a simple wooden stage that has been constructed in the center of the town. Spread around it are hastily constructed booths of all kinds, the mortals selling their hot pies, streamers, baskets, and any other random trinkets they have the limited skills to create. We push our way through the crowds. At first getting looks for our foreign appearance, but I've learned the simplest ways to manipulate the fear of the sheep, and within a few steps we are strange no longer. I take a deep breath, ignoring the stench of the grime that covers the skin and clothes and picking out the warm blood beneath it. A feast tonight. It makes being here to watch the fools dance bearable.

"Uncle, this is incredible," Rolix says, his eyes wide to take in the bustle and energy of the crowds. He points up at the stage, where a monster of a man has made his appearance. Dressed in a long blue velvet robe hanging open at the waist, with a bare chest and simple leather pants, he is easily the largest human I have ever seen, not just in height but in sheer mass, with enormous muscled arms and a wide barrel chest. Not just a human, I can taste it in the air. Divine. I see his eyes dance our way, and I give him only a slight nod of understanding. I know what he is, and I'm not afraid.

The man doesn't flinch, doesn't react. His eyes work their way across the crowd as though he had seen nothing he wasn't expecting. The meat still moves around me, unaware of the newcomer. Until he speaks.

"Ladies and lords." His voice booms across the crowd, stopping all of the conversation, all of the motion. They are like rabbits frozen by an oncoming fox, still and attentive in their surprise.

"Ladies and lords," he says again, more quietly. "It is my humble honor to be here before you today. My name is Tobias the Grand, master illusionist and strongest of the strong, and I'd like to tell you a tale."

"Let's get to the front," Rolix exclaims, pushing his way through the crowd towards the front of the stage. I'd rather keep my distance from this Divine, but I won't let the pup too far from my sight. I too approach the stage.

"This is a tale of good and evil, of the world above, and the world below."

He moves his hands, and flames puff out in the air in front of him. Another motion and wisps of clouds twirl around him like a cobra. The crowd 'oohs' and claps, and I see they are regaining their minds, shifting themselves for a better view of this Tobias.

"There are monsters that walk Britannia my friends," *he says, his voice grand and overemphasized.* "Monsters that would eat your soul and burp up dung."

His illusions follow his speech - casting a shadow of a were, and having it double over to expel something from its mouth. This gets a laugh from the gathering, but I don't react. There is no mistake he looks at me before beginning his next sentence, and I see the challenge for what it is. Not here, not now. Tonight. There will be no dining on sheep until the shepherd has been dealt with.

"He is a fool," *I say to Rolix. The pup is enamored with the show. He seems unable to understand how the hulk on stage is mocking us.*

"His tricks are amazing," *he replies.*

Tobias continues his show. He brings out puppets, a man puppet and a wolf puppet. The man tricks the wolf and destroys it, much to the amusement of the crowd. He laughs along with them, taking the wolf puppet and throwing it in my direction. Rolix catches it, laughing, oblivious. I've had enough. I grab the pup by the neck and pull him from the crowd. I can hear the 'oohs' and 'ahs' behind us as we retreat away from the gathering, reaching a small alley between a smithy and an apothecary.

"Do you understand nothing?" *I ask, ripping the wolf puppet from Rolix's hands.* "Do you not see what this Tobias is?"

Rolix backs away, his head down in submission. "He is Divine," *he says.*

"What kind of Divine?" *I growl, throwing the wolf puppet out of the alley and into the small thoroughfare.*

He looks up at me with dumb eyes. "I do not know Uncle."

I'm tempted to cut his throat right there, to spare his father the embarrassment of this imbecile. I had thought I could bring the pup to his senses, but I had been wrong. I snarl and raise my hand, changing it to a sharp set of claws. Rolix's eyes widen, and he drops to his knees.

"Please uncle," he says. "I don't understand."

I want to do it, but I pause. I can't return to the Delta alone. A fool the pup may be, but he may still have use. I lower my claws and reach out with my hand. "Come," I say to him. "Put your childhood aside Rolix. Tonight we hunt."

"Today you die," the voice says from the mouth of the alley. I recognize the sound, and I recognize the scent.

"Rolix, stay behind me," I say, pushing him away from Tobias and turning to face the man. I don't say anything. Instead, I shift, feeling the strength pour into my body, my face elongating into a muzzle filled with sharp fangs, my body sprouting fur, my hands and feet growing a complete set of claws. I growl softly.

Tobias smiles and reaches under his velvet cloak, dropping it to the ground. A single strap rests across his chest, and he reaches behind for a short handled, double-bladed axe that had been strapped to his back. When he brings it forward, I see the eye tattooed to his wrist.

"Templar," I hiss, crouching down, preparing for the fight. "Have sense and flee. I am no petty were, but Ulnyx, alpha of the Mekong Delta."

"You're all the same to me," he says, charging.

He comes at me, and his strength is overwhelming. I slip away from his blade, twisting past the forehand and the backhand, which lead me right into his fist. The force of it sends me sprawling backwards, and I kick up dirt and stone scrambling to maintain my feet. Tobias wastes no time, his massive frame propelling him towards me, his axe coming down from above. I slip aside, digging into the dirt with my feet and kicking dirt up into his face. He groans and stumbles, but rolls away before my claws can find his flesh.

"You're quick for your size," I say, returning to a fighting posture while he rises to his feet. The first effort is a draw.

"You're ugly, even for your kind," he replies, spitting onto the ground between us.

I snarl and charge, leaping towards him, twisting to avoid his axe and catching his wrist on my forearm. The force shatters my bones, but it shatters his as well, and the axe falls from his hand. I try to scratch his face, but his arms are too long, and his other hand grabs my face and pushes me to the ground. I manage to roll over, but as soon as I do a monstrous boot presses me to the dirt.

"Stay still," he says, pressing down harder when I struggle. "I'll make it swift."

He bends over, reaching for the axe. When he does, Rolix leaps from the shadows, landing on the Templar's back, raking him with his claws. He lets out a short grunt, and then throws himself backwards against the wall of the smithy, sandwiching Rolix between his muscle and the stone. A low cry is all I hear, and when Tobias steps forward again I see Rolix tumble to the ground, broken.

"No," I roar, moving to regain my feet. The pup will heal, but only if he has time. As for the Templar, his face is pale, the demon poison beginning to spread through his veins.

That doesn't stop him from putting his boot on my neck and forcing me back down. That doesn't stop him from picking up his axe and turning to Rolix.

"You care for this one?" he asks, right before he plants the blade in Rolix's chest.

The blessed runes flare, and his chest begins to smoke, small whimpers the only indication that he feels the pain of his demise.

My hands scramble against the foot on my neck, but a layer of chain hides beneath the cloth and I can't break through. The pain is clear on Tobias' face when he looks at me, his face twisted in anger.

"Next time," he says, removing his foot from my neck, his axe from Rolix, and running out of the alley. I assume he seeks holy water, and I hope he dies before he finds some.

The van was still moving when the memory faded, but I was slumped over, my forehead pressed against the dashboard. Zeek was on the phone, talking to somebody. Whoever 'm'lady' was, I supposed.

"Hey, he's awake. I'll see you soon. Of course, m'lady." He disconnected and tossed his own cell onto the dash. "Sorry, Landon," he said. "I didn't know that would happen."

I lifted my head and leaned back. "Me neither," I replied. I studied him for a minute, remembering the anger that guided the axe into the young were. "Why did you do it?" I ask. Ulnyx's pain, his shame in failing to protect the boy was still resonating through my emotion.

"My wife was named Katherine," he said, sadness filtering into his voice. "She was the sun that I revolved around, a perfect beauty, and a friend without equal." He paused, remembering her. "She was killed by a demon the year before. Even though I destroyed the creature, I carried the pain and anger of her loss with me still. When I saw the were, when I saw his arrogance, I wanted to kill him. Then, when I saw how he cared for the boy, I wanted him to suffer, the way I was suffering. It never should have happened. For whatever it's worth, I'm sorry."

He was being honest, but it wasn't worth anything to me. Ulnyx was silent, so I could only guess he didn't care either. "I thought the Templars were supposed to be looking out for Heaven's best interests? Never mind the reasons, why would you be sorry to have killed a demon?"

His eyes found the road again. "I'll let m'lady explain," he said. "The short version is because the story goes a lot deeper than you know right now. You haven't been around that long, not for a Divine. This is pretty new to you. There's an awful lot of others who find it all a part of ancient history."

I put my eyes on the road, trying to decide if I should push the conversation or not. A lot of questions were circling in the maelstrom of my mind. The one that wasn't present was the identity of 'm'lady'. If I pieced everything together, it all started to make a very convoluted sort of sense.

"There's a mattress in the back of the van, if you want to catch a few," Zeek said, motioning towards the rear. "But you probably don't sleep."

I slipped out of the seat and crept to the back.

"No, but I'm working on my zen," I replied.

The back of the van was barren save for the small mattress and a couple of boxes of junk food. If Zeek was a Templar, that meant he had drank from the Grail and gained an immortal life span as one of his new talents. Even so, he was still mortal, and still needed to eat. I guess it didn't matter what.

I dropped over onto the mattress and closed my eyes, not trying to fall asleep, but trying to shake the last vestiges of Ulnyx's memory from my soul. I was surprised by the level of emotion the Were had exhibited towards the boy; while his primary concern was the embarrassment of losing his charge and failing to kill Zeek, that he felt anything at all towards Rolix showed me that even with access to his past I had misjudged him as nothing but a monster. That didn't make him a good guy by any stretch, but it did show a semblance of humanity that I hadn't believed he possessed.

The key to being in tune with Josette and Ulnyx was letting myself relax and somehow easing off on my nascent defenses, so I laid there completely still and focused on my breathing, trying to let go of the state of alarm I had been in since Mr. Ross had dropped me on the Statue of Liberty. Five years, and I was only beginning to see the true depth of what I had become, and more importantly what I was losing. No wonder I suddenly felt so overmatched again.

I'm not sure how much time passed. It couldn't have been too long, because we weren't that far from the airfield. I lay on the mattress for some time before a single thought, a single word passed up and resonated in my soul as no more than a whisper.

"*Landon,*" Josette said.

I didn't open my eyes, but tried to stay calm and centered. I could sense a single fine thread snaking behind the blackness behind my eyes. I reached out for it, taking a gentle hold on the end.

"*Josette*," I said. My voice echoed in the dark hollow, but the thread vibrated in response.

"*I hear you*," she replied. "*It is faint, but I hear you.*"

"*Sarah*," I said. My hold was tenuous, and it seemed too much effort would blow it away like smoke.

"*She is diuscrucis. She can be saved.*" Her confidence was unwavering. It gave me comfort.

"*She may need to die*," a new voice interrupted.

Another thread, dark and hard to see. I didn't need to see it to know Ulnyx. I reached out again, splitting my attention, careful not to lose my grip on Josette. Before I could take hold of it, it latched onto me. Not an attack, but an effort to stay connected.

"*She might*," I admitted. I could feel Josette's sorrow wash through me.

"*You are not wrong, demon*," Josette said. "*But not without trying to save her. You have seen her goodness and charity. Such things cannot be lost so easily. Just ask Izak.*"

"*Izak is unique*," Ulnyx said. "*He was never meant to be one of us. Don't expect such softness from any other demons. You've seen it yourself with your vampire honey.*"

I wanted to be angry at the comment, but there was nothing. No emotion could travel through this connection. Only whispers. "*Who is he?*" I asked. "*I saw him visit you in your cell. I saw how you cared for him.*"

The threads didn't move.

"Josette? Ulnyx?"

There was no reply. I felt a lightness reaching across my flesh, and I opened my eyes. Zeek was standing in the rear of the van, the back doors thrown open. A light breeze was filtering in, and I could see the small aircraft waiting behind him, propellers already spinning. He had a pastry in his mouth, crumbs in his beard, and donuts in each of his hands.

"Time to fly," he mumbled through bits of danish.

.

CHAPTER 17

I spent the first ninety minutes of the two hour flight trying to recapture my calm and get back the threads of Josette and Ulnyx's souls. Between the shaking of the twin-prop while it winged its way past the Alps, and the crunching of candy bars and crackling of cellophane bags, it was an impossible task. I opened my eyes and cast a murderous glance over at the giant Templar, who I could swear was forcing the plane to fly slightly banked to the left. He was too busy consuming sugar to notice, so I looked forward to our pilot, a Spanish mortal named Javier. According to Zeek, the flight had been contracted by m'lady, and so the man had no idea what it was he was carrying.

"Have you been flying long?" I asked him. He had given each of us headphones so we could speak over the din of the engines, but Zeek had been cut out because the cans didn't fit over his skull.

"Affirmative," he replied, holding out a bony arm and flashing me the 'okay'. He was an almost comical inverse of the Templar, short enough to need a booster on his seat and thin enough to see the skeleton beneath his skin. "Thirty five years. I got my start in the Spanish Air Force, it was the easiest way to pay for flight training." He laughed hoarsely. "After that, I spent a few years doing cargo hauls, and then a few more as an instructor. The last five have been as an indie. I bought Bella here twenty years ago at an auction. Now I'm living my dream."

I couldn't see his smile, but I could feel it. It dug into me more deeply than I had expected. A man living his dream. *This* is what I was fighting for. I'd been avoiding the finite life for so long, I'd forgotten what it was.

"You resurrected her yourself?" I asked.

"Sure thing," he replied. "Took me almost twenty years of parts auctions, graveyards, and some of the oddest jobs you can think of, but I put her together piece by piece with these hands." He lifted them from the yoke to show them off. The calluses and wear on his fingernails made it clear how much time he had given to the task.

"She's a marvel," I said.

I leaned back in my seat and looked out the window to the right. There was some scattered cloud cover we were skirting on top of, and beyond that some of the taller peaks poked through like icebergs on a white sea. The moon was resting high in the sky, a thin sliver that didn't provide much light, not that I needed it. I was about to lean forward again to ask Javier about the mountains when my stomach lurched forward and I got super dizzy. The balance. Something had just happened to give it a bad push to the dark side. Remembering what Gervais had said he thought Rebecca and Sarah planned to do, it was an effort to keep breathing. Was she really going through with it? It seemed impossible.

A sudden explosion of heat in my Sight brought me out of my stupor. I lunged forward and grabbed the yoke from Javier, pulling it back and twisting it, praying that the pilot's loving workmanship would be enough to spare the craft. A gout of flame sped past the window, close enough for the heat to leech through.

"What the hell was that?" Javier cried, pushing my hands away from the steering. His expression was tight, and I could smell his fear.

"Landon?" Zeek was shoved back in his seat, a soda spilled on his lap.

I could See the fire demon out beyond, circling around for another pass. It was worse than that - three angels were angling on a direct path for the plane. Not fallen angels, but straight from Heaven angels, working in concert with the demon. It was Rebecca's promise, already being fulfilled.

"Sword?" I asked the Templar. He pointed at the back of the plane, where a small lockbox was resting.

I focused, pulling it to me and snapping the locks. "Javier, dive now," I said, flipping open the lid and pulling out the blessed axe. The same one that had killed Rolix. I could feel Unlyx's desire to plant it in the Templar's chest. It was a good thing he wasn't in control.

"I can't go too far my friend, or we'll crash into the mountains," he said, calm and cool in the face of something he couldn't possibly understand. He was a former military man, his training had taken over.

The plane dipped forward, forcing Zeek to put his feet up to keep him from slamming into the the pilot's seat. The maneuver threw the angels off, and they hung stationary for a few seconds before they followed the fire demon downward behind us.

"How did they find us?" Zeek asked.

I started to shake my head, then felt my stomach drop. "Sarah," I said softly. She knew where I was. She *always* knew where I was. If there was any remaining doubt she was helping Rebecca, it fled in that instant. There was no time to lament though. I had to act.

"What now?" Javier asked, pulling back and leveling the plane.

"Just don't fly straight," I said to him. "Try to be unpredictable."

I focused on the hatch and pushed it open, holding the freezing air to prevent it from rushing in. I walked over to the edge and looked out, seeing the fire demon behind us, its mighty wings pumping hard to keep pace with the craft. It didn't seem possible that something so large could move at such speed, but the laws of the mortal world had no bearing on the Divine, no matter how big and ugly they were. I took a deep breath and hopped out onto the wing, planting myself to the metal and pushing the door back closed. Even though the angels had started behind the fire demon, they were more like fighters, so much faster and more nimble. They reached me first.

I had to focus to hold myself on the plane against the buffeting wind. The angels shot into view, wings swept back like falcons, swords held forward at their chests like spears. I gauged the distance to the lead seraph and loosed the axe, feeling a bit like Thor when it shredded through a wing and I pulled it back to me. The afflicted angel turned over and tumbled from the sky. He would live and the wing would regenerate, but it would keep him out of this fight; not to mention hurt like hell. The other two slowed their pace, planning their approach more carefully.

Javier was an expert, and the plane jerked and skittered along the thermals, leaving the angels to make constant adjustments, their wings flaring in and out as they attempted to close the gap. I left my perch on the wing and started walking towards the tail, holding the axe ready to throw. The pilot was almost too skilled, making it difficult to line up a shot.

Just when I thought I had an opening, the targeted angel dipped from my sight, falling away. The remaining seraph deftly slipped her sword over her back and replaced it with a dagger. She pulled up, twisting and turning upright, leaving me a huge target, but getting in the perfect position for an attack of her own. The dagger sped through the air with an impossible velocity, leaving me just enough time to get the axe up to block it.

At the same time I did, the second seraph reappeared right behind me, pounding into me with the full weight of his body. I fell forwards, watching the fuselage of the plane speeding away. I jammed the axe into the tin, tightening my grip on the handle and preventing myself from being thrown out into the open air.

The second angel landed on the wing and drew his sword, a blank expression on his face. He started towards me, and I was considering how to handle him when I saw the cockpit door swing open and the end of a shotgun stick through it. Whatever Zeek was using for buckshot, it wasn't holy water. The angel screamed and tumbled from the plane.

I pulled myself back to my feet and focused on my Sight, searching for the fire demon somewhere behind us. The plane was diving again, drifting downward into the clouds. I could only imagine that Javier was doing his best to keep us out of view. If only that would be enough to stop the oncoming demon. I found him well back of the plane, a hundred yards at least and staying away. The action alone told me something wasn't right, and if recent history meant anything it was that my Sight wasn't completely trustworthy. I turned my head, looking around for enemies in the whiteout of the clouds.

It wasn't my Sight that saved my head; it was Ulnyx's sense of smell. I knew the scent of sulfur and dust that passed instantly in the stiff wind, and I jumped backwards towards the end of the wing just in time to avoid the heavy blade that slashed where my neck had been. At the same time I heard the crackle of breaking glass, and looked forward to the cockpit. A second fallen was smashing her way through the windshield, trying to get at Javier and bring the plane down.

I reached for Unlyx's power, feeling my body changing as I shifted, becoming the Great Were. The fallen angel on the wing came at me, his sword a toothpick to the thick hide of the Great Were. I slapped it away from him, and dug my claws deep into his stomach, lifting him up and throwing him backwards off the plane. With a snarl, I coiled and sprung, landing just behind the surprised fallen angel and using my momentum to throw her from the aircraft. I heard a snap when her body collided with the right hand propeller, and the plane began to list.

Javier's face was tight with concentration while he worked to keep the ship level and airborne. A thick plume of black smoke trailed from the afflicted engine, and in my Sight I knew the damage was enough to give the fire demon the extra boost it needed to overtake us. I turned and looked back down the length of the fuselage, to where the blessed axe still clung to the aluminum like Excalibur.

"This is crazy," I said out loud, reverting my form and dashing back along the length of the plane. When I reached the axe I focused, pulling it to my hand as I pushed off, launching out into the empty space beyond with the clouds a dreamlike mist surrounding and aiding to disguise my kamikaze launch.

The demon's massive body came into view out of nowhere, a mirage solidifying before me. I brought the axe up over my head and chopped it down on the creature's chest, slamming into its body with my own and planting the weapon deep into it. The demon cried out in pain and tried to smack me off with a huge claw, but I hopped onto the extruding handle of the axe and used it to launch myself upward over the attack. Once I had reached my zenith, I twisted and reached out, grabbing the demon's neck and swinging around to land on its back. Its wings were beginning to beat more slowly now, and I could smell the frankincense heavy on the air. The fire demon was dying, and I was stuck on its back at least a thousand feet in back of the plane.

I looked down, but all I saw were clouds. I could guess what was underneath me - jagged mountain peaks and a more than slightly painful landing. I wasn't so much afraid of the pain as I was of the possibility that I could find myself decapitated by a jagged edge, or crushed beyond my ability to regenerate. It wasn't the time for indecision.

I pulled at the flow of power running through me and focused, reaching out to Purgatory to make the changes there that would alter reality here; the changes that would either spare me, or destroy me. The fire demon was dying beneath me, and it groaned and gurgled while the last vestiges of existence slipped away. I unwrapped my arms from the demon's neck and pushed back, getting away from the carcass and beginning my free fall. My heart raced to my throat as I pushed harder, demanding the world to change in a way that went above all logic, and threw the laws of physics and gravity to the cold wind.

I flew forward like a rocket, my skin pushing back against my skull, my clothes rippling around me. Within seconds I had reached the plane, and I altered my direction and forced my velocity to shift and reduce. Too fast. I was going too fast. I could see the fuselage approaching in a hurry. I could feel Purgatory's energy slipping away. My head exploded as it rammed into the side of the aircraft and I dropped flat onto the wing, taking a desperate hold on Ulnyx's power and using it to shift a hand to a claw and dig it into the tin to secure me. What I had done had been a gamble, and I knew it was going to have consequences. Not only could I feel the small wobble I had just created in the fabric of reality, but I could also feel my consciousness slipping away. The last thing I saw was the door swinging open and Zeek reaching out for me. I could only hope he wasn't too attached to that axe.

.

CHAPTER 18

I knew where I was the moment I woke up. The Statue of Liberty, laying on Rebecca's bed. I could smell her perfume hanging in the air around me, and feel the softness of the sheets I had never lain on before, despite the days and weeks I had spent there.

I took a deep breath, and felt a tingle run along my spine and through my limbs. I knew where I was, but something was off. No, everything was off, just a little bit, just enough to tell me that I wasn't really where I seemed to be.

"Landon."

I sat up with a start. "Sarah?" Her voice was unmistakable. I looked around, but I didn't see her.

"I'm here."

Suddenly, she was right there in front of me near the foot of the bed. Like everything else, she was a little off too. It wasn't just that her eyes were whole, they always were in these places between. It was something else; nothing that I could see, or smell, or touch. It just *was*. She was wearing a simple lace dress that fell to her knees, simple black ballerina slippers and a red flower in her hair. She was smiling at me, her white teeth sparkling behind red lipsticked lips.

"Where are we?" I asked. I reached backwards, trying to remember how I had gotten here, but the answers were evasive. The last thing I could recall was having dinner at the Eiffel Tower with Rebecca. It had been a wonderful meal, and afterwards we had danced like the night of her birthday party. After that... after that I must have gone to sleep, because now I was here.

"We're inside your soul," she said.

She waved her arm languidly across her body, and one of the walls faded from view. I was bathed in a blinding luminescence, so bright it was impossible to look beyond. I knew it for what it was.

"The link to my Source," I said, rolling off the bed and stepping towards it.

She angled around to step in front of me. "It's beautiful," she said. She took my hand. "You're beautiful."

The way she said it was disconcerting. I tried to move away, but I was frozen in place.

"What are you doing?" I asked.

"Relax," she said. "I'm here to keep you safe. You've done your best to protect me, and now I want to protect you."

"Protect me from what?"

She brushed her hand across my cheek. It was soft, warm, and tender. "The world is going to change, brother. The world has to change. I know you've tried your best, but this is a war without end; a war that cannot be won. As long as Heaven and Hell remain you must be the gatekeeper, you must be the warrior, and the Awake will always be the casualties. Why should they suffer so that others can prosper? Why should you suffer for the sins of a vain god?"

"Sarah, I don't understand. You've always wanted to do good for others. To help them."

"I am helping them," she replied.

"How? Instead of outcasts they'll be slaves."

She shrugged. "Slaves or kings, it makes no difference. What they will be is equals. Accepted."

"In return for all of humanity?"

"No, brother. In return for so much more."

I looked right into her red-gold eyes. "So is that it? You want power? You want to be no better than your father?"

Her eyes swirled, the colors dancing and flaming into an angry orange. "You know what he took from me, brother," she said. "You know what he did. To my eyes, to my mind, to my soul. For what? To make me his pawn in this stupid game? To claim the power he doesn't deserve? You remember what I said to you, don't you, brother? They can't win if you don't play. Don't play their game, and *we* can win. *We* can decide the fate of this world. *We* can make everything whole."

My heart dropped, and I looked away. She was wrong, but I understood in that moment why she couldn't see it. "We can't make everything whole," I said in a whisper. When I looked back a moment later, she was crying.

"Sarah, you don't have to do this," I said.

She reached up and rubbed her eyes. "Yes, I do. I'm sorry, brother. I want power. I need power. Once the new lord has risen it will be up to me to impose order. I'm the only one who can. That's why he's waited so long to begin his ascension. I've seen this future, and I know it to be true. Things will be difficult for a time, but they will get better."

"Better for who?" I asked. "You're part human. You know what that life is like - filled with opportunity, filled with hope, and laughter, and love. Is it fair to take that away from billions to feed a world where the only hope of avoiding chaos rests on your master's ability to Command them?"

That's what it was. Not a panacea of demons and seraphs frolicking carefree in the tulips together, but a single overload using an inordinate amount of power to keep the Divine in line. I was wrong about one thing though. It wasn't the master who would be Commanding.

"There's no way you can do it, and keep your sanity," I said. "You'll lose yourself. You'll be no more than a puppet on a string." She wouldn't be Sarah. She'd be a conduit, a circuit. Nothing more.

"You can't Command. You know nothing about it. With help, I can keep them all under control. I can keep them all at peace. You won't have to fight anymore," she said. "You can have your freedom, your free will. It's been promised. All you have to do is join us."

I looked down. I could feel the tears forming on the edges of my own eyes. She waited patiently while I tried to find the words that could change her mind. In the end, I knew there weren't any.

"I'm sorry," I said, looking up. "If you won't stop this yourself, I'm going to have to stop you. I won't let you do this, Sarah. Not to yourself, and not to the people I've promised to protect."

People like Javier, who deserved to live his dream. The name sparked in my mind, and my memories came flooding back. Rebecca, Zeek, the fire demon and the plane. That's why I was here. I had overused my power and nearly killed myself. Whatever subconscious strength I had that kept Sarah out of my head was gone, and she was able to get in. Had that been the goal of the attack? She wouldn't come just to try to recruit me, not when Rebecca had already tried and failed. There was something else she wanted.

I tried to move, but I was rooted firmly in place, my limbs solid bricks cemented to the floor. "What did you really come here for?" I asked her, my voice an angry shout.

She smiled, reached out and cupped my face in her hand. "Shhh. It's okay, brother. Relax. I won't hurt you. I don't want to hurt you. I wanted you to join us, so we could be a family - you and Rebecca and I. She loves you, you know. She has since the first time she saw you. I love you too. I couldn't have asked for a better protector, a better big brother."

While she was speaking, her hand slid up from my cheek towards my temple. I felt a heat and charge of energy below it when it came to rest.

"What are you doing?"

Her hand was getting warmer, and I began to get dizzy, my eyes shuddering open and closed and my life playing through like a bad movie. The images danced around me, my first birthday party, my father before he died, the school play. She was Googling my existence.

I closed my eyes tight, and tried to fight against it. She wanted something, something I knew. There was nothing in my lifetime that she could possibly need, but there was one memory that came after. She wanted to know where I had hid the Grail.

"It's okay, brother," she cooed, using her power to Calm and removing my focus from her efforts. "I'm not going to…"

I heard her sharp intake of breath, and felt her hand fall away from my head. I opened my eyes and saw her on the floor in front of the bed, Ulnyx on top of her, trying to hold her down.

"What is it with you and women?" he growled, finding purchase on her wrists and pinning her to the floor.

Life returned to my body, and I started towards them. I never would have expected the demon to come to my aid.

"Let me go," Sarah said with complete calm.

Ulnyx stiffened, and then his hands dropped.

"Get off."

The Were was robotic, shifting and moving to a stand. Sarah pushed herself to her feet and looked at me. "Your pets can't help you, brother. You're too weak to control them better than I can."

"Sarah?"

Three heads turned at once. Josette was standing in front of the white light of my power, no less angelic in a simple white frock and bare feet. Her eyes were wet with a mixture of sadness and joy.

Sarah didn't move. "Do I know you?" she asked.

"Yes," Josette replied. "We've met before. A long time ago."

Sarah cast her eyes to the floor, trying to remember. Josette started walking towards her, eyes locked on her daughter, hands out to the side.

"I don't remember you," Sarah said, raising her head and meeting Josette's gaze. "You're so familiar to me, but I don't remember."

Josette smiled. "You were just an infant," she said. "I'm not surprised you don't remember me. But I remember you. I've never forgotten you, and I will never forget you."

She reached Sarah, putting her hand onto the girl's cheek. She was frozen, and I waited for the moment that she would find the commonality and make the connection, that she would know it was her mother standing right in front of her.

The moment came too soon. Sarah's eyes widened, and then narrowed, and she backed away. "No," she said. "You can't be." She looked at me. "Brother, tell me it isn't true. Tell me that my mother hasn't been right in front of me this entire time, and you've said nothing. Tell me you didn't kill her." Her voice rose to a shout, and the entire world around us shuddered in response to her pain.

"Sarah, wait," Josette said, reaching out again.

"No," Sarah screamed, still looking at me. "I trusted you. I believed in you. Why didn't you tell me? How could you do this?"

"Sarah, listen to me," Josette pleaded.

"No," she said, tears falling from her eyes. "I've seen so many things, but I never saw this. I never knew, and you never told me, and now I know why." She looked at Josette. "I'm sorry, mother."

She put up her hand, and Josette froze in place. Her attention returned to me, and I lowered my head.

"Sarah, I'm sorry," I said. "I wanted to tell you."

"Stop talking," she Commanded, and the words were too powerful to disobey. "You had five years to explain. Five years to tell me how you absorbed my mother's soul, to give me a reason and a way to understand. It doesn't mean anything once you're caught.

"I see things, Landon. Things that haunt my mortal dreams. Futures that may or may not come to pass, things that have been and may still be. In all of these futures you were there, and you took care of me. You looked out for me, and protected me from the darkness that threatens to envelop all of us. I believed in you, I loved you. I don't know how I could have seen it all so wrong. You killed my mother, Landon, and I'm going to kill you."

My body became frozen again, and it was just as well because the pain that echoed through me would have shaken it to dust. I should have told her from the beginning, but I always thought that either she already knew, or she would never have to know. It was a stupid thought, but being Divine didn't mean being perfect.

Sarah stepped up to me and put her hand back on my temple. "First, I need something from you," she said. "I was trying to do it without hurting you before. I hope it hurts like hell."

It did. It hurt more than hell possibly could. Every second of my life expanded and contracted in an instant, every emotion magnified and intensified, altered and twisted into nothing but direct agony that rippled throughout my being. The world around us trembled, the walls cracking and crumbling, a horrible, awful howling of emptiness and hurt unlike any sound any sane creature could ever produce.

I knew when she found the memory, because it was the one instant when the pain stopped. For just the barest fraction of time she lifted her hand. "Thank you, brother," she said with a hateful snarl. "Now, die."

The pain returned, doubled upon itself, causing my frozen body to defy even Sarah's commands and contort into a ball, leaving me fetal on ground that was rattling and shaking apart with every passing second. The howling intensified, a forlorn banshee wail that coated every molecule of my whole with distress.

Sarah's eyes were wild, blinding in orange fury, her own face mangled by her pain and anger. She poured it all into me, transferring it in a stream of power unlike anything I could comprehend. I lay on the floor, curled up in indescribable agony, just waiting for it to end.

The last thing I saw was Josette frozen in her own spot, a single tear tracing its way along her cheek and tumbling in slow motion to the floor.

CHAPTER 19

I was still screaming when I woke up, my voice hoarse from all of its efforts. Still weak, still cold and shivering as a result of my excess, I couldn't see right away. My eyes took in only a blurred vision of reality, lots of red and gold all around me, an arm reached out to my forehead, a face, black hair, a huge black blob of mass. The scream sputtered out into a cough, and another hand held out a glass of water.

"As mortal as you'll ever be," she said. "Try to relax and accept it. You'll heal faster that way."

I knew the voice. Charis. At least I had been right about something. I took the offered glass in a shaky hand, spilling some of it as I brought it to my lips. It felt like glass trailing down my throat. I coughed half of it back up.

"Easy," she said. "You've forgotten what it means to be alive. Your body doesn't know how to react."

My eyes were beginning to focus, and I could see a little more clearly. It was definitely Charis positioned next to me on the king sized bed, laying on her side in a sharp white suit with a red blouse underneath. She smelled like fire and roses. I recognized Zeek now, standing at attention at the edge of the bed.

"What do you mean, alive?" I asked.

"Ezekial told me what happened, about how you flew. It was a gutsy move, but you knew the risk; although I guess you didn't understand the specifics. When you over-exert like that, your physical self loses its connection to your Divine self. For all intents, your body becomes mortal again. You feel cold, you tremble, you need to eat and drink. Remember what I told you would happen? You lost your sense of living, and now it's forcing itself back on you. It's a shock."

I tried the water again, with a little more success. "Why didn't you tell me more? About what would happen? About Rebecca?"

She smiled, a sad smile. "I would have, if I had known. There's so much we need to talk about, Landon. So much you need to know. Most importantly, I'm as human as you are. I make mistakes, I misjudge people, I put my trust into the wrong hands. It sounds like a punishment, but it makes us strong. It makes us unpredictable."

I couldn't argue with that. "What you did tell me, about the balance. I understand."

She nodded, and took her hand from my forehead. I missed its warmth immediately. "Lay back and rest while we talk." She turned to Zeek. "Zeek, you've done a commendable job getting him here. Why don't you go downstairs and get a bite to eat?"

The big man bowed. "Of course, m'lady," he said. "See you around, Landon. You owe me for that axe." He laughed his way out of the room. A moment later I heard a more distant door close.

"So you've found the texts?" she asked.

I laid back onto the softest pillow I had ever felt. "Most of them," I said. "I'm not really sure what they mean." I looked at her. "If you knew about them, why weren't you collecting them."

"If I had taken them, what would you have been searching for? I needed to know when you were ready, and to see what you would do. You're an amazement to me, Landon. It took me nearly two hundred years to reach the same point you're at today."

"You didn't have anyone to throw what you were back in your face, I guess," I said.

"No, I suppose not," she replied. "Believe me when I tell you, I think you had it easier in that regard."

"So now what? I'm still missing one of the strings. Everything else is useless without it." I paused, thinking of what had just happened with Sarah. "Besides, that's the least of my concerns right now."

She shrugged. "I agree. The texts can wait. Tell me what was happening to you. Zeek carried you in here screaming. He said you'd been at it non-stop since before he brought you through the rift. I know something was attacking your mind."

The thought of it still hurt. "What else do you know?"

"Rebecca returned from Hell stronger than I could have imagined any vampire to be," she said. "At first, I thought she was just going to work on consolidating her power within her kind, but her actions have been... erratic. I found out she was working with Gervais, and that she had you in her sights. We've had Templars watching the archfiend for weeks. When you turned up in Paris, I kept Ezekiel tailing you at a safe distance.

Everybody converged on the Eiffel Tower, and you know the rest."

"So you don't know about Sarah?" I asked.

She shook her head."Who's Sarah?"

"It's a long story," I said, closing my eyes and taking a deep breath, trying to calm down. "The short version is that she's the demon Gervais' and the angel Josette's daughter. She's a true diuscrucis."

Charis' entire face changed, and every sense of her turned cold. "Tell me everything," she said, her voice flat, scared.

I couldn't stop my eyes from tearing up as I tried to put it to words. I told her about my relationship with Sarah, how we met in the sewers below New York, how I had cared for her at her mother's request. I told her about what Gervais had said, and what Rebecca had told me. Finally, I told her about what she was doing to me, trying to kill me in anger over her mother. When I was done, she sat there in silence, her expression grim.

"I should have told her," I said. "It was bad enough she was buying into Rebecca's promises, but maybe I could have changed her mind. Now, there's no way."

Charis put her hand on my shoulder. "You did what you thought was right, what you thought you needed to do to keep her safe. We can't always know the consequences, or whether they will come back to bite us later. We can only do the best we know how. If you did what you did out of love, there is no shame in the outcome, no matter how much we might want it to be different."

"Except most of the time the decision doesn't have the fate of the world hanging on it," I said. "She thinks I betrayed her. She was angry before. I'm afraid of what she's going to do now."

"I know," she said, no longer talking to me, but some other invisible presence. "You warned me this could be the endgame. We couldn't have known, not this soon. Yes, I know. We should have been more careful."

She turned her attention back to me. "What's done is done, Landon. Be strong, and stay hopeful, because this isn't over yet," she said. "Ezekial got you to us on time, and Vilya was able to ward your mind. Sarah will be able to See you as soon as you leave the ward if she's looking, but she won't be able to get back in once your strength is returned."

She motioned upwards, and I noticed for the first time that I was laying in a round four-posted bed, with a huge, ornate canopy hanging over me, and tied back drapery flowing around us. The wood of the canopy was scarred with an intricate pattern of demonic runes. The sight brought me to understanding, and I sat back up to look into Charis' eyes. The maneuver was easier this time, my energy slowly returning.

"Vilya," I said, searching my counterpart. Her red eyes flared. "I should have realized sooner. Thank you."

"You're welcome," Charis said.

"There's more," I said. "It's already started. I'm sure you felt the balance shift too. Sarah's started Commanding angels."

"Three so far," Charis replied. "The three that attacked you. Rebecca summoned the fire demon. It was all part of their plan to weaken you."

"I know. We have to stop them."

"We can't," she said. "Not yet. You need to get your strength back, and then we need to prepare. You may have learned a lot in the last five years, but you're still raw. You've only scratched the surface of what a diuscrucis, even a second-hand version like us, is capable of."

She leaned forward, and kissed me lightly on the forehead. "Go to sleep for a while, and be at peace. I know you'd probably like to talk to your angel, but the wards will prevent any other soul from communicating with you. Don't worry though, I'm going to teach you how to speak with them, the way I speak with Vilya. I'll be back in a few hours."

She smiled the warmest smile I've ever seen, and slid gracefully off the bed. I laid back down on the pillow, and then remembered something. "Charis," I said, causing her to come back to the bed.

"Yes?"

"My clothes. Can you grab my cellphone?"

"Landon, you should rest."

"I need to check on my friends. I'm not going to be able to rest until I do."

She nodded and made her way over to a massive ornate armoire resting against the wall. She opened the doors and pulled out my jacket, unfolding it and retrieving the phone. As she did, Avriel's Box tumbled to the ground.

Charis bent over and picked it up, looking at it in wonder. "Where did you get this?" she asked in a whisper. She turned it over in her hands, examining every surface.

"Rebecca tried to trap me with it."

Her head snapped towards me. "This prison already has inhabitants," she said.

I shook my head. "They've been paroled," I replied. "Avriel and the demon Abaddon. The last time I saw them they were in the sewers beneath Paris."

"She released them?"

"She needed the Box to catch me."

She held the Box in her hand and brought me my phone. "First things first, but a scourge like Abaddon can't be allowed to stay in this world for long. None of this will mean anything if he remains."

I had witnessed the demon's power. I didn't doubt it. "Agreed. Do you know how it works?"

"No, but I think I may know someone who does. Make your call, and go to sleep. I'll return soon. If you need anything, ring the bell on the nightstand. Ezekiel will hear it, no matter where he is."

I twisted my head so I could see the small golden bell on the nightstand. It was sitting in front of an ivory lamp.

"Where are we anyway?" I called out to Charis' retreating back.

"Thailand," she shouted back, and then she was gone.

I actually had two phone calls I wanted to make. I fought against a sudden overwhelming fatigue and navigated my way to my call log. I found the last number and dialed it again.

"Landon?" Lylyx asked, answering the phone on the first ring.

"Yeah, it's me," I said. "I was just checking in on you. Did you do like I asked?"

"We're safe for now," she said. "It took some work to get Izak away, and we barely made it out in time. A freaking army of demons stormed the gates about ten minutes after I talked to you. If it hadn't been for Gervais I think we would have been toast."

Wait... What? "What do you mean Gervais?"

"You shouldn't be surprised, after what he did to Izak. It was only fair."

"Izak branded him?"

"After he flayed him a few times and cleansed all of his scars. He made his own, with his brand at the center. I've never seen anything like it. He sent him out to fight them while we made our escape."

She was right, I shouldn't be surprised. "Lylyx, I need you and Izak to go back to New York. Find somewhere safe to hide, someplace far enough away from the city that Izak won't be spotted. Just wait there, and I'll find you when I can."

Hopefully before Rebecca did, but I wasn't going to tell her that. I didn't want to move them closer to the oven, but I needed them to be ready for whatever might happen.

She hesitated. "Landon, are you sure it's safe?"

There was no point in lying. "No," I said. "It isn't safe anywhere, but there's strength in numbers. Just get there."

I hung up the phone before she could say anything else, and considered Izak. The demon could be a huge problem if he decided to follow Sarah over to the dark side. I would have to put my faith on his love for Josette being greater than his love for her offspring. Nothing felt safe about that bet, but I was hanging onto the memory of him resting his head in Josette's lap.

One more call to make. I pulled up my contact list and hit the call button.

"Ben's crematory," the voice on the other end said. "You kill 'em, we grill 'em."

"Bad time for fire jokes," I said.

"Sorry, man," Obi said. "Hey, you sound like crap."

"I feel like crap," I said. "I'm getting my ass kicked out here, so please tell me you have something."

"I'm working on it," he replied. "I do have Thomas here though, and his initiate, Melanie."

"Melody!" I heard her shout through the phone.

"Melody, right. We've been poring through the stuff you had in your trunk. Thomas thinks he knows what you're missing. You're never going to guess what it is."

It was the way he said it that clued me in. That and the fact that the angel knew what I was missing. "The bible," I said. I should have known.

"Wow, I didn't think you'd get that one. Yeah, but not just the bible. *The* Bible. The first one, and I'm not talking about the first one penned by some monk somewhere, or written down by one of the prophets. We're talking the original, written by the very first of God's angels."

"The first? As in?"

"Yeah, the Devil himself. According to Thomas, the Devil's Bible is a rumor among the seraph, but he believes in it, and he's sure your missing text is inside."

"Why?"

"Hang on," Obi said. I could hear the rustling as the phone was handed off.

"Landon?" It was Thomas.

"Thomas, why do you think the text is in Satan's Bible?"

"The marker," Thomas said. "Do you know what it means?"

"No. Do you?" I had spent hours trying to discover the meaning of the symbol that was left wherever a piece of text was found. I had never been able to determine its significance beyond the obvious.

"There has been talk for centuries among the seraph. Some call it a myth, some a fairy tale, some a rumor. Others believe it to be true. It is about the First Fallen, his bible, and the mark of the beast. They say that while most mortals have interpreted the reference to the beast to mean Lucifer, the term has nothing to do with him at all. In fact, it is said that the mark is mentioned in his bible, in reference to something else entirely, a creature with no name or identity that possesses the power to bring the downfall of all of God's creations. To be honest, I never believed in it, until I opened your trunk and saw all of these marks for myself."

I swallowed hard. "You're telling me that the trail I've been following…"

"Is the mark of the Beast," Thomas finished. "Yes, that's my belief. My guess is that deciphering these texts will lead you right to it."

The truth hit me hard. All of a sudden, I wanted to be ignorant again. Rebecca and Sarah were talking about a new lord, a new god who would overthrow the old one. A power that could destroy everything that had been created; the Beast. One whose whereabouts had been scattered across the world but tracked and kept safe by a collection of angels and demons alike. One who already had followers, including the Demon Queen and the world's only true diuscrucis. One whose location was likely known to at least two of those followers. There was a reason I hadn't been able to find the final text. I had a good idea who had it.

"Thomas," I said.

"Yes, Landon?"

"We're in pretty deep on this one. Rebecca is back from Hell. I think she plans on waking the Beast."

There was a long, tense pause. "Are you sure?" he asked, sounding as meek as I felt.

"Not completely, but it's a pretty safe assumption. I met with her over dinner, and she tried to recruit me to their new world order. She was talking about replacing God."

"I've got to go," Thomas said. "I have to tell the others, and send a message to the archangels."

"Thomas, wait," I said. "You can't tell anyone else. I don't know who we can trust. To be honest, I'm taking a risk trusting you."

Another pause. "I understand. You can trust me, Landon. There's a reason the Lord brought us together. There's a reason Josette sacrificed herself to you. I will follow you in this."

There was no lie, no deception. "I know," I said. "Tell Obi that he needs to find Rebecca, but he has to do it without ruffling any feathers. I know she's been using cellphones to communicate, so tell him to start there. Stay with him, and do what you can to keep him safe. Do you trust Melody?"

"Of course," Thomas said, almost automatically. "Well... no, I can't say I do, not with what you've just said. But I also can't just walk away."

"You've got to keep an eye on her," I said. "And make sure she doesn't hear anything that could give us up to Rebecca."

"I will," Thomas said.

"Thank you, Thomas," I replied. "Can you put Obi back on?"

"Yes..."

My ears rang with the sound of gunfire through the receiver, the unmistakeable whoomph of the Desert Eagle unleashing silver fury. "We've got to get out of here," came the shout through the line.

"Thomas," I shouted, as loud as my tired lungs will allow. No response.

"They're on the roof," Melody screamed.

"Thomas," I repeated. "If you can hear me, find Izak. He'll be somewhere outside the city."

"Come on," Thomas yelled. "Obi, light it up and let's go."

I heard the clatter of the phone falling to the floor. I heard growling and more gunfire, and the crackle of flames. The texts, they had burned the texts. Without the strings, we wouldn't be able to follow the mark. We wouldn't be able to stop them from setting the Beast free.

Footsteps echoed in the receiver, along with muffled voices. I heard the floor creak, and the sound of someone lifting the phone.

"Landon, is that you?" Cho asked. "You're missing all of the fun."

I fought to get up, to move my body from my position in the bed. My limbs felt like lead, and my head began to spin.

"Landon, are you there?" he laughed.

"Laugh while you can," I said, my menacing threat falling flat in a hoarse, croaky voice.

"Oh, I plan to," he replied. "All the way to the end of your world, and the dawn of ours."

The phone clicked. I tried to throw it across the room, but even that ended in failure. I fought to get up again, my body resisting every effort, my power useless in my current state. I couldn't even scream in anguish and rage. I started reaching for the bell, but halfway there I realized it was hopeless. There was only one way to get back in the game, and that was to rest. My mind was racing a mile a minute, but as soon as I let my head go back to the pillow my physical fatigue overwhelmed me. I fell asleep instantly; a dreamless, empty sleep.

CHAPTER 20

Charis was there when I opened my eyes, sitting on the edge of the bed, watching my every movement. I must have been thrashing in my sleep, because I found myself face down, my body splayed out across the expanse of the mattress, the blankets thrown haphazardly around me. I knew by the draft that certain parts of me were bare, but I found that modesty didn't seem that important in front of her.

I closed my eyes again and reached for my power, finding comfort in the feeling of energy flowing into me with renewed vigor. I had been asleep for nearly twelve hours. It was way too long.

"How long have you been sitting there?" I asked, rolling over and sitting up. She had changed into a pair of yoga pants and a pink sports tank, her raven hair tied back in a single long ponytail.

"A few hours," she replied, reaching behind her back and tossing me my clothes. "Did you make your calls?"

The question made me remember. I could only hope that Thomas had heard the last thing I had said. I grabbed the clothes and jumped off the bed, out from under the wards for the first time.

"She can See me now?" I asked while I pulled on my pants and shirt. Charis was still watching me, her expression flat, but her eyes dancing along my outline.

"Yes," she said. "If she is looking for you."

I nodded. "I figured as much. Tell me about the Beast."

I could tell she was surprised. "You didn't know about that when I left," she said.

"Phone call," I said. "Look, Charis, I'd love to keep playing this game we've got going, because you're so darn intriguing and super sexy, but my friends are out there, and they've got a big red 'X' painted on them. You have to get me up to speed in a hurry, because if you don't they're going to die, and I have a bad feeling that will only be the start."

She smiled. "That's the spirit. Much better than the first time you woke up."

I recoiled. I had come out of it a little battered the last time. I don't know if it was the renewed memory of what it was like to be human, or a general feeling of pissed off that was fueling me, but I had reached my limit of self doubt and guilt. Charis had been right when she said I had done my best with Sarah. If she was going to be a brat about it, I was going to put her back in her place. Dante had put me in charge of protecting mankind from the bickering of the Divine. As far as I was concerned that extended to any Beast that could destroy, well, everything.

"I'm committed," I said. "I assume you already were, or I wouldn't be here."

"Follow me," she said, slipping off the bed and walking towards the door. I trailed behind her. "Like I told you earlier, it took me a long time to catch on to the secret war... the *real* secret war. I spent years following Dante, listening to his advice, going along with his instructions. I didn't question it, because I loved what I was. I loved the power that came with it."

We exited out of the room into a small antechamber with an elevator. She pressed her palm against a flat part of the wall and the invisible doors slid open. We stepped inside, the doors closed, and the elevator began to plummet.

"I was a spy during my mortal life," she continued. "I worked in espionage for King George during the American Revolutionary War. My role was to get in with the American Generals and convince them to share their secrets with me. I used everything at my disposal; sex, violence, blackmail. I suppose that was what made me so balanced. I did a lot of questionable things, but my motives were always pure, my goals always honest. I was loyal to a fault."

"No offense," I said, "but the British lost."

She cast me a glare that was both amused and offended. "One can only do so much," she replied.

The elevator finally slowed to a stop, and the doors slid open. We were underground, in a long passageway that led out into the distance, too far to see what waited at the end. The corridor seemed as though it had been created by compressing the dirt outward in a way no machine could manage.

"You did this?" I asked.

"It took me a few weeks, but yes," she replied. "It's nothing you can't do. As I was saying, one day I was hunting an archdevil, one of the

First's many offspring. He had decided to make a run on this world. I thought I had him in my sights, but he was a tricky one, with thousands of years of experience. I found myself trapped, my neck nearly severed. It would have only taken one little cut to end me."

"How did you get out?" I asked.

"The archdevil was strong, but he had been reckless. He had attracted the attention of the Templars. That they showed up when they did was pure luck, nothing more. That they surprised him enough to keep him from making the final cut was just as lucky. Sometimes, Landon, luck is the only thing that saves us. A millimeter here, a millisecond there. Yet, I'm still not sure that luck is random, or if it's engineered by something bigger."

"You're talking about God?"

"I was never a religious girl, even after going to Purgatory. I'm still not in favor of God's overall design, especially when it comes to the balance. I was going to die, and the Templars saved me. At the last possible moment they saved me. He saved me. Not God, the Templar, Joseph. I'd always used emotions to my benefit, a tool to meet my aims. It was the first time I truly fell in love."

I could hear the sadness in her voice. "I'm sorry," I said. I really was.

She stopped walking and looked at me. "I don't know why I told you that part. I feel like I can tell you anything."

At least it wasn't just me. "We're cut from the same cloth, aren't we?" I asked.

She tilted her head. "I'm not so sure," she replied. "Maybe more of a mirror, like we're reaching the exact same point from two completely opposite sides and reflecting one another."

"Balance?"

"Yes."

Our eyes caught for just a second, but so much passed between them in that short period of time. I felt a comfort I hadn't known before, as though a missing piece of me had been put into place.

"So, the Templars weren't created to protect the Grail," I said, getting us moving forward again.

"They were, in part," she said. "After Joseph saved me, he taught me about their history. He showed me his world, and I learned more about humanity, even my own humanity, than I had known even when I had been alive. I left my dreams of power behind, and took the oath of the Templars in secret."

"Why in secret?"

"When Dante found out how I felt about Joseph, he had one of his little hissy fits. He tried to convince me that the Templars were servants of God, and needed to be held to the balance just like the angels. He warned me that if I kept up with Joseph it could only end in tragedy. They are servants of God, but it ends there. Unfortunately, he wasn't completely wrong."

She grew distant then, and I could feel the coldness run through me. We stopped walking and stood silently together while she made peace with the memory. I didn't say anything until we starting walking again, but I knew what she was getting at. Everything was making so much more sense with every word she said.

"The Beast," I said.

"Yes. The Templars were founded by the son of God and tasked with preventing the Beast from ever being given a new foothold in this world. In a sense, while you and I were charged with being the bodyguards of humanity, the Templars are the guards of everything."

"It sounds like a tough job," I said.

She laughed. "I know you're making light of it, but it's harder than you think, especially since nobody is supposed to know their true purpose. They have to fight demons as though they are no more than servants of the seraphim, while being careful not to throw their weight too hard and make waves with the likes of you and I."

"Okay, so I assume that the Templars have been following this 'Secret Society of the Beast' for thousands of years, and that's how you knew about all of the texts you had me going around and collecting?" She nodded. "You made sure to arrange our meeting five years ago so you could drop your hint about it, and start prepping me, because you knew you would need me one day?" Another nod. "And you didn't clue me in before now because you wanted to be sure I would side with the Templars when the time came?" She nodded a third time. "And Dante can't know any of this, because frankly, we can't trust anybody right now?"

"One hundred percent," she said. "To be honest, I wasn't expecting much from you when I found out you had been chosen, but I have to say, I'm glad I blew you up."

As stupid as it seemed, I was too. "About that," I said. "According to Dante, you killed a lot of Templars that day."

She sighed, her posture turning heavy, her eyes dropping to the ground. "We decided to put the Grail out into the public so that I could take it as the Demon Queen. The goal was to get it into possession of someone that both sides feared more than the Templars, without giving away my true identity. I was going to hold the Grail until a new diuscrucis entered the world, and I was expecting to do it for a long, long time. It was a surprise to me that you came along as soon as you did, but I felt it the moment you were brought into this world. I contacted Reyzl and started making the amulets, creating a situation that I knew Dante would throw you into. The rest was just a little bit of luck and a lot of hope."

When she looked up, her expression was fierce, proud, and infinitely sad. "My involvement with the Templars is secret, and had to remain secret. I couldn't have convinced anyone otherwise without their sacrifice. The Templars have pledged their lives to this, Landon. They know what failure means."

"I'm not judging you," I said, reaching out and putting my hand on her shoulder. "We do what we think is right, don't we?"

She surprised me, turning into my reach and wrapping her arms around me. She buried her head in my neck, and I could feel the wetness of her silent tears against it as I finished the embrace. Holding her while she cried, I could only hope that hadn't been the day Joseph had died.

I gave her a few minutes to mourn, and I hated to force her back to the present, but time wasn't on our side. "Come on, Charis," I said. "We have work to do."

She pulled away and looked up at me, her red eyes flaring. "She likes you too," she said, her entire demeanor changing. "Let's go."

We reached the end of the corridor. I found myself standing in front of a small wooden door that looked completely out of place down here. It was old, it had to be, the wood stained and faded, pieces of it chipped and cracked. It reminded me of the giant door at the Catskill Sanctuary, only at a much smaller scale. It too was covered in runes, similar to those of the seraphim, but with a flourish and tightness that made it illegible to me.

"Templar script," she explained. "It's very similar in style because its origin is closely related. The power is what really differentiates." She flicked her eyes at the door, and it swung open without a sound.

She motioned me in, and I moved ahead, stepping through the doorway. I found myself in a place that betrayed all sense of time and space. A cave, with uneven surfaces, stalagmites dripping from the ceiling, and veins of crystals catching the small amount of light and reflecting it in iridescent shimmers. It was beautiful to behold, but what made the space truly amazing was the Templar script. It covered every available centimeter of the ceiling, walls, and floor, tightly wound in a pattern of order and chaos that defied all understanding. It ran everywhere I put my eyes, and I beheld it in wonder as one of the most complete and amazing works of art I had ever seen.

"What is this place?" I asked.

Charis pulled the door closed behind us. As soon as she did, the network of runes began to glow softly, the light reflecting from the crystals, the resulting vision taking the room from unbelievable, to mind-blowing. When I turned around, the door was gone.

"Somewhere else," she said. "A place outside of all things. A place beyond. Science might call it a pocket universe, or maybe a fractal dimension. Neither of those things is accurate, but they'll suffice."

"How?"

"This is the true inheritance of the Templars," she said. "And of the faith. This is the cave where Jesus Christ was buried, and rose from the dead."

I looked around, my upbringing creating more than a little shock, awe, reverence, and guilt. I didn't feel like I belonged here.

"Shouldn't this be near Jerusalem?" I asked.

"It was, once," she replied. "I moved it. It left me in a coma for a week, but we felt it had been compromised."

I kept turning, in circle after circle, trying to soak it all in. "Tell me more," I said.

"Catholic teachings say that Christ was buried and rose on the third day, which is true enough. To any observer on the outside, only three days passed. But Jesus was the son of God, he couldn't take the mortal path to Heaven. He also had some of the power of God, and bringing him here brought him closer to his Father. It was in this very spot where he learned to harness that power, to use it to return to his birthright. How long it took - weeks, months, years, millennia - is irrelevant. Time is irrelevant here. A hard concept to grasp, but one that we can use to our advantage."

I put my fingers on the wall, feeling the power thrumming along the surface in smooth vibrations, like a well-tuned engine. "The runes. Who created them?"

"The second. An archangel named Malize."

"I thought that was Michael."

"Most do. Malize is the forgotten, and he prefers it that way."

"That's where you got the blood from?" I asked. "For the Grail?"

She nodded. "Yes. This is his home."

"He isn't here," I said.

She smiled. "Remember, there is no time here, not the way you're familiar with it. He has been here since the day he finished the final rune and connected this realm to ours. For us it has been many thousands of years. For him, either millions or the blink of an eye. He will experience it as he chooses."

"Will we see him?" I asked.

"I don't know. He will decide. We don't have much time, not out there, but there are things you need to know, things we need to accomplish."

"What kinds of things?"

"I told you I would help you communicate with your angel. That is part of it. There is more, but it would be impossible to explain." She looked away, before she brought my eyes to hers. "I know I'm asking a lot, but I need you to put your complete trust in me."

Trust? I stared at her. I had put my trust in Rebecca, and she had run away with it, all the way to Hell. Now I was trapped in another universe, and the former Demon Queen was asking me to trust her? I looked into her red eyes, trying to find a hint of deception, a hint of insincerity. She was like me, she could lie all she wanted and I'd never know. How could I be sure she wasn't plotting to leave me here?

I had always felt a kinship to Charis, an understanding. We were so alike, yet so different. A mirror, she had said. Balance. Rebecca and Sarah were a serious tag-team. Nothing short of that would have even the smallest chance at stopping them. This wasn't just about learning to communicate with Josette and Ulnyx, I realized. This was about a union to create the balance that was demanded, because without it everything was already lost.

"I trust you," I said, making my decision. The words flowed from my lips like molasses, my experience of time suddenly fluctuating.

She moved in slow motion, her smile growing wide, her face set in resolve. The cave was small and we were already pretty close, but she moved in closer to that our chests were touching, and I could feel the heat of her body against my own. She was a little bit shorter than me, so she had to tilt her head up to keep eye contact.

"I promise I won't tell anyone," she said, her eyes sincere. I didn't know what she meant, but I had plenty of time to watch her tilt her head, lean up and forward, and press her forehead to mine.

I took a single breath, the inhale pulling in the warmth of her, the smell of her, the touch of her skin against mine. The exhale felt like it took forever, and it plunged me into a cold darkness, like a cannonball into a frozen river. In an instant I understood what was happening, and my first reaction was fear.

The darkness subsided, and I was a small girl standing on the street, watching a horse and carriage tumble by on a cobblestone road. My mum grabbed my hand and pulled me along, I was already late for lessons...

I was a teenager, at a fancy party arranged for the children of the upper crust. My dress was so tight I could barely breathe, but I moved with confidence, the belle of the ball, my beauty undeniable...

I was a young adult, in service to the King, laying unclothed in bed with a high ranking American official. He was sleeping, and I rose quietly and went over to his desk to rifle through his possessions, in search of anything that could be of help to His Majesty...

I was laying on a table in a hospital, blood pouring from the hole in my sternum where the musket ball had entered. I don't know why I tried to save the General from assassination - we weren't on the same side after all. Now I would pay with my life...

I was in Purgatory with Dante, and he was talking to me about the history of Purgatory, and about the role of balance in keeping mankind from the edge of oblivion. He told me I was special, and promised to teach me everything I would need to know to return to life as a champion to humanity...

I was in the midst of the American Civil War, fighting the demons that aimed to take the lives of the wounded in the night, and the angels that sought to save them...

I was trapped by an archdevil, my neck nearly severed, about to die. The door burst in an the most beautiful man I had ever seen stepped in, wielding a sword that seemed to make him immune to the devil's power. He cut the demon down, and set me free with a gentle hand that I would forever remember...

I was standing over the body of my love, ravaged by the archvampire and the now fallen angel who had worked together to lure him into an elaborate trap. I swore then that I would have my revenge…

I was struggling against the archfiend Reyzl, cursing him for his betrayal, fighting to remove the dagger he had planted in my back. I couldn't focus, couldn't breathe. I was powerless as he shoved me into the Hell rift…

I was trapped in Hell, in a prison of bone and anguish, crying out in pain while my keeper methodically cut away at me, over and over again as I regenerated, the pain unbearable and unending…

I was laying broken on the floor, my bonds severed, my body feeling relief for the first time in ages. My captor stood over me, her dark face an empty mask of curiosity…

I was in her arms, and she was professing her love for me. She was begging me to take her soul, to escape this place before another could be sent to take her place. She said she was sorry she had hurt me, and she handed me a dagger. I asked her name. 'Vilya', she said…

I was in the cave, alone, sitting prostrate on the floor, focusing on my breath, on letting go. I called her name, and heard her weeping. 'Are you sad', I asked her. 'I have never been happier,' she said…

Trust. That was why Charis had required it. It was her life, and I lived it, from the beginning to the present, every breath, every word, every feeling. I knew every instant of her existence as though it had been my own, from her greatest triumph to a trip to the bathroom with a bout of diarrhea.

Trust. She had lived my life too; every embarrassing moment of my own, every failure, every success. She knew me at least as well as I knew myself, and probably better. She had that perspective that I would never have, just as I did for her. It was a frightening, incredible experience that left me feeling more bare than any nakedness could, yet more fulfilled than I could have imagined. When her forehead separated from mine, and she moved back far enough to look into my eyes I could see myself reflected in them.

"I don't know what so say," I admitted, struggling to catch my breath. Such a deep understanding of another was a difficult thing to resolve. Knowing Charis, everything that made her who she was, and every decision she had made - I hesitated to call it love, but it was something like it.

"You don't need to say anything," she replied. "Focus, and tell me how you feel."

I did as she asked, reaching out for my power. I grasped it easily now, and so much more securely. I could almost visualize it in a corner of my mind, not only able to touch it, but also pick out individual fibers like strings. I could see the way Josette and Ulnyx's power entwined around my own, and with a thought I could begin to release them. As I did, I felt the clarity of their souls coming into focus, moving forward in my consciousness.

"Josette?" I whispered tentatively.

"*Landon,*" she replied, her voice clear in my soul. "*I can hear you. I can feel you. You've changed.*"

My eyes were open, still looking at Charis, but I could see her in my mind, standing against a blazing white backdrop. I sharpened my focus, pulling Ulnyx forward.

"*Sucker,*" he said, materializing next to Josette. "*Are you sure you want to give me so much control?*"

That was the trick. In order to communicate with them, I had to extract them, at least in part. The more I let them go, the more will they could exert upon their surroundings, upon my soul.

"*Behave yourself, creature,*" Josette said, smiling at the Were.

He laughed and winked at her. "*Not a chance,*" he replied.

Satisfied, I returned my attention to Charis. "This is what he wanted, isn't it?" I asked her. "Dante?"

"Yes. One diuscrucis is powerful, but adding a second and having them connect increases the output. It is because of our humanity, our unique strength that the other Divine don't possess. That was why I told you I needed you, and why we need each other if we are going to stop the Beast."

I nodded and delved into her eyes. "Vilya is a daughter of Belial," I said. "Yet she fell in love with you, and helped you escape."

"All creatures have the touch of God, and all creatures are capable of love," she said. "Love and hate are how the universe balances. Sometimes people confuse these words with good and evil, but they aren't the same, and they are all subjective. Her love saved me to be here with you now. What the effects of that decision will be remain to be discovered, but it has no doubt altered the course of all time."

I knew it was true, and I had seen it before with Izak. "But that means…"

She put a finger to my lips. "I know what you're thinking, Landon, and it may be true. It also may not."

It was a weak hope to pin the future of everything on. "Then I guess there's only one thing left to do."

"Fight," she said.

"Fight," I agreed.

"You may want to know what you are fighting," the soft voice said from behind me.

Charis and I turned as one to greet the archangel. He was a slight young man with dark olive skin and shiny black hair, a sharp, pointed nose and deep set, dark eyes. He was wearing a simple black cossack sashed with a rope belt, and a sword hung from his hip. He regarded us with interest and curiosity.

"Malize, the time has come," Charis said. "The Pure One walks, and the servants seek to free the Beast."

He didn't look surprised, maintaining his soft calm. "It is sooner than I had expected, but we knew this day would come. No secret can be contained for all time. Still, it is only a fool who goes into battle without knowing their enemy, and so I shall tell you what I can."

He turned his back to us and waved his hand, and we were transported in this universe to a world newly born, covered in verdant green but devoid of any other life.

"There was a time before time," he said. "When this world was newly created, and mankind did not yet exist. My Lord looked down on what he had wrought with pleasure, for He knew how good it would come to be. There were no angels then, nor man, nor beast. Only the promise of life, and His love.

"He began to lay the seeds of humanity, bringing life to this realm; the creatures of the sea and the land and the sky. He prepared this world, stocked it for those He would create in His likeness, to bestow His love upon them and to follow His own nature as a creator. The world was young, but it was vibrant, and He was very pleased indeed."

The scene changed, to dark skies filled with smoke and clouds, and fires raging as far as I could see.

"There would have never been a need for the seraph, if it hadn't been for the Beast," he said. "Perhaps even Lucifer would still call us brother." He shook his head sadly. "It matters little. At one time, there was no Beast, and then there was. It saw what my Lord had created, and it was intent on destroying it, for that is its nature."

"Where did it come from?" I asked.

"Another place," he said. "Perhaps like this one. My Lord is the Lord of all things, but there are an infinite number of all things, and as such he cannot keep a constant watch on them. It has been said that it revealed itself to Him and begged Him for amnesty and protection; that it had been exiled from this other place for attempting to defend the name of the Lord. It claimed that others like it, but calling themselves the true gods would follow after were it not hidden.

"My Lord, His heart filled with mercy granted its request. He allowed the Beast to settle in your world, to hide under His wing. Ages passed and all was good, until one day this realm began to burn, and the Beast rose up to challenge Him."

The scene changed again, now showing Malize and another seraph, an incredible figure of beauty and light, dressed in golden armor, their wings spread in magnificent white glory, standing before a dark figure. It didn't really resemble a beast. It looked like a man, but even in the recreation of the history I could feel the coldness and despair.

"We were the first of the seraph, Lucifer and I. We met the Beast in battle, and we lost. Other seraph were made, and in time we had an army. We marched on the Beast, but it had created its own army from the remains of the dead, and again we lost. As we died, its power grew, using our casualties as soldiers, feeding off the destruction of the world. We were nearly helpless against it."

This wasn't making me feel any better. "You trapped it," I said.

He nodded. "Yes, but it required a new way of thinking. When my Lord would grant His power to us, the Beast would know, and it would grow its own, such that we would fall against it. So we devised a new weapon - a language. A special language that could siphon its power too quickly for it to adjust. This was the Templar script, the first language from which the scripture of the seraph is derived, and the runes of the demons derived from that. This was to be our path to victory."

Now we saw the battle. We watched as legions of angels fought against legions of the dead, knitted together in haphazard fashion, a grotesque motley of flesh and bone.

"There were thousands of us against it. We accepted the casualties, we accepted the loss. We moved in, Lucifer and I, getting past its armies and confronting it one final time. Lucifer tricked it into chasing him, and led it straight into a trap. A cage of words, symbols, and numbers, not unlike this cave, where my Lord's power overwhelmed it and held it in His grasp. There it has remained, trapped for all of eternity."

A final image of the Beast, curled up on the floor, quaking in fear, surrounded by light. I shivered, chilled by the visage.

"Time passed. Lucifer sought to record the history of the seraph, and so he created the angelic scripture and wrote the first book, that of the origins of the angels. In his book he included the symbol that the Beast had given as its name; to serve as a warning so that we would never forget all that we had nearly lost."

"Satan's Bible," I said.

"That is what they are calling it?" he asked. "The scroll was lost when Lucifer was cast out. They have said it fell to the mortal realm, and there it must remain."

"The servants of the Beast have used Lucifer's words to encrypt their own," Charis said. "They may have located its cage, but without the Bible, we cannot follow."

"The Pure One," I said. "You're referring to Sarah. Where does she fit in?"

"There is only one way to open the cage," Malize replied. "One who is mortal, who possesses the power of both the Lord and the First Fallen must spill their life's blood into His cup, which must then be emptied into the seal. Know this now, if the seal is broken, it can not be replaced. It will take some time for the Beast to regain its former strength, but when it does, there is no soul on this world or any other that will be able to stop it."

"Their life's blood?" I asked. My own began to run cold. "You mean..."

"She must be destroyed for the Beast to escape," Malize said. "It feeds on destruction."

I looked at Charis, whose face had gone white. She hadn't known, or I would have already. "How much do you want to bet Sarah doesn't know?" I said. "They are betraying her too." I had no proof, but I was sure of it.

"Malize," Charis said. "How can the Grail be used to break the seal? It didn't exist when the cage was created."

The archangel shook his head. "It has always existed. It is made from the soul of the Lord made tangible, and was delivered to His son to aid him on his path to join his Father. The Lord's power holds the Beast, and only the Lord's power can release it."

Charis took my hand in hers. "Landon, it's time to go."

"Wait," I said. "I don't understand. If the Beast is such a threat to God, why would He make it at all possible for it to be freed?"

Malize said a single world in reply. The word I should have expected.

"Balance."

CHAPTER 21

"Landon, help me seal the tunnel," Charis said. We had left Malize and the cave behind, the door returning to our vision through her focus. "We can't afford for the Beast's servants to find this place."

"Right." I focused on the rock above the tunnel, pulling at it, ordering it to expand and collapse. Charis brought it up from below, and together we buried the entrance in no time.

"Not enough," Charis said. "That door leads to one of the most important artifacts in existence. We have to bring down the entire tunnel."

"I see why you needed my help," I replied.

We moved back along the corridor, pulling and lifting the rock down behind us, until there was just enough space left for the two of us to stand in front of the elevator doors.

"It's going to be weird for anyone who comes down here," I said. We had boarded the lift and finished filling in the tunnel, leaving the doors to open on a wall of rock.

"There shouldn't be anyone else coming down here," she replied.

We returned to the room at the top of the tower, and Charis called for Zeek while I tried to get a hold of Lylyx. The phone shunted directly to voicemail. It could have meant anything, so I tried not to worry about it.

I had lived through Charis' life in the cave, and although in my mind it had seemed as if over two hundred years had passed, in this universe it had been little more than thirty seconds. It was strange to be back where I had started so soon after I had left, yet having experienced and learned so much.

"We're going to save her," I said.

"*I know,*" Josette replied.

I smiled. I had always been able to feel her soul, to touch it and use its power. It was nothing compared to her actual presence. If anything could bring me comfort, it was her.

"Are you okay with this?" I asked. "I know what Charis did to you, to your fellows."

"*It is difficult, but I will accept it as His will, if you believe her actions were righteous.*"

She had done it in order to begin her pursuit of the Demon Queen title. Being sent to Hell hadn't been part of the plan, but it had worked out to her advantage.

"I wouldn't say righteous," I replied, uncertain that there wasn't another way she could have accomplished the same thing. "For whatever it's worth, her intent wasn't grounded in evil."

The door to the suite opened, and Charis walked in with the huge Templar trailing behind. She had a blessed sword across her back, and a cursed dagger at her side. She offered me the same.

"These belonged to Joseph," she said.

I knew it as soon as I took hold of them. I remembered the first time I had seen the simple longsword, stabbing into the chest of the archdevil. I accepted the blades in silent reverence, and altered my clothes to better accommodate them - combat boots, a pair of paratrooper pants, a black t-shirt, and a rig to hold the weapons.

"Don't lose them," Zeek added. He had a shotgun slung over each shoulder, and an axe that looked eerily similar to the first showing behind his head. A utility belt with boxes of shells attached to it caused his coat to bulge out at the sides.

"Can't we just rip his throat out?" Ulnyx said. *"It would be my pleasure."*

I ignored the Were. "What about the rest of the Templars?" I asked.

"They're willing to die for this, of course," Charis said. "But we're few enough in number. I'm not going to just throw away their lives."

I nodded. I knew from her memories how much they had lost. "We have no way to track Rebecca and Sarah unless they reveal themselves," I said. "We know they want the Grail, and we know they need Satan's Bible. I think our best chance right now is to stop them before they can get the Chalice."

"If they go after it first," Zeek said.

"They will," Charis replied. "They know that Landon knows they're after it. They'll want to get their hands on it before we can react. They have a huge head start though. I don't know if we can catch up."

I flashed her a sly smile. "Do you think I would make it that easy?" I asked. "They'll get the Grail with enough time for sure, but hopefully we haven't reached enough time yet."

She reached back for the memory and returned my smile with one of her own. "You are a clever boy," she said.

My face flushed at the compliment. "If we don't catch them, we need to get to the Bible before they do, plus we'll need Obi and Thomas if we're going to have any hope of decrypting the strings." I could only hope that they had known what they were doing when they had torched my collection.

"It'll make it a whole lot easier if we can cut them off instead of chasing them," Zeek said.

"I don't know if 'easier' is the word I would use," I replied. "But the Beast needs Sarah to get out, which means we need to get to Sarah first. If we fail at that, we find Obi and get the Bible."

"Sounds like a plan," Zeek agreed.

"The rift is on the rooftop," Charis said. "I disabled it to prevent us from being followed, but Vilya and I can put it back together. It won't take long."

"Let's go," I said.

Charis bypassed the elevator and led us up to the roof via the emergency stairs. We emerged into a gray gloom and a stiff buffeting wind. The roof was large and flat, with a helipad in the center and a radio spire rising to the south. The transport rift was tucked into the space below the spire, hidden from view of the Divine by the physical obstruction.

"It will only take a few minutes," Charis said when we approached. I could see that some of the runes had been scraped clean.

"Nothing to do but wait," Zeek said.

I scanned the sky with my Sight, my hackles raised. If Sarah was keeping a lookout for me, she would know right where I was. Somehow she and Rebecca had managed to get the angels and fire demon on our tail mid-flight to our original Swiss destination - I didn't doubt they could do the same, or worse, again.

The geography around us was clear, at least as far as I could tell. Someone in Hell had taught Rebecca how to make herself and others invisible to Sight. Someone who was clearly a servant, and clearly powerful; but who? Was there an even stronger enemy out there, just waiting in the wings in case she failed? If there was, with any luck they were trapped in Hell.

I felt the change in the transport rift before Charis had a chance to announce that it was ready. It was a strange sensation, like being tickled by the edge of a flame, and one that I hadn't felt, or at least noticed before. A few seconds later the flames ignited around the circumference of the rift.

"Come on," Charis said, motioning us through.

Zeek went first, a shotgun cradled in his arms, just in case. I didn't hesitate to follow, finding my focus as I stepped in.

I was greeted by the strong smell of burned wood and the sight of a flamed out husk of a structure interspersed among the small army of Divine that greeted us on the other side. My Sight flared in response to the heat. A trap? Or just an obvious immersion point? Either way, we had just walked right into an ambush.

The first wave of demons had pounced the moment Zeek had appeared, but his initial salvo of holy water laden shells had managed to slow the advance. Even so, I found myself ducking and jiving out of the way of vampire claws even before I could pull my right foot all the way through. I dropped to a knee and whipped the sword from my back, planting it into the demon's chest and using it to shove it away. The blade slid free through a cloud of smoke, but I watched it sizzle and heal over in a matter of seconds. Not good.

"Zeek," I shouted, reaching out and grabbing the Templar before he could move too far from the rift. We had two choices, stay and fight or go back through. I was going to pull him back, but then Charis appeared and all hell really broke loose.

Her sword came to her hand like magic, flashing in the light of the rift and severing the claws that grabbed for her, circling back around and decapitating the first vampire that tried to touch her. She crouched low and kicked out, hitting a second vamp in the groin and launching him backwards a good twenty feet.

"Come on, Landon," she spat, her eyes on fire. "It doesn't matter if they've been suckling from your girlfriend if you take their heads."

Her words hit me. I was stronger, faster, better than before, and I shouldn't be letting their healing factor psych me out. Renewed, I slipped around a shorter female and grabbed the dagger, using it to pin her while I took her head with the sword. Another vampire was coming at Zeek from behind, and I tossed the dagger into its forehead. The move only slowed it long enough for it to reach up and remove the blade, but that was all the time the Templar needed. His axe swung cleanly through the demon's neck.

"*You fight like a girl,*" Ulnyx growled from below the surface, his voice clear in my mind.

I felt him reach out, asking for control. I could see the threads of power now, and understand them. I knew I could keep him contained, and so I let him take it. His power poured into my body, his soul capturing a portion of my mind and beginning to issue commands. My body moved like a marionette, sheathing the blades, hands shifting to a nasty set of claws, reaching out and ripping the head from one of the demons. I observed through shared eyes, my heart beginning to beat wildly at the scene of the destruction the Were created.

No longer participating in my physical motion, I focused, reaching out to the splinters of wood around us, sending them airborne and planting them into the enemy masses. It didn't do much damage, but it was a distraction, and it gave Charis and Zeek time to dig in with their blades.

"*A little better,*" Ulnyx said, his gravel voice filled with bloodlust. "*I'm starting to like you, meat.*"

"*Then you'll love this,*" I said, shifting my focus downward. The ground began to tremble, and pointed berms of earth shot up below the feet of the demons, spearing them through the legs and groin. Ulnyx pounced on one, grabbing its head and twisting, taking pleasure in the crack of the separating spine.

I couldn't use my eyes, so I focused on my Sight, using it to find Charis and Zeek both taking advantage of the chaos I had caused. I felt Charis' attention shift towards me, and a moment later a lance of heat reached through my body.

The pain was intense, and I recoiled, the lapse in concentration forcing Ulnyx from my nerve center, causing my body to revert to human form.

"*What the hell?*" he cried, at the same time I glared wildly at my counterpart. I saw her own expression turn to one of shock as she realized what I was thinking.

Before I could say anything, I caught the sickening stench of burned flesh, and I spun around. Lurching towards me was another vampire, charred from head to toe but healing fast. Without a second thought I pulled the dagger and brought it around, severing its skull in one smooth stroke. By the time I turned around again, Charis had moved on.

The enemy ranks were thinning, and it only took a few more defeats for them to break off the attack, the furthest edges of the army fading away into the darkness at a full run. The demons may have fed on Rebecca's blood and become harder to kill, but these weren't trained fighters, these were chafe, and they weren't all ready to lose their lives to the cause. The victory was a meek one. We'd routed the weakest soldiers, but we'd also given them a lot of information to take back to their master.

"Nice work," Zeek said, sidling up to me with his axe still in hand.

"*That sucked so hard,*" Ulnyx cursed, pushing against me, desperate to get back into the saddle. I felt the threads of my power and brought them around to wrap his up again. His voice faded from my consciousness, still kicking and screaming.

"*Thank you,*" Josette said. "*I was growing irritated with his whining.*"

I laughed. I couldn't help it.

"Landon, I'm sorry," Charis said, walking up and putting her hand on my shoulder. "I was only trying to protect you."

I put my hand on top of hers, holding it out between us. "It's okay," I said. "I know."

We lingered like that for a few heartbeats, and then she pulled away. "This group wasn't intended to win," she said.

"I know that too. Sarah could tell her when I arrived, but I bet she wanted to know *who* I arrived with. Do you think she knows whose side you're on?"

Charis shrugged. "It doesn't matter. She does now."

"So, where to?" Zeek asked.

"St. Patrick's," Charis and I both said as one.

The rift had been located at an old warehouse on the Chelsea waterfront, a two and a half mile walk from the cathedral. It was a cool, calm morning; still early enough that the streets weren't too crowded with people, but late enough that the sun was beginning to peek above the horizon. We were running, the Templar keeping up remarkably well considering his bulk.

My thoughts had taken me back to the morning after the events at the Statue, and I related the history to Zeek while we ran. I had returned from the Island and had been wandering the streets of New York, my mind whizzing at a million miles per hour, my heart scalded by the outcome, the Holy Grail clutched in shaking fingers. I had been looking for a place to rest, some relief from the twist and pull of Ulnyx and Josette on my soul, a respite from the guilt and sadness. I had wandered back towards the

Waldorf, and had landed on the steps of St. Patrick's.

It was there that I had collected myself for the first time, gaining a semblance of lucidity that had led to inspiration. It may have seemed counter-productive to have stashed the Holy Grail in a place like St. Patrick's Cathedral. After all, there was no other place in the Northern Hemisphere that shouted 'Heaven' as loudly as the structure. In that moment of verisimilitude, I realized that was what I could count on to keep it safe.

I had approached the door, but before I could enter I noticed the series of seraphim runes running along each edge of the archway, and I felt the power radiating off of them. I made an effort to step inside, but the pressure was overwhelming, and my body halted mid-step. I focused, pushing back against the runes, and tried again to no avail. This was no way in.

After circling the structure, trying every door, and enhancing my eyes in order to examine the frame of every window, I realized that I wasn't going to be able to enter. What was more, I knew from the experience with the demonic runes under the Statue that if the goal had only been to keep demons out, I would have felt the pressure but have been able to enter. The fact that I couldn't meant the scripture was blocking *all* Divine.

"But if you couldn't go in, how did you get the Grail inside?" Zeek asked between huffs of air.

"I had to find someone else who could. A mortal." I had known exactly who to go to. A priest in a small church near the Belmont. The one who had given me the holy water to heal Josette. He knew enough about the Divine to accept my story, and while he had been less than thrilled to see me again, it hadn't taken too much effort to bring him around to my way of seeing things. I had helped him sneak into the buiding, and he had hid a glamoured Grail. I didn't know where, but he had promised that it would be safe, sure as he had seen a leprechaun.

"It was a good idea," Charis said. "The cathedrals were built for the mortal worship of God, free and safe from Divine intervention. It was also close enough for you to keep an eye on it, and sneaky enough that it would have taken quite a while for any Divine to figure it out. It isn't your fault Sarah ripped it out of you."

Literally. The choice of words brought the pain back. I winced and shook it off.

"I get that," Zeek said. "But how come they haven't gotten to it yet? Isn't Sarah a mortal?"

"Yes, but I couldn't tell her exactly where the Grail was, because I don't know. She's probably still in there, rooting through the Cardinal's drawers."

When we reached St. Patrick's, I found out how wrong I had been. The cathedral rested heavily in the morning sunlight, at first glance a peaceful vision of the strength and power of religion and faith. That was until my eyes settled lower on the structure, on the dozens of men and women who had fallen chaotically across the steps.

"*No,*" Josette cried out in my mind, sharply enough to force me to a knee.

Zeek knelt down beside one of the people, a young woman with long red hair. He put his hand to her neck and shook his head. "Dead," he said.

"They're all dead," Charis confirmed. "But they're still warm."

I got back to my feet and looked up. The door to the cathedral was hanging open, only silent darkness beyond. I fought back against the anger that was creeping up my spine, refusing to believe what I knew was true. I climbed the steps so that I could see inside.

Sunlight streamed in weakly through the stained glass windows, casting an eerie light on the ransacked interior of the church. Pews had been thrown aside, the floor had been dug into, the statues smashed. It would have taken an army to do so much damage in so little time. An army that had been decommissioned once they were no longer needed. Still warm. We hadn't missed them by much.

"*How could she do this?*" Josette asked, her voice raw. "*I know Izak raised her with kindness. I know he would never have taught her this.*"

I could have kicked myself. She did it because she knew we were getting close; that her time was running out. We had been wasting our time fighting Rebecca's minions while she had Commanded regular men and women to go into the cathedral and find the Grail. Against their will she had made them defile the house of God until they found what she wanted. Once they had, she had killed them. Each and every one of them.

"How could they die?" Zeek asked. "There isn't a scratch on them."

"She was Commanding them," Charis said. "She probably told them to stop breathing."

The world started spinning, my emotions climbing their way back from the depths where I had learned to contain them. More and more they had been finding their way out, escaping the prison I had constructed to hold back the torture of loss and betrayal, but now they burst free in an explosion of guilt, anger, sadness, disappointment, and fear.

"Sarah," I shouted, focusing my energy on the word, casting it upwards into the sky and downwards into the dirt. The power of it was a shockwave that sent the air flowing out around me, pushing over the corpses and shaking the world. In my mind, I felt a recoil, a coolness that I hadn't noticed before. She had heard me, and fled.

"She has the Grail, and we don't know where they are, or where they're going," Zeek said.

Charis walked over and put her arms around me, pulling me down to bring her face level with mine. "Landon?"

I hadn't realized I was crying until I tried to look at her through tear-coated eyes. "I don't know if I can save her," I said in a whisper. "I don't know if I can kill her."

She cupped my face in her hand, her eyes fierce. "You can save her," she insisted. She looked down. "If you can't, I'll kill her. We can't let them free the Beast. I know you care for her, but she's still only one person."

"*Landon, she's right,*" Josette said, her words heavy. "*If she has lost her way and we cannot help her find it, there is no other choice. We cannot sacrifice everything.*"

I took a deep breath and looked around at the bodies, taking in each face, remembering them all. This would be the fate of every man, woman, and child if the Beast were set loose. Used up and tossed away.

"They have the Grail. Let's hope we can get to the Bible first," I said. "Strength in numbers. We need to find Obi. I think I know how."

CHAPTER 22

Rachel's office was downtown, but her home was on the upper west side, a huge brownstone that was mixed in with the residence of other popular New York dignitaries. I had stayed there for a couple of weeks a few years ago, living in the high class of a wealthy Manhattanite while I poured my heart out to her about everything and anything. I had hoped the exercise would have been cathartic, and she had done her best to listen and offer comfort, but in the end I had come away with the understanding that I was powerless against the true undercurrents of the Divine existence.

It was that realization that had started me down the path that Charis had shown me, so it seemed fitting that the same path had led me right back to Rachel's door. If only it could have been under better circumstances.

Rachel's housekeeper Celia was the one who answered it, pulling it open just enough to peek out at us. When she saw me, she smiled and opened the door the rest of the way.

"Landon," she said, coming out onto the steps and giving me a huge bear hug. Celia's build and attitude were more appropriate on a linebacker, but she had the heart and soul to be anybody's grandmother. Her white hair was pulled back in a short ponytail, and she was dressed in a simple black maid's uniform. She had been with Rachel for over twenty years, and had been nothing but warm and kind to me, and to anyone I had ever seen her meet. Even though she was Awake, and knew exactly what I was. She told me that the way she saw it, the only way to end any disagreement was through kindness. I had tried picturing myself hugging a fire demon, and wished I could have agreed.

"You look like you haven't eaten in weeks," she said, pulling back and giving me the once over. Her eyes flicked over to Zeek and Charis. "Oh, you brought friends? Boy, I didn't think you had any friends." Her laugh was boisterous, and she gave each of them the same hug she had given me.

"What did your momma feed you?" she asked Zeek after releasing him. Her arms had barely gotten around the huge man's sides.

"Spinach," Zeek said, laughing.

"My, you are a looker," she said to Charis, the hug for her only slightly more gentle. "Mmmm, demon inside you, eh? I'll let it slide, since you're friends with my boy."

"I appreciate that," Charis said, uncomfortable with the woman's attention.

"Celia, the big one is Ezekiel, we call him Zeek. The pretty one is Charis," I said, introducing them. "I assume Rachel isn't here?"

She put her hands on her hips and glared at me. "You know full well she isn't here," she said. "When has she ever been here this time of day?"

I *had* known she wouldn't be there. As much as I wanted to, right now I didn't trust Rachel either. What I *did* trust was that her computer would be safeguarded from eavesdropping and tracking.

"Okay Celia," I said. "You figured me out. Actually, I was just hoping I could borrow Rachel's office for a few minutes. I promise I won't snoop around into anything I'm not supposed to."

She laughed. "Like anyone could stop you if you wanted to," she replied. "Go ahead, but I'm going to call Rachel and tell her you're here."

I had expected as much. "Of course. Charis, Zeek, if you wouldn't mind waiting downstairs with Celia?"

"I've got some fresh brewed iced tea," Celia said. "And I was just baking cookies for my grandson's school fair, but I'm sure I can spare a few."

"Lead the way," Zeek said. "I could never say no to a cookie."

Celia brought them inside, through a simple marble-floored foyer and into the living room. Rachel's taste had always been understated. Instead of the crowded, ornate decorative taste shared by the wealthy, she had a standard sofa, love seat, recliner and ottoman, a painting of her parents, a fireplace, and not much else. The kitchen was to the right of the living room, and Celia led Charis and Zeek that way while I climbed the steps on the left side of the room.

The door to Rachel's office was locked, and I knew it was both protected by angelic scripture that would alert her to anyone entering, and under the watchful eyes of a number of hidden cameras. I figured Celia was probably dialing her right now, so I didn't hesitate to unlock the door and let myself in. I looked directly into one of the cameras and waved, and then focused on them, pinching off the flow of electricity and disabling them. I knew she would get on me about why I didn't want her to see what I was doing, but right now I didn't care.

Her office was standard fare, a near clone of the one downtown. I took a seat behind the desk and turned on her monitor. The computer was locked, but it just so happened that I knew the password. I had pulled it from the keys once when I had been here with Rachel. I typed it in, and then opened up a web browser. For all I knew, Obi hadn't gotten away from Cho, but if he had I could only assume he would have sent me a message. That meant SamChan.

I would have preferred to use a VPN and a darknet to visit the site, but I didn't have much time if Rachel decided to head home. She didn't know about SamChan. As far as I could tell none of the Divine did. It made it the perfect resource for secure communication.

My heart lurched in excitement when I saw the first message subject.

Don't cross the lane over the divider

It had been posted by Oblitrix, two hours ago. I knew it was meant for me. I clicked into it.

Friends don't let friends drive blind so txt me

The string was a code for the phone number. I pulled my cell out and started typing.

"*Still kickn?*" I wrote.

The message came back a few seconds later. "*u bet. feelin advntrus?*"

"y cu soon"

I smiled and pocketed the phone, and then dug into Rachel's computer to clean out the history and the cache. It wouldn't stop any serious snooping into my activity, but it would at least cause it to take a few hours.

I was reaching for the power button on the monitor when I noticed the dead pixel. It was such a tiny, inconsequential thing that most people would never have seen it, and even if they had would never have given it a second thought. I wasn't most people, because I knew how fastidious Rachel was with keeping things in order, and so I did give it another look. Squinting, I tried to discern it with my eyes, but failing that I forced my will on it, examining the diodes that made up the pixels and looking for one that was unlit. There weren't any.

I stared at it for a few seconds, and then grabbed the mouse and navigated over to the tiny dot. I clicked on it. Nothing happened. I waited a few seconds, clicked again. No result. Almost satisfied, I started reaching for the power button again but then reconsidered. I double-clicked, and felt my pulse pick up the pace when a fresh window popped up.

Staring back at me from the monitor was an icon that was all too familiar. It was replaced a moment later by a login screen.

I slumped back into the chair, my mind reeling. Rachel was a servant? My pounding heart was breaking at the thought of her deceit. I had known her database had held a message that was intended for me to find, but I had trusted in her, and assumed it had been planted by someone else. Now.. Had she put it there herself?

What about the ambush I had interrupted? Was I as much of a fool as the witch had said I was? I had thought the demons were there to flex some muscle. What if the ambush was no ambush at all, but a meeting? Alyle had joined up with the angels to fight against me. What if it wasn't out of self-preservation, but because he was already working with them?

"*You've been punked,*" Ulnyx said, his rough voice in my head, pushing my confusion closer to rage. I closed my eyes and clenched my fists, trying to make some kind of sense of it.

"*Landon, wait,*" Josette said. "*You don't know that. She could be trying to help. Maybe she got her hands on some information, and she was going to share it with you. After all, she has been Touched for many years, and I know her well.*"

I took a deep breath and let my body relax. Josette had a point, and it helped extinguish some of the anger. I looked at the login screen. Maybe she *was* trying to help, and my dealings with the Divine had left me so jaded I wasn't able to see it. I leaned forward and started typing.

First, I tried Rachel's standard username and password combo; the same one that allowed access to the machine. Of course, it didn't work. Why would she use the same password for both anyway? I sat back down and stared at the login screen. What would she use?

My fingers flew along the keys as I put in as many possible passwords as I could think of. I tried her birthday, her parent's birthdays, and her anniversary. I tried her favorite author and her favorite book, the names of her deceased pets, and even my own name. I had software on my laptop that would have been able to brute force it in a matter of hours, but I wasn't so lucky here. Instead, I was taking stabs in the dark trying to guess the right key press combination.

At least twenty minutes had passed when I decided to give up.

Time was in short supply, and we needed to go meet Obi. I could always bring him back here and set him on cracking the system if necessary. I typed in one last word, 'balance', and watched the red error text pop up yet again. It was worth a shot.

"Can I help you with something?"

I had been so involved with the computer, Rachel's voice caught me completely off guard. She was standing on the other side of the desk, hands on her hips, a stern expression on her face. When had she gotten here? My initial reaction was to push myself back from the desk and start to utter an apologetic explanation. I remembered what Josette had said and I tried to stay calm. Seeing her standing there, her posture accusing me; it didn't work. My emotions were too raw, and in the back of my mind I could hear Ulnyx calling me a sucker.

"Yes, you can," I said, pulling strength into my body and leaping across the desk. I had the demonic blade against her throat before she could react. "You can tell me the password to that little hidden app you've got. You know which one I mean."

I had nearly shouted, and I could hear the chairs in the kitchen shifting downstairs. It was followed by a herd of footsteps, and a moment later Charis and Zeek stormed into the room, with Celia right behind.

"Landon, child, what are you doing?" Celia cried, shoving herself between the two Templars.

"Celia, stay back," I said, pushing the blade against Rachel's throat as tightly as I dared without breaking the skin. "I'm sorry, but she's been keeping some pretty major secrets, and I need her to tattle."

Zeek took hold of Celia's arm, keeping her in place. As strong as she was, she was no match for the massive Templar.

I pulled the dagger away and gave Rachel a soft shove towards the computer. "Put in the password," I said.

Rachel looked at me, fear and tears in her eyes. "Landon, wait. Please. It's not what you think. I'm not…"

I was hoping she would defend herself, and tell me I was wrong. Part of me was counting on it. Too bad she was lying. It only made me more angry.

"*Told you so*," Ulnyx said. I came down on him like a vice, pushing him from my conscious stream.

"Not what I think?" I shouted. "Not what I think? What I think is that you're a servant of the Beast. Am I wrong? Tell me I am, and remember that you can't lie to me."

I could smell every bit of her fear. I could practically taste it on my tongue. She backed away from me, towards the chair behind the desk. She looked at the ground. "What are you doing here?" she asked me again.

"I came to borrow your computer," I said. "I was looking for Obi. I found more than I wanted to. Now answer the question, or I swear I'll put this dagger into your heart."

She flopped into the chair, her eyes downcast. "I'm sorry, Landon. I never wanted to hurt you."

She was telling the truth, at least as she believed it. "Then why?" I asked, my surfaced emotions bounding chaotically. "You're a Touched; a shining example of what it means to be compassionate and giving and to walk the holy path. You were also like a mother to me. Why would you do this?"

I could see the tears drip from her eyes and land between her legs, splashing on the leather of the chair. Her hands moved slowly to the keyboard, and she whispered between breaths. "It was no accident I was the one who took you in, after you defeated Reyzl," she said.

What? My mind shot back to the day we had met. It had only been a few days, and I was still in a fog. She had found me walking the streets, I had never questioned how or why. We had started talking, and she invited me to dinner. No judgement, no anger, only compassion. Had it all been an act?

"I was supposed to keep an eye on you, and help you where I could without stepping over the line. The balance is very important to our work. You're an easy person to care for, Landon. You have a strong soul. There was a time when I began to question what I was doing, because I had grown fond of you. Except, I thought when the time came you would join us. I thought you would go with Rebecca. She loves you, and the way you talked about her, I thought you cared for her too. Don't you see, Landon? Everyone who cares the most about you - Rebecca, Sarah, and I; we want to set you free, to set everyone trapped in this stupid war free. This is the only way to do it."

I walked around the desk so I could see the screen. She began typing in the password, one slow character at a time.

"You want me to believe you're doing this for me?" I asked. She thought she was, which made me sick to my stomach. "How could you be, and believe it? You were a servant before you ever met me."

I didn't know if the last part was true, but she didn't deny it. "None of us are free," she replied. "We've been at war for thousands of years. We will *always* be at war. I used to believe that I could make a difference. I used to believe that God cared, and would help us win, so that the faithful could rise up and get the heaven that we deserve. I've realized that it's never going to happen. The Beast *can* happen. Change *can* happen. I *am* doing this for you, and for me." She pointed at Charis and Zeek. "I'm even doing it for them. The Templars think they're so righteous. Maybe they just enjoy all of this war mongering?" She shrugged. "I don't. I'm done. It will never, ever end, Landon. Is that what you want?

She finished typing, and moved her hand to hover over the enter key, waiting for my response. For the first time since Sarah had disappeared, I gave pause, and that pause led me to doubt. What if she was right? I had been tired, empty, and emotionless. I had been acting on instinct, keeping the balance, and feeling nothing. I had sought out the mark, searched for it in hope of finding some kind of salvation. I looked up at Charis, her face a bunched mess of worry at my hesitation.

What if my path had led me here not to fight the Beast, but to help set him free? My emotions were a tangled nest that I couldn't sort. I looked back to Rachel, pleading with her eyes, begging me to listen to her reason. I couldn't deny I had been unhappy, drained by my position in the universe. What if I did free the Beast? What if it destroyed everything? I would be free from the prison I had put myself in. We would all be free of the constant battle, the so-called balance. Did it matter if everything else was gone too, if I wasn't around to know it?

My anger began to fade. I leaned in and kissed Rachel on the

someone would be me? One thing at a time.

Charis' power began to fade as she relaxed her grip, heaving a deep sigh at my words. Rachel's eyes locked onto mine, and I could feel her fear and sadness.

"You have a choice, right now," I said. "Forget about everything that's gone before. We can make a difference. You can make a difference. It can start right here."

"I don't, I can't," she replied. "It's too late for me. I've already sworn myself to the Beast. I can't escape it." The tears were flowing more freely now. "I'm sorry, Landon. I'm sorry I lied to you, and tricked you. It wasn't supposed to be this way, but I'm just so tired."

"The Beast is still caged," I said. "I'll protect you. Rachel…"

Before I could react, she shot forward, her hand reaching out and finding the handle of the cursed dagger. She pulled it, getting just enough metal to slice her other hand open. The veins of poison began spreading instantly.

"Celia, holy water?" I asked, frantic in the moment.

"No," Rachel said. "Landon… the Beast… the cage… is imperfect." She closed her eyes, the poison spreading quickly up her arm. It didn't matter, because she was already gone. She had acted to take her own life, and had fallen, dead.

CHAPTER 23

"What did you do?" Celia cried, pulling her arm free and rushing around the desk. "Rachel?"

She bent down and put her hands on Rachel's face, a face wracked with the pain of death and loss. I stood motionless, trying to come to terms with what she had done, and what she had said. 'The cage is imperfect'. What did it mean?

"You did this," Celia said, turning on me. "You couldn't just leave it alone. You couldn't just use the computer and go. Why did you have to be so snoopy?" The anger fell from her, and she collapsed onto the floor.

"I'm sorry," I said, kneeling down and putting my hand on Celia's back. "I didn't want her to die. I just wanted her to see the truth."

"What truth?" Celia said through the sobs. "Folks don't understand what they're getting into when they sign up to fight a war. Folks never see themselves as a casualty."

"*Just leave her,*" Josette said. "*She needs her time to grieve, and you have work to do.*"

She was right. I didn't say anything else. I stood up and headed for the door, averting my eyes from Charis and Zeek as I passed.

"First we get Obi, and then I have to go talk to someone," I said. "At least we got lucky with finding Satan's Bible." I didn't feel lucky. I remembered what Charis had said earlier, and it gave me chills.

"Landon?" Charis said, trying to touch my shoulder on the way by. I shook it off.

"Not now. Just give me a few minutes, okay?"

They followed me out of the room, downstairs and away from the house. My mind was still a whirlwind of thoughts and possibilities, and I didn't speak until we had walked a few blocks.

"Obi is at the Intrepid Museum," I said, not slowing or turning to look at them. "We go and pick him up, make sure he's safe, and then we move on."

"Landon, you know who the keeper of Satan's Bible is," Charis said. "We don't need to go to your friend. I'm pretty sure he can take of himself."

I stopped walking and turned on her. "I've already lost most of the people I care about over the last two days," I said. "I'm not going to leave him behind. Cho is sure to be looking for him, because it's likely he doesn't know who has the Bible and he still wants to keep us from getting it. He *does* know Obi and Thomas are our best shot."

"It won't matter if Rebecca and Sarah free the Beast," she said. "Every second we waste makes that even more likely. The Templars have the texts, we just need to get the Bible and go back to Thailand."

I put my face close to hers, feeling the flush of our anger intermingling. "Would you have left Joseph behind? Besides, I would think you'd be awfully keen to get a shot at Cho, after what he did to him." It was a cheap shot, and I knew I had gone too far. She reacted as though I had hit her in the gut.

"You son of a bitch," she growled, her spittle a coldness across my face. "How dare you?"

"Guys," Zeek said. "Let's just take a breather here."

I fought to reign myself in. This could have gotten out of hand in a hurry, and it was the last thing I wanted. "I dare because I need you," I said, my voice calm. "I need your help, and you need mine, and I'm going to the Intrepid Museum to collect Obi before Cho does. You can come along and help, or you can hang out at Starbucks and wait. Either way, I'm going."

Her red eyes flared, but she smiled, her anger subsiding. "Okay," she said, leaning up on her toes to press her forehead against mine. "I do need you, and I trust you. If you hadn't found that hidden file, we'd be severely up the creek, instead of just treading water in it."

I returned her smile, keeping my head against hers. "Thanks for seeing it my way," I said. "I'm sorry for being an asshole."

"You're welcome, and I forgive you, asshole," she replied with a smirk.

"If it matters to either of you," Zeek said, "I'm in."

I didn't typically like to rely on cabs to get around the city, but we were on the upper east side, and the museum was to the midwest, resting on the Hudson. Our driver was a middle eastern man who drove with all the pizzazz of a legendary NYC cab driver, careening us through every back alley shortcut imaginable to get us to our destination in no time. There

266

wasn't much room in the rear, with Zeek shoved into the first half of the back seat, and Charis and I sharing the other half between us. We were squeezed in pretty tight, so it wasn't all bad.

"Intrepid," the driver announced, tapping his meter. "Twelve seventy five."

I reached into my pocket and found a twenty. "Keep the change," I said, handing it to him and pushing open the door. We spilled out onto the sidewalk.

The Intrepid towered above us, a hundred feet of American steel casting a long shadow on the seaport. I had been here once before, on a school field trip when I was a kid. It was my story about how I had wandered off into a restricted area and wound up getting booted off the ship that had probably given Obi the thought to meet up here.

I focused and reached forward with my Sight, in search of Obi's familiar signature. I found him near the center of the ship, towards the flight deck. Thomas and Melody were with him.

"Up there," I said, pointing. Charis nodded, she had Seen them too.

I looked around in search of any other Divine, not expecting to find anything. If Cho were here, he and his crew would be hiding themselves anyway, and we didn't have time to do a careful recon. I had nearly finished my sweep when Charis pointed off to a restaurant across the street.

"Over there," she said. "It's small. A messenger, I think."

I followed her aim with my Sight, feeling the light touch of heat that gave the demon away. I recognized this one too. "Could be a problem," I said. "Wait here. Stay ready."

The people parted around me as I jogged across the street, not even trying to disguise my approach. When Yuli saw me, he waved.

"Good evening mastersss," he said, flapping his wings and bowing deeply in the air. "What bringsesss you to thisss part of the city?"

My relationship with Reyzl's former familiar could only be called interesting. After the events under the Statue, the demon had sought me out, offering me his services in exchange for an occasional bit of raw meat and the promise of my protection. I had taken him up on it, and his status in the city had been a great benefit to keeping tabs on all of the potential Reyzl replacements. That wasn't to say I trusted him though. I knew he would sell me out at the drop of a hat. If he was here, he already had.

"Just came to meet some friends," I said. "What are you doing here?"

His lips drew back from his snout in a wide, leering smile. "Justsss came to meetsss your friendsss," he said. "It'sss just businesss."

"Cho?" I asked.

"Yesss. He promisesss Yuli twice the meat, and a girl if I tellsss himsss when you arrivesss."

"Sounds like a good deal," I said. "Is he here yet?"

Yuli cackled. "Maybe. Maybe notsss." I reached out to grab him, but he swooped away with ridiculous quickness and started laughing. "Good luck. Call me if you needsss my servicesss again."

I didn't stand around to watch him fly away.

"Cho is on his way," I said, grabbing Charis' hand and pulling her behind me as I ran towards the Intrepid. "Obi doesn't stand a chance alone against him."

We burst up the ramp and onto the hanger deck. It was early enough that the museum was still pretty empty, with just a couple of local schools herding their students through the exhibits. I located the stairs up to the flight deck and focused, giving myself extra speed to sprint to the steps and glide up them. Charis was close behind, but Zeek just couldn't keep up.

I spotted them as soon as I exited the stairwell, all three standing near the front of the Blackbird spy plane, one of the prizes of the museum's collection. Melody saw me first, and she immediately grabbed Thomas and pointed my way.

"Landon, wait," Thomas shouted as I ran towards them. "It's a trap!"

I felt my body float into the air, vaguely aware of the heat and noise when the aircraft next to me exploded in a ball of flame. I heard the screams of the people scattered around the deck, smelled the sickly scent of cooked meat, and then landed perpendicular to my friends, face down on the smooth surface of the vessel. I knew by the pain that half my side had been ripped away, but I could already feel it healing.

Charis had been thrown by the blast too, and she shouted curses from somewhere behind me. I pushed myself up onto my hands and knees and tried to turn around, but before I could a thin wire dropped down over my head and tightened on my throat. I felt the serrated edges dig into my skin, and then I felt the wetness of blood running down my neck.

"It's so good to see you again, Landon," Cho said. He pulled on the wire so that I was forced to turn around to face him. He was still wearing that same fancy suit, clean and pressed and smelling like cologne. "It is especially wonderful of you to be so utterly predictable."

"What B-movie did you steal those lines from?" I asked.

He laughed, and then spun me so I could see Charis, similarly tied, along with a small army of vampires who didn't seem to mind the bright sunshine blasting them. Another benefit to feeding on my blood, I was sure. Zeek had also finally made it up the stairs, but he was powerless with both of us being held. He dropped his shotgun and surrendered without a fight.

"Now, I have to assume you wouldn't normally be so stupid and reckless to rush to your friend's aid without ensuring it wasn't a trap first, so I must conclude that you're in a bit of a hurry. Which means Rebecca has the Grail, and is on her way to meet our destiny."

There was no point in denying it. "She does," I admitted. "But it won't do her much good when she doesn't know where to take it."

"I wouldn't be too sure of that," he said. He must have noticed my shocked expression, because he laughed again. "Ah, I guess you weren't expecting that little tidbit. Not that it will do you any good in your current situation. I guess there's just one more loose end to tie up, and we can get on with changing the world."

He reached forward, sticking his hand in my left coat pocket, and then my right. "Where is it?" he asked.

"Where is what?"

"Avriel's Box," he hissed. "What did you do with it?"

I didn't have it. Charis did. "Sorry," I said. "If I had known you needed it, I would have brought it with me."

That smart-ass remark earned me a punch in the face, and the wire noose tightened enough to cut into my trachea. I could feel the blood pouring down my neck.

"No matter," he said. "I can adjust." He pulled me along with the noose, leading me to where Obi, Thomas, and Melody were standing. He motioned for his cronies to bring Charis and Zeek over too.

"Hey, boss," Obi said when we approached. "A little help?"

"I would love a little help, thanks," I said. He smiled. Even in the face of death, he kept his sense of humor. His eyes shifted to Charis.

"Man, you get all the hot girls," he said.

"She's hotter than you know," I replied.

"Enough," Cho said, tightening the noose even more, opening my neck wide enough that I couldn't get any air to speak. "Such a brave soldier," he said to Obi. "A joker right to the end." He reached behind me with his free hand, taking hold of the cursed dagger. He held it up to Obi's face, trying to get him to flinch.

"I'm not afraid of you, man," Obi said.

"You should be," Cho snapped. He took the dagger and jabbed. I winced at the pain as it sunk into my flesh. "Be a good man, and hold that for me while I drain your sidekick." He smiled, his eyes flashing black and his teeth elongating.

"Who, whoa, whoa, hang on one second," Obi said. "You can't suck my blood!"

Cho's laugh was throaty. "Why not?" he asked.

Obi glanced at me, and winked. "Because you don't have any teeth," he said.

I saw the glint of light reflecting off the dagger an instant before it smashed into Cho's face, shattering his jaw and teeth, the force of the throw dropping him and causing him to relinquish his hold on the noose. I didn't waste any time getting my hands on it and pulling it off my head.

There was a flash of heat, and another explosion as a second plane went up in flames. The force blasted a couple of the vampires and threw us all to the ground. I was on my feet in an instant, and I rushed to Charis' side, decapitating her captor before he could get his hands back on her noose. I looked up at the ship's island just in time to see a Great Were make the thirty foot leap to the deck, landing almost gracefully and charging a pair of vamps. They didn't stand a chance.

A hand touched my shoulder, and I whipped around, coming face to face with Izak. Where the hell had he been hiding? He greeted me with a feral grin, and then reached out and put his hand on the face of an incoming enemy. The vampire cried out as the flesh and bone rotted and collapsed below Izak's touch, leaving a disintegrating, headless corpse behind.

"An ambush of an ambush," I said. "I love it."

The flight deck erupted with the sounds of growling, and hissing, and the clang of steel against steel. These weren't the meat that had greeted us at the transport rift. These were the Beast's true soldiers.

"Landon, look out," Charis cried.

Izak and I both turned. The dagger cut deep into the fiend's neck, and the follow up kick sent him tumbling away from me. I barely got my own sword up in time to block Cho's attack.

"She wanted you alive," he said, his blade and claws almost too quick to follow. He reached past my defenses and dug into my side. "Forget that. I want you dead."

I twisted away, taking him on from the side to reduce the size of his target, following the muscle memories that I had inherited from Josette. Cho came at me, his assault a frenzy of steel and bone, his mouth wide in a toothy leer. Josette was the best, but he was an archvampire, and he was fast, insanely fast. I struggled to keep up, until I couldn't anymore, and his blade sliced deep into my jaw, disabling one of my eyes and cutting off half my face.

I jumped back, landing a dozen feet away, and focused, trying to keep an eye on him through the blood and pain. His approach was intercepted by a jet engine, slamming into him and throwing him away. I focused again, healing myself and enhancing my strength, leaping to him in one step and bringing the sword down. Somehow, he managed to wriggle just out of the path of the blade, and then the engine came up and hit me, sending me to the tarmac.

"I'm not just some prissy vampire," Cho said, getting back to his feet. I rolled and stood, facing off against him again. "I've been to Hell, just like Rebecca. I learned some things there too." He held his palm out, and a jet of hellfire erupted towards me. I had fractions of a second to try to evade the flames, and fractions weren't enough.

"Ullie!"

The cry came from my left, and I was shoved aside just in time, Lylyx's massive form taking the hit. She howled in pain, her fur catching fire. Her screams were torture, and she dropped to the deck engulfed. She was ash within seconds.

"*Noooooo*," Ulnyx cried, his energy exploding with such strength that I couldn't hold onto him. His power overwhelmed me, furious and feral and unstoppable. My body changed and grew as he pulled me into his Great Were form.

"*Josette, help me*," I said, trying to focus and regain control.

"*This one is mine*," Ulnyx growled, his voice dripping with rage. "*Don't you dare take this from me.*"

I felt Josette in my soul, ready to challenge the Were. I gave her pause with a thought. "*Fine*," I said. "*But you'd better win.*"

He roared, a massive sound that vibrated the steel we were standing on. Cho gazed at him, unconcerned. He crinkled his brow and put his hands forward, prepared to send another round of flame towards us.

Ulnyx was ready for it. He rolled to the side, bunching his hinds and pouncing. The move was fast, but Cho was faster, skipping away with ease. At least, he would have, but I used the opportunity to pull some of the spilled blood below his feet. He slipped on it, teetering over and landing on his back.

We turned on a dime and reached out, great claws raking the archvampire across the chest. He cursed his pain and shoved himself backward, sliding along the deck away from us. Ulnyx followed at a charge.

"*Ulnyx, wait,*" I cried, guessing the move before it came. A wall of fire sprouted up right in front of us, too close to avoid. We tumbled through it, the hell-birthed flames scalding us with intense pain. I focused, trying to heal it, or at least reduce the pain. Ulnyx didn't even seem to notice.

We rolled back to our feet in time to catch Cho's claws with our own, our strength wrenching his arm back with a loud snap. The follow up nearly caught his neck, but he got the dagger up to block, and jabbed it into our hand. I couldn't hold back the scream when he kicked the burn on our chest and we flopped backwards.

"*I said you better win,*" I shouted to the Were. The pain was making me dizzy, and I could feel my body dying.

"*Shut up,*" Ulnyx replied, forcing me back to my feet. We were set for round three, but it never came.

Charis landed between the archvampire and us, her sword alight in white flame, her body covered in blood. She was a blur of steel and flesh, stabbing, kicking, and spinning, launching her all out assault.

"*No! He's mine, bitch,*" Ulnyx cursed.

I knew what he would do in his bloodlust. I focused inward, finding the strands of his power and taking hold of them, pulling him back. He fought me, and in his anger and despair he might have won, but Josette added her power to my own, and together we pulled the demon from control. My body shifted immediately, reducing me back to my human form and leaving me weak on the ground, a huge burn across my midriff. Between that and Ulnyx's desperate efforts to regain my body, the pain was almost unbearable.

"Landon." Thomas was at my side. He rolled me onto my back and pulled a flask from the pocket of his pants. He spoke the beautiful language of the angels as he poured the holy water over the wound and the burn slowly began to heal. I wasn't going to die, so I turned my attention to Charis.

She and Cho were still locked in melee, but I could see the archvampire was losing. Even with the strength he had gained from my blood, even with his speed, he was struggling against the blinding light of the blessed sword. He cringed every time it came near, shying away from its brightness and losing the motion of the attack. He tried to defend himself with fire, spreading it across his body the way Reyzl had, giving Charis a small measure of pause.

The sword was immune though, and she was relentless against his defenses, each failed deflection opening a wound on the demon that shined with white light. He had a dozen scores on his arms, and he screamed in anger and agony while she pounded against him. Then, it was over. The blade made it past his arms and claws, digging in and cutting him open from chest to pelvis. The white light was an infection spreading quickly across his body and reducing him to ash.

"That was for Joseph," I heard her whisper, standing over the pile of dust. She spit on it, and then waved her arm. A sudden gust of wind scattered it off the side of the ship and out over the water. The white flame on the blade expanded out and vanished.

276

She rushed back over to where I lay, a satisfied smile creasing her face, her eyes moist. "Are you okay?" she asked me, leaning down and looking outward with a protective gaze.

I pushed myself to a sitting position, feeling the last of the burns fade away below the holy water. My strength returning, I focused on Ulnyx, smothering him with my power, ensuring he would stay buried and promising myself to work it out with him later.

"I will be, thanks to Thomas," I said. I used my Sight, finding Izak, Obi, and Melody scattered on the other side of the deck. Where was Zeek? "Zeek?" I asked, feeling sick.

Charis shook her head. "He didn't make it," she said, fighting further tears. "He saved my life."

"I'm sorry," I said.

"I'm sorry as well," Thomas said.

"That thing with the sword, what was that?" I asked.

"The light of Heaven," she replied. "This sword belonged to Malize. He traded with me long ago, but warned me not to use it except to fight against the Beast. He said the archangels would know if his blade had been used, and they would be watching. You already know what could happen if they were to decide to intervene here."

A strange idea, Heaven watching us from above. I wasn't quite ready for them to come down and start Armageddon yet.

"They're all dead," Obi reported. He and Melody approached together, the angel helping him support his weight.

"What happened to you?" I asked.

"It's just a scratch," Obi replied. "It'll heal. Mel already treated it." Mel? He looked at her with a big smile. The angel blushed and looked away. "Bastards destroyed my Eagle though."

"I'm sure you can get another one. Izak!" I shouted the demon's name when I saw him approach through the black smoke of the smoldering aircraft wreckage. His shirt was hanging in tatters, but he was otherwise unharmed. "So, will somebody explain what I missed?"

Obi gently extracted himself from Melody. "Cho showed up at the Belmont, looking for you, I think. Or maybe just looking for your books - he didn't bother to say. Thomas here had already gone through the trouble of memorizing all of the important text, and he had Mel do the same in case he didn't make it."

"You can do that?" I asked him. He nodded. Impressive.

"Yeah, so we burned all the stuff in case he wanted it for himself, and we took off. His demon friends were chasing us, and man, I didn't think we were going to get away, but then Mephistopheles over there shows up with another big nasty furball in tow and lays hellish waste to them."

I tilted my head. "Whoa, hold up. What did you just call Izak?"

Obi looked at the fiend, who nodded. "Man, you didn't know that Izak is Mephistopheles? Did you actually *read* any of those books?"

My head was spinning. I had only been interested in the mark. I *hadn't* read the rest of the books.

"You had a text from the 12th century that translates to 'A History of Devils'",Thomas explained. "There was a sketch in there of the demon Mephisto that had a pretty uncanny likeness."

"But isn't Mephistopheles a direct servant of Lucifer?" Charis asked, looking at the fiend.

"He was," Thomas said. "A very powerful, intelligent, and sly agent of the First Fallen. If you're familiar with Faust, you have a good idea of his position in Hell. It's not wholly accurate, but its close enough."

I remembered the memory of Josette in her cell, with the fiend's head resting in her lap. No wonder he reacted the way he did. He was an angel once, and couldn't be redeemed by God. He had redeemed himself to me.

"*And me,*" Josette said. "*No matter what he once was, he is not that thing today.*" I could feel her heart burning for him, wishing for an end to his suffering, and joyous at his salvation.

"So, you returned to this world as an archfiend, until Gervais tricked you, and branded you?" I asked. He nodded. "He fell in love with Josette while she was being held captive, and then with Sarah. That's why he's here now, helping us. She saved him."

"Yeah well, he saved me," Obi said. "Heck, he saved all of us. Like I was saying, Cho had us dead to rights until he came along. After that, I told him where I was going to tell you to meet, and he and Lylyx disappeared for a while. She said they'd gone to convince that little guy you work with to tell Cho where you would be. He and Lylyx made themselves scarce, and Cho came and collected us to use as bait. He never had a clue Yuli was double-crossing him."

"How much did you have to give him?" I asked the fiend.

He put his palms out and pushed up. A lot. Of course.

"Well, I'm glad you're with us," I said. "Who else knows who you really are?"

He pointed at us.

"Good. They know you're a badass, but they don't know how badass. We can use that to our advantage." I held out my hand. "In any case, it's nice to meet you, Mephistopheles."

Izak started to reach out for my hand, but then scowled and waved his hand. I could guess at the meaning.

"You prefer Izak?" I asked. He nodded. I could understand why. Once it had been a curse, a name given to him by his captor. Now it was a blessing, the name spoken by his savior.

"So, now what?" Charis asked. "We need to get the Bible and decrypt the message. Landon, you know who knows where it is."

I smiled. "I do, and it's time I paid him a visit," I said, closing my eyes. I focused on the energy flowing from Purgatory, taking hold of it and letting it pull me in.

CHAPTER 24

I found him sitting on a beach, the warm sun shining down on him, reflecting off his nearly bald head. He was wearing a pair of simple white linen pants rolled up to his knees, and he had his toes dug deep into the sand. His chest was bare, with a small patch of wispy white hair vibrating in the soft sea breeze.

"Satan's Bible?" I asked him as I approached. He didn't move from his position, or acknowledge me at all. He just sat there, staring out at the ocean. I took a seat next to him. "Dante?" Nothing. "You know what I'm talking about, don't you? A history of the angels, written in Lucifer's own hand?"

He still didn't move. He just stared out at the ocean. I leaned over so I could see his face more clearly. It was pained.

"Damn it, Dante, talk to me," I yelled. "I did everything you asked me to do. You owe me that much."

I watched his adam's apple slide down and back up. He licked his lips. "Signore," he said. "Mr. Ross has told me what is happening in your world. I have been sitting here for some time, waiting for you to return; trying to find some way to explain, and some way to repent. But God doesn't hear me. Neither does Lucifer. Nobody hears me."

"I'm listening," I said, releasing my anger. There was no point to it.

He turned his head at last, but he wouldn't look me in the eye. "I don't know how familiar you are with the history of my life. There was a time when I was exiled from my home of Florence by the Black Guelphs. It was a very difficult time for me, and I spent many months fighting the injustice that had been done. In time, my goals brought me to the Tuscan city of Lucca. It was there that I met Gentucca."

He closed his eyes, remembering her. "As a mortal, I did not know it at the time, but she was a Turned. She had made a deal with a demon in exchange for great beauty in both the body and soul, and it was this beauty that lured me in. I fell in love with Gentucca, or at least I believed I had.

"One night as I was writing, she brought me a scroll. It was an old scroll, made of papyrus, but somehow untarnished and in perfect condition despite its age. She taught me to read its language, the language of the angels. She said her master had taught her to read it. She showed me the mark.

"She spoke to me of the injustice of the world. The suffering I had been through, and the suffering of others. I was a Godly man, and I argued against her words, refusing to believe in her twisted truths. That was the night that I left her."

He sighed deeply, picking up a handful of sand and letting it slide through his fingers, watching each grain trickle back to their place on the beach. "She planted a seed of doubt in my mind. I set upon learning all that I could about the Beast, and its servants. I travelled, seeking more proof, more texts, while at the same time desperately trying to restore my name and heritage and living a life of Godly piety.

"Then, one night while I was at my desk, a man came to me. He did not tell me his name, but he asked me if I would like to go on the journey of a lifetime. It was this night that I learned the truth about the Divine, this night that I was touched by the caretaker of Purgatory." He closed his eyes, thinking back on that moment. A moment he had described to me once before, under a completely different pretense. "It was this journey that became the foundation of my Comedy." He chuckled lightly. "Of course, I took some poetic license, but I *did* meet God, or at the very least some part of Him. I asked Him about the mark, and about the Beast, but was denied."

"Who was the man?" I asked him. "Not Virgil."

He shook his head. "No, not Virgil. I do not know who he was, for he would give me no name. I have never seen or heard from him again. He was a powerful Divine, I know that for sure, to be able to travel to each of the realms."

I was curious, but it didn't really matter. "So you came back to the mortal world inspired to write the Divine Comedy. How did you wind up in control of Satan's Bible?"

"That is simple, signore," he said. "I stole it."

"What do you mean, you stole it?" I asked.

"I did not know it was Lucifer's Book when I took it," he said. "The night I left Gentucca, I packed the scroll with my belongings and left with it. As I said, she planted a seed, and the seed began to grow."

"They didn't come for you though," I pointed out. "They let you keep it. They let you protect it."

"They did after my visit to Heaven. After He refused to answer my questions about the Beast. After I learned about the balance, and His intentions for mankind. I was angry with Him. I wrote a letter to Gentucca, and told her I wanted to become a servant. It was the worst mistake I've ever made."

"Not the worst mistake," I said.

"I did not know what Sarah was, signore. You never told me. I did not know they would use her to free the Beast. I was a servant, it is true. Even after I died and came to this place I was a servant. I tried to go back to God. I begged for entry, to speak to Him of the balance, and of the Beast. He rejected me, refusing to grant me an audience. Even His son rejected me. For many years I believed that He did not care. Not about me, not about mankind, not about anything. I wanted to see Him be forced to care, to fight, to possibly die or lose all that He had created. It was a blackness in my soul.

"Yet the embers of that hatred cooled, and I no longer wished to see the Beast reborn. I focused my energies instead on protecting mankind, by searching for Charis, and then you, and by keeping the secret of the Bible locked with me here. You see, signore, if nobody could get the Bible, and nobody could get me, then the Beast could never be freed."

"I don't know how, but you must be lying to me," I said. "Rebecca knows where to find the Beast. From what I understand, she and Sarah are on their way there right now. How would they know where to find it, if you didn't tell them?"

He hung his head. "Yes, Mr. Ross has told me this. He is out seeking a way to stop them. But, signore, I do not lie to you. I have never lied to you. I have omitted things, and I have altered the sequence of things, but I have not lied. I never told Rebecca what was in the Bible, and she could not have discovered it for herself."

"You have lied," I insisted, growing frustrated. "You told me Mephistopheles' Collectors had come for me, the day we met. They tried to decapitate me right in front of you. I just met Mephistopheles. Actually, I've known him for a while under a different name. He's been in the mortal realm for at least three hundred years."

"Yet I knew them best as his Collectors," he replied, getting angry. "No matter what they were when they appeared, that is how I identified them. You think things that are truths are lies because you do not understand them, but there are many ways to lie, and many ways to not lie. Such a power is useful, but it is not all encompassing. I did not tell Rebecca where to find the Bible, and I did not tell her what it contained."

"Then how?" I asked, backing down. "How could she know where to go?"

He shook his head. "I'm sorry, signore. I do not know."

"I need the Bible," I said. "I need it fast, or the Beast is going to escape."

"It will do you no good without the rest of the texts," he replied, defeated.

"I have the texts. I've been collecting them for the last three years. Tell me where to find the Bible."

He seemed surprised, but pleased. His whole woe-is-me demeanor changed, and he sprang to his feet. "Then there is still time?" he asked.

"If we hurry. Where is it?" I asked again.

He laughed. "Where do you find any book, signore? You go to the library."

"What are you talking about?"

"The library, signore. It's a place where they have many books. The Devil's Bible is sitting on a shelf at the Library of Congress in Washington, D.C."

Hiding in plain site. I should have known. "Wouldn't a scroll stand out a bit?"

"It was a scroll then," he said. "It isn't a scroll now. It is glamoured to look like a United States income tax law book. I placed the glamour myself with the full power of Purgatory. It is invisible to others, mortal or Divine."

Again, I wondered how Rebecca knew where to go. Had she somehow found the Bible without Dante's knowledge?

"Okay," I said. "I'm in New York right now, but I should be able to get to D.C pretty quickly, as long as Charis has a rift handy. Once I'm there I'll come get you, and you can show us which book it is."

His face turned more pale than it already was. "Wait, signore. Did you just say Charis?"

I had, without thinking anything of it, but Dante thought she was dead. Or did he? Truth and the truth were two different things. "Yes. She isn't dead, you know."

"I know," he said. "But she has abandoned the balance, and fights for Hell. You know what she did to get the Grail. How can we be sure she isn't a servant?"

It took me a few heartbeats to decide how much to tell him. Charis had warned me not to trust him too far, and with all of his sly manipulations of truth, and the fact that he had never bothered to mention his involvement with the Beast, I was inclined to agree.

"I'm sure she isn't," I said. "We connected."

His eyes widened. I could sense the storm of his anger growing behind them, but for once he managed to hold it at bay. "You connected?"

"I thought you would be happy about that. Isn't that what you wanted the diuscrucis to become?"

"There was a time when I did. A time when I had put my faith in her." He put his hand on his chin and looked thoughtful. "Perhaps this is good news after all. She abandoned the balance, but maybe you can bring her back to it. She is helping you to stop the Beast?"

"Yes."

"It will be interesting to see her again," he said. "We did not part on good terms."

I was sure they didn't. I put my hand on the poet's shoulder. "We've all made mistakes," I said. "But we need to drop all the crap for now and just deal with the Beast. You two can have a heart-to-heart, or rip each other apart, or whatever later."

He nodded. "Of course, you are right, signore." He changed then, his bare chest and linen pants replaced with a black t-shirt and combat fatigues. He looked like a skinny, old Rambo. "Only one change. You don't need a rift to get to Washington. I will take you there."

He had transported me before, but only a few blocks. This was a bit further. "You can do that?"

"It will not be easy for me, and it will put a strain on the equilibrium of our realms, but I can take you. Desperate times, signore."

"Can you take others too? I don't have the texts myself. The angel Thomas has them in his head."

He didn't look happy about that piece of information. He sighed. "I can only take those who are pledged to Purgatory. I'm sorry."

"What about if you bring me there, we grab the Bible, and you bring me back?"

He shook his head. "No. It cannot be moved out of the mortal realm. You can't imagine how much time and effort it took for me to get it to its hiding place this way."

"Then I guess we're back to plan A," I said. "It will take more time, but hopefully we'll be fast enough. I'll be in touch."

Before I could leave, he reached out and put his arms around me, squeezing me in a fatherly embrace.

"Good luck, signore," he said.

I didn't hug him back. Instead, I let go of my hold on Purgatory, and allowed my soul to travel the path back to my physical form.

CHAPTER 25

"The Library of Congress?" Charis asked. "Are you serious?"

"That's what he said," I replied. "We need to get to D.C, and we need to get there fast."

"Are you sure?" she asked. I started to reply, but I realized she wasn't talking to me. "Then there is no other way? Okay." She looked at me. "The closest rift is the one we came through earlier, but neither Vilya or I know of any near Washington. The best we can do is Virginia."

"That's a little closer at least," Obi said. "Only a couple of hours."

"Right now a couple of hours is a long time," I said. "Dante offered to give me a lift, but the Bible is useless without the rest of the texts."

"So let him take me," Thomas said. "I can match the strings."

"Can you decrypt them?" Obi asked. The angel shrugged.

"It doesn't matter," I said. "He can't take angels. Come on, we need to get to the rift."

I made my way past the gang, headed for the stairs. I could hear the fire engines in the distance, finally reacting to the mess we had made. With so many Divine clustered so close, there hadn't been any people up on the flight deck, so at least the damage had been limited to machinery. I'd kind of had my fill of causing innocent people to die.

"Landon, wait." Thomas rushed up to me and grabbed my arm. I turned around to face him. I knew what he wanted by his tentative but excited expression.

"No, Thomas," I said. "No way."

"Come on," he said. "We both know I'm not very good as an angel. I've been pushing the boundaries since I met you, and this is my chance to really do something good, not just for the faithful, but for all of mankind. Heck, for all of us Divine too."

"I can't," I said. "Not because you feel pressured. You'll regret it in the end."

"*I've never regretted it*," Josette said, making herself known in my mind.

"*You didn't have a choice*," I reminded her.

"I won't regret it," Thomas said. "I'm not cut out for this. I thought I was, but I just can't follow the rules the way they are, just so black and white, and I don't have my brother around to keep me in line. I mean, I was supposed to be mentoring Melody. Instead I've dragged her into your world, and now she's making eyes at Obi. You saw her at the airport. She was so enthusiastic about the rules that Mephi… Izak nearly fried her."

I looked past him to where Melody was standing. Obi had finished healing, so she was no longer supporting his weight. That didn't keep her from staying right by his side, her arm around his waist.

"*If this is what the Lord wants for him, you cannot deny it*," Josette said. "*I believe this is as it is supposed to be."*

I took a deep breath. There wasn't time to argue. "Fine," I said. "If this is what you want?"

He smiled. "It is."

"You know you won't be able to fly anymore."

His shirt moved as he flexed his wings beneath it. "I've never really gotten used to these anyway," he said.

"Kneel down."

Thomas got on his knees, and I put my hand on his forehead. I'd never tried this on an angel before. Actually, I had only done this once before, to Obi. I let my power flow through my hand and into Thomas, focusing on infusing him with energy. Unlike with Obi, I could feel the power already in him. I concentrated on wrapping my own around it, trying to keep as much of it from leeching away as possible. His wings were folded tight on his back, but I could see the shirt loosening on him as they shrunk away to nothing. A moment later he began to moan, and I knew I had done enough.

I took my hand away, and Thomas opened his eyes. He looked thoughtful, and then got to his feet. "I think it's better this way," he said, stretching his arms and back. "Although I will miss Heaven."

"You feel okay?" I asked.

"Yes. No regrets," he said.

"You are quite skilled at bringing people to your cause," Dante said from over the back of my shoulder, surprising me. I hated when he did that.

"Dante," I said. "Meet Thomas."

Thomas held out his hand. Dante took it and shook vigorously. "It is my pleasure, signore. Now, I will take you..." He stopped speaking, and his eyes jumped. I was spinning around enough to get dizzy, and now I saw that Charis was headed towards us.

"Ms. Stone," Dante said, circling around us to greet her. "It has been a long time."

"Dante," she said, her voice as hard as her name. "Not long enough. All this time, you knew about the Beast, and you said nothing. Do you know what I went through, that you might have been able to prevent?"

I stepped between them. "Charis, I know how you're feeling, but we need to do this later, okay? Please."

Her eyes spat venom, but she nodded. "You're right. He's not worth it anyway."

Dante's face was pale, and he looked like he wanted to be anywhere else but standing there with us. "Are we going then?" he asked, his voice weak.

"Obi," I called. "Come on."

He came over with Melody and Izak. Dante bowed slightly when the demon reached us.

"It has been a while, has it not?" he said. Izak nodded. "It is good to see you are free from that one." Izak nodded again, and smiled. It left me wondering what their history was, that they were so cordial with one another.

"This is Melody," Thomas said, motioning to the angel. "Melody, this is Dante."

"I know who Dante is," she said, her voice cool.

"Ah, still rooting for Heaven?" he asked. She turned red. "No matter. I cannot take you with us, unless you'd like to follow in your mentor's footsteps."

Melody shook her head. "I can't."

"Of course," Dante said.

"Melody," Thomas said. "Please promise me you won't tell the others about this. Remember what I told you, we don't know who we can trust."

"I know," she replied. "I promise on His name that I will not reveal anything to them about the Beast, until you tell me I can."

Thomas walked over to her, gave her a hug, and kissed her on the forehead. "Thank you," he said.

"Izak," I said, facing the demon. "Thank you for everything. Especially for saving my ass, and Obi's ass. We'll meet again, and when we do, I'll have Sarah with me."

He didn't look too sure of that, but he nodded again.

"Tell him I love him, and that he is a true spirit of goodness in my eyes," Josette said. I relayed the message, and a tear rolled down the fiend's cheek. He grabbed my arm, and looked deeply into my soul. I could feel his power

reverberate through me as he expressed himself to her without a word.

"Let's go," Charis said.

"So, do we have to hold hands and sing cumbaya or something?" Obi asked. "I'll see you around Melody." He winked at her, and she blushed.

"We do have to be touching," Dante said. I put my hand on one of his shoulders, Charis the other. We all joined from there. Dante closed his eyes and muttered something. I felt a cool breeze, and when I opened my eyes we were standing on the steps of the Library of Congress. That was such an awesome trick.

"Tax laws, right?" I asked Dante. I felt him wavering under my shoulder, so I shifted my grip to hold him up. His eyes looked a little glassy, and his skin was nearly translucent. "Are you okay?"

He put his bony hand on mine and patted it. "I'll be fine, signore," he said. "I've never done so many at such a distance before. Follow me."

I had never been to the Library of Congress before. I had seen some pictures of the inside - the huge round reading room with the desks arranged in concentric circles around the center, the grand exterior with the columns and steps. That wasn't where we were. This building was more flat, edged, and modern. It looked more like a military bunker than a library, at least to me.

"I thought you said Library of Congress?" I asked.

"This is the Law Library," Charis replied. "All of the law books are here."

"Over two million," Dante said. "Come."

Dante pulled us through the building at a furious pace, dashing through hallways and corridors too quickly for me to get my bearings. The next thing I knew, we were stopped in front of a huge shelf of books that all looked nearly identical, save for the volume numbers printed on the spine.

"See, signore. The Bible is still here," he said. "If Rebecca had found it, I doubt she would have left it for us." He reached in and pulled a book from the shelf. It was identical to those around it.

"Heh, I guess nobody ever actually bothers to read the tax laws," Obi said. "Best hiding place, ever."

"The Sleeping don't even see this book," Dante replied. He held it in his palm, cover up, and placed his other hand over it.

"I thought it was a scroll?" I said.

"This book was made by the first angel, Lucifer himself. It is not bound to any single form." He closed his eyes and whispered foreign words. The Bible caught fire in his hand, though the flames did him no harm. The original binding burned away, revealing a simple black lacquered wood cover beneath. It bore no writing, no markings or indication of what it was, but now that the glamour had been removed I could feel the energy leeching off of it.

Dante opened the book, and then set it in front of him, hanging stationary in the air before us. "Here it is," he said, pointing at the mark, set in gold on the page. "This is the Book of the Beast." He began thumbing through the pages. "It is a history of the war."

We all looked on in amazement. Despite all that I had seen and done as a Divine, the fact that we were looking at text penned by Lucifer himself, before he was cast down to Hell was mind blowing.

He came to the final page, and rested his finger next to the final passage. "Here is the final passage. The servants used these words to encrypt their code."

Thomas approached, getting close to it and looking down. "I need a piece of paper, and a pen," he said. "I'll write a few of the strings, and hopefully you can help me decrypt them."

"I'll get it," Obi said, racing out of the room.

"What does the final paragraph say?" I asked.

Dante cleared his throat. "For in those final days it came to pass that the Beast was thus defied, the might of his essence imprisoned for all time by the will of God and the sanctity of His creation. We hail the honor and glory of our Lord, and we mark this day as a day of Blessing. Let all of Heaven remember. Let all of Heaven remain. Thanks be to God."

He glanced up, the power of the words etched across his face. My limbs tingled in response, and I could tell by Thomas' and Charis' expressions that they were sharing the experience.

Obi came back in with a sheet of copier paper and a pen. He handed it to Thomas. "Amen," he said. "Now let's find this thing so we can shut him up once and for all."

Thomas took the paper and pen, and wrote out three strings. One was in angelic scripture, two were demonic.

"How are we supposed to decrypt something that's written in different languages?" I asked.

Obi was staring at them intently, his eyes flicking from the Bible to the paper. "Shh," he said. "Thomas, write out a few more. Make sure you go in order."

The former angel complied, writing out a dozen more strings.

"They alternate," Obi said. "One demonic, one angelic. It's not much, but it's a start."

We scanned the strings, we looked at the passage, we scanned the strings again. Thirty minutes passed. An hour.

"This is going to take forever," I said. "I don't think the idea was to create a code that could be cracked in minutes, and every minute we spend could be the last minute we have without the Beast in this world."

"Obi," Thomas said. "Can you get me more paper? Grab as much as you can find."

"Sure, man," Obi replied, heading out again.

"Thomas, what is it?" I asked.

"A passing thought. There is a room in the Lord's palace in Heaven. It is a map of the universe, the breadth of His domain. It is a sight to behold, both in its size and scope."

"I have seen it," Dante said. He looked at the passages. "Could it be?"

Thomas shrugged. "The map is not a series of dots for planets and stars and the like. With something so large, it would quickly become unreadable. The points would be so close together as to create nothing but a screen of white." Thomas turned the paper over and wrote the first letter from the Bible in the center. He then carefully etched the first and last word of the first two strings over it, being sure to connect the lines with great care. The result was just a small piece, but it did have a familiarity to it.

Obi came back in, dropping a ream of copier paper on the floor. "Is this enough?" he asked.

Thomas nodded. "I'm sorry to say, this will take some time. Dante, can you put the book on the floor. I'm not comfortable touching it."

"Of course, signore," Dante said. The Bible slowly lowered itself to the ground.

"Each letter in Lucifer's Bible is the center form of a larger shape," Thomas explained. "The larger shapes together will form an even bigger shape. My feeling is that what we will have is a map."

"With a big red 'X'?" Obi asked.

Thomas smiled. "Almost."

He set himself to the work, starting with the first letter and the first few passages. Obi leaned over his shoulder, observing. When he reached the tenth letter, Obi stopped him.

"That's not right, man," he said. "The shapes are too out of whack to fit together."

"Are you sure?" Thomas asked. He examined the papers, then pushed them aside. "I'll start again." And he did.

Another hour passed. Charis and I sat against the wall in silence, though at some point she had leaned in and put her head on my shoulder.

Dante had hovered over Thomas for a while, but now he came over to us.

"My friends," he said. Charis lifted her head and gave him another icy welcome, which the poet ignored. "I'm afraid I must return to Purgatory now, or I will lose the way back. My thoughts and prayers go with you, as well as any offer of apology you may choose to accept. I know I have caused much harm with my decisions, and some have been made out of no more than anger, jealousy, and fear, and for that I am eternally sorry. Please, know that I am proud of you, and honored to have met both of you. I believe we will meet again, and I will anxiously await that moment."

He held out his hand. I looked at Charis. Her expression had softened only slightly. Just because I knew her history, that didn't make it mine. I took Dante's offer of peace. "I'll see you soon," I said.

Charis got to her feet. She stared into Dante's eyes, her own flaring red and then fading to a warm brown. It was the first time I had seen their original color. How did she do that?

"I can spend eternity hating you for your mistakes, or I can praise you for your sacrifices. Today, I'll simply accept that you are as a flawed as the rest of us, and call it even."

She took his hand, and pulled him to her, wrapping her arms around him. Dante looked bewildered beneath the embrace. "I too will see you soon," she said.

Dante reached up and wiped away a tear as he smiled, looking every bit the part of a doting old grandfather. A moment later, he vanished.

"I think we've figured it out," Thomas shouted.

Charis and I went over and leaned in, looking at the scattered mess of shapes written across over a hundred pages.

"How do you know?" I asked.

"We just have to arrange them," Thomas said. He picked up the stack, and began laying them out on the floor. "I'll need one of you to hold some of these in place." He placed a sheet at hip level, where it would need to levitate to remain in position.

"I've got it," Charis said. Thomas let go, and the paper didn't move.

The former angel continued to move around the room, sometimes swapping sheets out, sometimes shifting their positions slightly. How he knew where to put them, I couldn't guess, but he worked with such purpose he had to be onto something.

"Wait," Charis said suddenly. The hanging pages shivered at her voice. "Landon, doesn't this look familiar to you at all?"

I looked around at the symbols. "No," I said. I examined them more closely, my mind picking me up where my eyes were failing. "Oh, crap."

Charis reached her hand out towards Thomas. "Give me the pages. I know where they go."

She took the remaining stack, and threw them up into the air. They danced around one another, swirling in an invisible wind until they were floating around us.

"It isn't enough to just put them out," she said. "They need to be tighter. Obi, Thomas, wait over there."

The two of them backed up reluctantly, leaving her and I standing alone in the center of the papers. I could feel her power as she focused, and the ink lifted itself from the pulp, remaining neatly scrawled but floating in midair. She pulled them in, contracting them until they began to overlap. Moving them closer and closer to the two of us.

"Landon," she said. "I need your help. We have to move them faster."

"You know what this is going to do?" I said to her, tapping into my power and focusing on adding velocity to the whirlwind.

"Yes."

"You know I don't have a good feeling about this?"

"Yes."

I looked past the ink to where Obi and Thomas were standing. "I'm sorry guys," I said. "But it looks like this is a one way ticket on a two man train."

"You get to have all the fun," Obi said. "Be careful, man. You too sexy lady."

Thomas held us his hand. "Godspeed," he said.

Charis and I pulled the runes in tighter. I moved closer and put my arms around her, squeezing in so we could both make the journey. I had recognized some of the symbols from the Cave of Christ, and had discerned their purpose based on that.

The runes spun faster and faster, rocketing around us as we fed them more power. They started to glow in a soft blue, and then the ink began to melt. I looked out of the spaces between to where Obi and Thomas were standing together, until the spaces were filled in and vanished. Within moments were were surrounded by a solid light, and I could sense the universe around us moving and shifting. Charis looked up at me with tenderness and determination. I returned her gaze with admiration. We held onto one another while we traveled to the unknown.

The blue light was replaced with darkness. We had arrived.

CHAPTER 26

Wherever we were, it was nothing that any mortal eyes had ever come across before, and it was nothing that could be easily explained. A streamer of blue light gave some bit of luminance to the place, running along either side of a crystalline black wall in no specific pattern, branching and coalescing as though it were a river cutting its way through the geography. It snaked around as it travelled, following the sides of the containment downward beyond our feet.

We were on a platform, I could tell, made of the same black, opaque crystal substance and lifted some distance above the ground. The floor was covered in runes, Lucifer's runes, etched into the material and shimmering slightly against the blue light. Looking up, I got a feel for the immensity of the area. The ceiling was at least another four hundred feet away. Towards its center, there was a bright white light like a miniature star, pulsing in a gentle rhythm.

I could feel the power of this place as heat and energy that raised the hairs on my arms. I could probably charge a Tesla by touch alone. It was nothing I had ever experienced before, but rather than foreboding, the sensation was intoxicating.

I focused, attempting to use my Sight to find Sarah or Rebecca, but as soon as a I tried a searing heat and constricting tightness held me in agony until I was able to let go. I looked over at Charis, and knew by her face she had experienced the same.

"This can't be good," I whispered to her.

"Let's hope that we aren't the only ones being cut off," she replied.

I wasn't sure if we would even regenerate here. I stepped over to the edge of the platform with extreme caution, getting on my knees and peering down over the edge. The bottom of the room was far enough below as to be invisible, but there was a set of steps off the north edge. What freaked me out was that the steps weren't attached to anything, each one stuck in the air, spaced evenly apart. What really freaked me out is that the platform wasn't attached to anything either.

"Lucifer always was a show-off, wasn't he?" I asked Charis, sliding away from the edge and getting to my feet.

"What do you mean?"

"Everything is just floating in the air, like its suspended in ice. The steps are that way."

"Interesting." She followed my finger, looking down when she got to the edge. "If we don't stop them, we're dead anyway, so there's no point in being afraid of heights."

She bounced off the platform, and her head quickly disappeared. I could hear her feet tapping on the steps, descending in a hurry. She was right about the heights. I took a deep breath, and started down behind her.

The steps spun in an odd spiral, sometimes closer together, sometimes further apart. The distance between them altered variably as well, and there were a few places where it took a true leap of faith to make it from one to the next. When we got down far enough to finally see the ground below us, we came to a total pause.

The blue light was originating there, all of the tributaries feeding into the center of the floor, where a fountain rose from the ground. It looked as though a huge chunk of the black material had been pulled up from the surface in a single block to be carved out. It was seamless and massive, rising up a dozen feet or so. Chiseled into it was what I took to be the scene of the Beast's defeat. Two angels, wings spread, dressed in rune covered breastplates, swords held high over a massive, hunched form. I recognized the face of Malize in an instant. The other had to be Lucifer, but the profile looked as though it had never been completed, with only the hint of a contour of eyes and nose and mouth. As for the Beast, it was a true mastery of stonework, for it held nearly no shape, yet elicited so much definition and emotion. To look on the carving was to fear.

The blue light spat up from the top of the fountain, spreading off into myriad lines of energy that cascaded over, illuminating it in a rich, heavenly glow before tumbling back down and running out again. It was a sight to behold, and I couldn't help but stand there and marvel at it.

"The essence of the Lord is held within this place," Josette said, her voice reverent.

"More than that," I whispered in reply. I could feel the energy. It was like oil and water, yet somehow it was entwined. "The Beast's essence is trapped here. I can feel it."

"As can I," Charis said. "The question is, where are Rebecca and Sarah?"

I looked around. There was enough light running along the floor that I could see the walls, two hundred feet or so in the distance on all sides. There were no doors, no entries that I could define.

"Maybe they haven't arrived yet," I said.

"Or maybe this is a trick," Charis suggested. "Look around. There are no doors. We're trapped in here too."

The thought hadn't occurred to me. I fought back against sudden panic. Did we just doom ourselves to spending eternity trapped here? I tried to focus again, but was once more greeted with the intense pain.

"Now what?" I asked. I started walking around the room, looking for a seam in the wall. There had to be an entrance somewhere. How else would Rebecca and Sarah get in?

"I don't know," Charis replied. "Maybe we wait?"

"For how long?" I asked.

"Not long," the voice responded. It came from everywhere. It echoed throughout the room. It was deep, and smooth. Like jazz.

I spun on my heels, but I didn't see anything, or anyone. "Who are you?" I asked, edging back towards the fountain, to where Charis was standing.

"I'm the past," the voice said. "I'm the future."

The words ricocheted around the room, overloading my hearing.

"I'm nothing, and I'm everything."

It was closer now. It seemed like it was sinking towards us.

"I'm the beginning, and I'm the end."

Whoever was speaking, they should have been right on top of us. Charis and I both threw our heads around the room, seeking the source.

It was a whisper, softly into my ear.

"I'm a prisoner, but you're going to help set me free."

My eyes closed, not because I wanted them to, but because they had to. I felt a rush of heat and my limbs locked up tight. What had we just wandered into?

"Open your eyes, kid," he said. I knew that voice, so much clearer now that it was centered in a single spot. My eyes opened on their own, but I already knew who I was going to see. That didn't stop the revelation from taking my frozen head and slamming it hard into frozen air.

It was Mr. Ross.

He was still dressed in his pinstripe suit, sunglasses over his eyes, big grin on his face. Flanking him on either side like a pair of backup singers were Rebecca and Sarah. They were both wearing too-revealing, short, thin dresses; Rebecca's in red, Sarah's in white. Sarah held the Grail in her hands, her face a wall of stone.

"Ta-da!" he said with a laugh. "I bet you didn't see this one coming." He punched me in the gut, and allowed me to double over coughing. "A cheap shot, I know, but come on - you deserved it."

"Go to hell," I croaked.

"Believe me," he said. "I've been there. And I have every intention of returning, once I'm done with this realm. Payback is a bitch, and I owe Lucifer big-time."

Mr. Ross was the Beast. I tried to wrap my head around it, to get it processed in my mind. Mr. Ross, who had shown up on the shores of Purgatory out of nowhere. Mr. Ross, who had the amazing ability to travel to every realm, to get information from anyone, anywhere. Mr. Ross, who had taken me from Purgatory and left me on the torch of the Statue of Liberty, where I had run into Rebecca. Where I had run into Rebecca...The truth was a ton of bricks, an anvil, and a sandbag. He had been playing me from the first note.

"Aren't you supposed to be trapped?" I asked, trying to keep my emotions centered while I regained my breath and straightened up.

"Funny story," he said. "Lucifer and Malize, they were smart. They used the essence of your so-called God to trap me here. They were so careful to not leave any seams in the stone, which is infused with energy from Heaven itself. They were so clever to create the perfect patterns in the flow - the mathematics are so exceptional, I still don't know how they figured it out.

"Your so-called God on the other hand, He wasn't so smart. Or maybe, He was just a tad bit ignorant. The angel's trap, it was perfect. I was stuck like a pig on a spit. My physical incarnation melted to nothing right where that cute little statue is, and all my power and consciousness was left floating in the blue ether, too dispersed to form any kind of coherent thought, every moment an exceptional, intimate agony."

His lip curled, almost into a snarl, before he brought himself back and began smiling again. "Time passed. Then one day, God and his bff Lucifer got into a little spat, and He realized how royally He had screwed up. He covered his ass by creating Hell, which almost got things back in balance. Do you know what happened next?"

"Purgatory," I said. Dante had told me this story.

He clapped his hands. "Purgatory. I love Purgatory," he shouted. "So close to this realm, sitting right below the proverbial surface. Too close. The perfect prison sprung a leak."

I remembered what Rachel had said. She'd tried to warn me, but I hadn't understood. If I had caught on sooner, maybe I could have confronted Ross on a better playing field, where I would at least have power of my own.

"Drip, drip, drip," Ross said. "I began leeching out into Purgatory, too slowly for anyone to notice. It took thousands of your years for me to take a new form. Do you like it? After that, it was so easy to get things moving in the right direction again. I even found out I already had a fan club! Once I convinced Dante to trust me, everything just came together so nicely."

I looked over to Rebecca, and then Sarah. They were calm and patient while Ross delivered his monologue. I tried to get Sarah to make eye contact with me, but she almost seemed to be in a trance of her own.

"God wasn't stupid," Charis said. "He knew. He knew that against all odds you would find a way to escape, that someone would try to set you free. It was balance, as you say."

Ross looked thoughtful. "You may have a point," he said. "It doesn't matter, because in the end it's come down to this moment, this time, and there's nothing you can do to stop it."

"Sarah?" She wouldn't look at me. "He's going to sacrifice you. He's going to kill you."

Her eyes found me then, so sweet and innocent, so mortal. "I know," she said. "My soul will go to to Heaven, or more likely Hell, and he will find me there and free me."

Ross laughed. "Was that your great hope, Landon? That you could talk her out of helping me? I'm sorry to disappoint you. Take them."

Rebecca and Sarah stepped forward. Sarah took Charis by the arm, tugging her towards the center of the room until she was standing under the light cascade of the fountain. Rebecca reached for me, but put her hand to my face before guiding me into position.

"I'm sorry it came to this," she said.

"Not sorry enough," I replied, turning my head away. After everything, she looked hurt.

She shoved me forward, moving me until I was standing below the fountain with Charis on my right. We were angled towards one another, and below us was a small pool in the center of a triangle. Sarah took the spot at the third point, and held the Grail out over it. When she let go, it hung in place.

"What are you doing?" I asked Ross. "Why not just kill us?"

"Kill you?" he asked. "Kid, it's taken quite a bit of luck just to keep you alive. Some of my servants have been, shall we say, a little over-enthusiastic. No, no, no, I never wanted to kill you, at least not yet. Did you think it was a stroke of good fortune, or the Hand of God that made us wait for you to arrive? Do you think an angel needed steps to get down from that platform?" He waved his hand up at the place where we had arrived. "It's taken quite a bit of work to get you here, especially with how stubborn you've been about the whole thing. It would have been so much simpler if you had just gone in the goddamn Box."

So, we were part of this somehow. "Why? Why do you need us? You have Sarah, she can set you free. Why go through so much to bring us here?"

He walked over, standing just outside the falling light, pacing back and forth as he spoke.

"Balance," he said. "You see, it has taken thousands of years for my power to leak into Purgatory. Thousands of years for me to gather enough to create this form and begin to manipulate the world. Even after I break free of God's stranglehold it will take time before I can fully realize my goals. By making sure neither army was too powerful, I've given myself the time I need."

I felt my heart racing. My body refused to follow my commands without Ross' consent. Was that why trying to focus here caused so much pain? It was too many revelations, too soon.

"Our power," I said. "It didn't come from Purgatory. It came from you."

He clapped his hands again. "Yes! I convinced Dante we needed soldiers of our own, to maintain the balance and keep humankind from becoming manburger helper. The best part about that one is that it's not even a lie; the future of your species in this realm does depend on keeping

Heaven and Hell on equal footing. I never cared about that. What I did care about is that they wound up too equal and confused to stop me. Dante agreed to my advice, and I started trying to imbue my power into the freshly dead, into the ones I thought would be the most agreeable slaves." He laughed and shook his head.

"It didn't work," he said. "My power would go in, they would scream, and they would vanish. Poof! Like they never existed at all." He shrugged. "The trick was that you had to be a diuscrucis to be able to absorb it, and you had to be in perfect balance to be able to use it. Trial and error, you know. Anyway, what I gave up was only ever meant to be a loan." His face turned dark, and his eyes flashed with a coldness I never wanted to experience ever again. "I want my power back."

He grinned from ear to ear, reached out and took Rebecca's hand, pulling her away from the three of us. "You're a good kid," he said. "Too good, actually. If you would have just gone with your honey in the first place, I would have let her keep you. I'm sure you would have enjoyed it." He gave me a suggestive wink and slid over to Charis. "As for you, I knew you'd find me sooner or later, even if it was just to tag along after that one over there. You're more of a goody-goody than he is, even if you like to think you aren't. Working for a God you don't believe in? If that isn't ironic, I don't know what is." He put his hand to her face, lifting it up so he could look her in the eyes. "I'll tell you what, sweetheart. I'll give you one chance to join the winning team."

I could see the fear in her eyes. I could almost see her shaking. Ross stood over her, waiting, but she didn't respond.

"No?" he asked. He let go of her face and backed away. "Don't say I didn't offer. You can't fight a god, Landon. Be honored that for a time you held even a drip of the power of one. Sarah, it's showtime."

CHAPTER 27

She looked over at him and smiled. "Don't keep me waiting too long," she said.

"Don't worry, I won't," he replied.

She reached out and took hold of Malize's sword, pulling it from the scabbard on Charis' back and looking it over. "I was going to use a regular knife, but this will add to the irony," she said. The blade lit up in the white heavenly light.

"Sarah," I said. "Sarah, please. Don't do this."

She looked at me. "Do not be afraid, brother. This is my destiny, my fate, my purpose. I was born to free the Beast. After all, it was the Beast who convinced Gervais to rape his own sister. Why do think he did it?"

"*Sarah, no,*" Josette's voice fell into my mind, frantic.

"You aren't some puppet on a string," I said. "It doesn't matter what anybody says you were born to do. You don't have to do anything you don't want to."

"But I do want to," she replied. "Everything I've felt for so long, everything that's happened to me. It has all led me here, to this moment. I'm so sad, and so tired, and so angry. I've seen it all happen, I know how it ends."

"Those are possible futures," I said. "None of them have to be."

"I'm sorry brother," she replied. "I have seen no other path. No other way to find relief." She took the blade, and stabbed Charis in a flare of white light. She gasped in shock and pain, looking down to watch the blood spill from her. The Grail floated over, placed under the wound where it collected her blood. The scene was too familiar. After Sarah had enough, she removed the sword. The wound closed over, but Charis looked pale and sick. Her eyes closed, and she passed out.

"*Landon, you have to do something, please,*" Josette cried, desperate.

"I can't move," I said.

"No, you can't," Sarah replied. She turned towards me and readied her thrust, the blood on the sword burned off by the light.

"*Landon,*" Josette shouted in my mind. "*Don't let her do this.*"

I tried to focus again, but the pain was unbearable. The more I pushed, the worse it got. "There's nothing I can do," I said in a whisper, choking on blood as the blade pierced my flesh. It was hot and cold at the same time, and I felt the blood passing out of me, watched it pour into the cup. Again.

She pulled the blade out. "There's nothing you can do," she agreed.

"Sarah, please," I said, my body weak, my eyes fighting to stay open. "What about your mother? She would never have wanted you to do this."

"My mother? My mother is dead because of you, her soul trapped with yours. Better for her to be one with the universe, than to be enslaved."

She took the sword and turned over her wrist. It was awkward with such a long blade, but she managed to make the vertical cut that would bleed her out. The blood poured from the wound, down into the Grail.

"*No*," Josette said, her frantic panic turning to resolute strength. I felt her power overwhelm me, her energy taking hold of my body. She couldn't be controlled by the Beast. Her power came from somewhere else.

She pushed me forward, reaching out and grabbing the sword, pulling it from Sarah's hands and throwing it away. She tackled the girl, throwing us both out of the fountain and onto the floor, moving my hand so that it locked around the wound, putting pressure on it and stemming the flow of blood. The geometry broken, the Grail fell to the ground with a soft clang, and the collected blood began to spill out into the pool.

"No!" I heard Ross cry. "It has to be all of it."

I heard the boots on the floor, Rebecca coming for us. Sarah wriggled beneath me, trying to get free.

"Sarah, listen to me," Josette said. Her voice was coming out of my mouth. I don't know how she was doing it, but she couldn't have picked a better time. "Listen to me."

I was laying on top of her. Tears were streaming from her face, and I could feel the warmth of her blood below my hand. She stopped struggling.

"Landon didn't kill me," Josette said. "I gave myself to him. I saved his life, so that he could protect you. I sacrificed myself so that you would be able to live a normal life, a mortal life. It doesn't matter why your father did what he did. To me you were a gift. You have always been my gift."

Rebecca was nearly on top of us. My body moved like lightning as

Josette grabbed the dagger at my side and flung it into the demon. It planted itself right between her eyes, and she fell backwards. It wouldn't keep her down, but it bought us more time.

"Sarah, I love you," Josette said. My own face was getting wet, my body responding to her emotions. "I've always loved you. I've tried so hard to protect you. I know it hasn't been easy for you. I know you've suffered, and I'm sorry. I've given all that I could. I've done all that I could. Please, it isn't too late."

The tears continued to fall, and she began to whimper. "Mother," she cried. "Mother, I'm scared. It hurts so much. It all hurts so much."

"Help us," Josette said. "Help Landon. Stop the Beast, or your hurt will never end. He knows nothing of love, or sacrifice. He knows only destruction. Please."

She flailed beneath us, her body writhing in an invisible agony. A piercing scream escaped from her then, a sound that reverberated from the walls and rocked the entire enclosure. Even Ross trembled at the noise. Then she stopped struggling, and I could feel the change.

"Landon," she said. "Help me."

I still couldn't move, the Beast wouldn't allow it. Josette could. She tore my shirt and quickly wrapped it tight around Sarah's wrist, staunching the flow of blood. We looked up. Ross had moved over to the fountain. He grabbed Charis' unconscious form and flung her like a sack of potatoes. She landed motionless on the floor.

"He's regaining his power," Sarah said. "I'm sorry. It was enough to set him free. It is too late."

"No, it is not too late," the newcomer said, appearing right in front of us. It was Dante. "You have freed some of his power, but it is not complete. Not while you live," he said to Sarah. He looked at me. "I am sorry, signore. I should have seen this sooner, but the leak was so small. I only found it because his power is being pulled through so strongly. He fooled me."

"He fooled all of us," Josette said for me.

Ross leaned down and dipped his hand in the pool of light. An inky blackness washed off and began spreading through it. At the same time, I could feel his energy growing. He looked up at us, his face menacing, his eyes crackling with dark power.

"Dante," he said. "My friend. Stay a while." He reached out, and Dante's body contorted into a sitting position. "We have a lot to talk about. A lot to plan. You can definitely be useful. In fact, I could never have gotten this far without you."

The poet groaned in pain, the stress evident on his face. He settled back and relaxed, easing himself straight, overcoming whatever Ross was doing to him. "I'm afraid I'll have to decline, signore," he said.

Josette got me up and reached out, pulling Sarah to her feet. The motion drew Ross' attention.

"You! I trusted you!" he shouted. "How could you?" His voice boomed throughout the entire structure, shaking the walls. The blackness was still spreading slowly through the rivers of light. He held out his hand and creased his brow in concentration, but nothing happened.

"He can't affect you," Dante said to Sarah. "Not without his full power.

We need to get out of here, now. Landon, get closer to Charis and I will try without touching." He didn't sound too confident, but he did sound determined.

"*Josette, we have to get Charis,*" I said.

She launched us forward towards her. Her eyes had opened, and they burned with a fierce red intensity. As we approached, she held up her hand.

"I am in control," Vilya said. "Do not touch me."

"Dante," I cried,"We're ready."

He nodded and took Sarah's hand. He had just closed his eyes when the sword point blossomed through his stomach.

"You aren't going anywhere," Rebecca said, pulling the blade out and shoving him to the side with her foot. "Not until the Beast is free."

I glanced back to Ross. He removed his hand from the pool and started walking towards us. "Thank you, my pet," he said. "Now, we have some uninvited guests who are gumming up the works. I think it's time to remove them."

He held up his hand, and I felt Josette twist inside of me, her cry of pain exploding in my soul. My body was instantly frozen again, and I could feel her being ripped away. I focused, desperate to hold onto her, doing my best to ignore the searing agony.

Rebecca held the sword point up to Sarah. "If you won't kill yourself, I'll do it," she said, reaching out and taking her by the hair. She pulled her towards Ross, ignoring her screams and struggles.

My eyes were the only thing I could move. I swung them desperately from left to right, in search of anything that I could use, doing my best to stay conscious over the double whammy of Josette's extraction and my efforts to use the Beast's power. Was he feeling the same pain? My eyes finally found it, Malize's sword, resting on the ground only a few feet from Sarah.

"Sarah," I cried, forcing my lips to move, forcing air through my lungs. I could only pray that she would know what to do.

The sword teetered, then launched from the ground towards her. She stopped her struggling, reaching out and catching the hilt, swinging it wildly over her head at Rebecca. The demon let go of her and ducked away, coming to her feet and deflecting the first of Sarah's strikes.

I had taught her what I could of her mother's skill with a blade. She had been a fast learner, but her lessons were nowhere near complete. She put up a good fight, the sword a strong extension of her arm, moving and flowing along with her as she put all of that practice to the test. Rebecca had a lot more experience, and it showed. She easily outmaneuvered Sarah, twisting and bringing her blade up and across, using it to rip the sword from Sarah's hands and send it tumbling away.

"Enough," she said, hissing in frustration. She reached out to grab Sarah again. "Let's get this done with."

"No," Sarah said. Her voice was calm and composed; the scared young girl replaced by someone strong and confident. Rebecca froze, as though she had been turned to stone. "You will not harm me," Sarah said. Rebecca lowered her sword.

"What are you doing?" Ross asked. "Bring her here."

Rebecca's arm started to rise again.

"No," Sarah repeated.

"Rebecca, do it!" Ross cried.

"No," Sarah said a third time. Rebecca's hands dropped as she heeded the Command. "Kill the Beast."

Her eyes widened, but she was powerless to resist. She turned on Ross, raising her sword and charging. Ross barely had a moment to react before the vampire was on him. The distraction set me free, and I pulled back on Josette and started running towards Dante at the same time. Charis followed my lead, and we all reached the stricken poet together.

I leaned down over him. "Dante," I said. His eyes fluttered and opened. "You've got to get us out of here."

I looked back at Ross and Rebecca. The Beast had flipped her over and pinned her to the ground. One hand was tight against her neck, the other was holding Malize's blade. Her head flopped over, and I saw the pain and fear and sadness in her eyes.

"Landon, help me," she croaked, her voice half curse, half sob. "Help me, please. I love you."

Again, she wasn't lying. My heart pounded as my pulse quickened even more. Dante had closed his eyes, and was murmuring and tracing runes in the air. One effort, one strong pull, and I could bring her to us. Except... she couldn't make the trip. I winced when Ross brought the sword down into her heart, causing her body to arch up and a horrible moan to escape from her lips. As she took her last breath, he looked at me, and smiled - a smile I'd never forget.

"I'm sorry," I whispered, hoping beyond hope that she could hear me. For the second time, I felt my heart shatter.

"See you around, kid," Ross said. The air shimmered around us, and everything went black.

CHAPTER 28

The world faded back into view. We were grouped together in a field, surrounded by stalks of wheat. It was nighttime, and I could hear a cacophony of crickets calling out in the darkness. Dante lay on the ground below me, coughing up blood and breathing erratically. His shirt was a sopping wet mess. Sarah and Charis kneeled on either side, their hands still on his shoulders.

"Dante?"

He opened his eyes. "Did we make it, signore?" he asked.

I nodded. "Yes, thanks to you."

He tried to take a deep breath, and wound up coughing again. I leaned in and put my arm behind him, helping him to sit up.

"I think you won't be thanking me soon," he said between coughs. "The Beast may not have his full power, but he has enough to start wreaking havoc on this world. He will not rest until he has finished what has been started."

I figured as much. "How long do we have?"

"It will take him some time to collect the energy that has been released, and I have cut him off from Purgatory. A few weeks? A few years? Who can say? He cannot launch an assault on the other realms without his full strength. He cannot get his full strength while any of you live."

"So, we have some time to figure out how to destroy him?"

Dante tried to laugh. It was a miserable failure. "You can't destroy him, signore. He *is* destruction. No, we must find a way to entrap him once more. There is no other choice."

I wasn't relishing the thought. "What are the odds that we survive this?" I asked.

He shook his head. "What are the odds that you will want to?" he replied.

The question gave me chills. I tried to shake it off. "Will you be okay?"

"I will be fine. The wound will heal as soon as I return home. It takes more than a demonic edge to put down Dante Alighieri."

"Then you should head back," I said. "I'll be in touch soon."

"Yes. I will rest, but only just long enough. Time is not on our side, signore."

"Dante," Charis said sharply, before the poet could disappear.

"Yes, my dear," he replied.

A tear dropped from her eye, onto the old man's shirt. "Thank you."

"For you, anything," he said, and then he was gone.

I got to my feet, rising up above the wheat, and looked around. We were in a huge, open expanse, but there was an old stone farmhouse about half of a mile away. I recognized the place. It wasn't an exact match, but it was close enough. Dante had delivered us to Tuscany.

"I guess he's still afraid to go back to Florence," Charis said, putting her hand on my shoulder.

"It seems that way," I agreed.

"I'm going to go check out the farmhouse," she added. "I don't know about you, but my head is killing me."

She wasn't alone. Ross' efforts to extract Josette had taken its toll. I focused, finding the threads of our souls. Right now, they were in tatters. "We'll be along soon," I said, taking her into a strong embrace. "Thank you, for everything you did."

I didn't hold her long, but when I let her go she was crying. "Thank you, Landon. You saved our lives."

I shook my head. "We all did our part, together. Besides, the Beast is yet to come." I gave her a stupid smile, trying to ease the moment. She couldn't hold back her laugh.

"That was really bad," she said.

"So bad it was good," I replied.

She didn't say anything else. She just started walking towards the farmhouse.

Sarah's empty eyes were already soaked before I lifted her up in the biggest hug I had ever given anyone.

"Landon, I'm so sorry," she cried. "I'm so sorry."

"Shhh," I said. "It's okay. It'll be okay."

"I ruined everything. I killed so many people. I was so angry. I just wanted the pain to stop. I just wanted the world to stop. I'm sorry. I'm sorry. I'm sorry." She clung to me tightly, burying her face in my neck. I held her close and stroked her hair.

"It's okay," I repeated. "We'll make it right. Don't worry."

"I'm evil. I'm so evil. I don't deserve to be alive. I don't deserve to have a brother like you, or a mother like mine."

Her words twisted the knife that was already planted in my heart. I picked her up and kept her close, carrying her all the way back to the farmhouse. In that moment, she was ten years old again, and all she needed was someone to protect her, to look out for her, and to care.

I used my foot to push open the door to the house. It was old, and not in great shape, but it was more than good enough. Charis was sitting in a dilapidated wooden rocking chair in front of an empty fireplace. It was clear to me she was mourning the loss of Ezekiel, but she still glanced over at us for just an instant, and I could feel the warmth of the caress.

I carried Sarah up the stairs in search of a bed. She had stopped apologizing, and was sobbing quietly into my shoulder.

The master bedroom had an old four-posted queen in it. The mattress was barren, and looked worn well past its time, but I'd never been so grateful to have it. I put Sarah down as gently as I could, and slid onto the bed beside her. As soon as I leaned back, she scooted over to me, putting her head on my chest. I rubbed her back, feeling her breathing even out. A few minutes later, she was asleep.

"Sweet dreams," I whispered to her, hopeful that she could escape the nightmare for a little while at least.

Left alone in the dark, my mind flashed back to Rebecca. She was crying out for me to save her, Malize's sword stuck in her heart, burning her in its heavenly light. My own tears ran freely while I remembered her, and all that we had gone through together. Did it matter that she had betrayed me? We had all made mistakes. Hadn't we only done what we believed was right?

I saw Ross' face then; the sick, wicked smile he had given me as he cut her down. He was the Beast. He was destruction. He was the universe's answer to God in a game that would never end. "They can't win, if you don't play," Sarah had once said to me. The trouble was, neither could you.

Game on.

ABOUT THE AUTHOR

Michael Forbes is mobile and web application engineer and author of science fiction and fantasy. He has a degree in fine art, and loves animals, the outdoors, good user interface and industrial design. Michael lives in the Pacific Northwest with his wife, a cat that thinks she's a dog, and a dog that thinks she's a cat. If you like what you've read, he'd love to hear from you!

Mailing List:
http://bit.ly/XRbZ5n

Website:
http://www.mrforbes.com/site/writing

Goodreads:
http://www.goodreads.com/author/show/6912725.M_R_Forbes

Facebook:
http://www.facebook.com/mrforbes.author

Twitter:
http://www.twitter.com/mrforbes

ABOUT THE COVER

Credit goes to the following for the royalty free stock imagery used in the creation of the book cover. All graphics licensed under Creative Commons 3.0 Attribution: http://creativecommons.org/licenses/by/3.0/

Design Elements Collection (fire):
GoMedia.us
http://www.freevector.com/design-elements-collection/

Japanese Fighter (sword):
Rockagraphics.de
http://www.freevector.com/japanese-fighter/

Creepy Werewolf:
VectorOpenStock.com
http://www.freevector.com/creepy-werewolf/

Silhouette
GotemCZ
http://www.freevector.com/fashion-models/

Eiffel Tower
LogoOpenStock.com
http://www.freevector.com/landmarks-vector/

Grunge Background
ImaginaryRosse
http://imaginaryrosse.deviantart.com/art/Grunge-Textures-117555400

Cityscape
Stockgraphicdesigns.com
http://www.freevector.com/cityscapes-vector-graphics/